BLINDING **LIGHTS**

BLINDING LIGHTS

ON STAGE TRILOGY

BOOK ONE

NAMIAR TOPIT

Content Warning

This book, and especially the trilogy as a whole, contains themes that might not be suitable for all audiences. Including and not limited to: profanity, nudity, explicit sex, mental health issues such as PTSD, violence, and substance abuse.

Please proceed with caution.

Edited by L. Jo King
Cover design by Fay Lane

Disclaimer: This is a work of fiction. All names, characters, places, businesses, and events are a product of the author's imagination or used in a fictitious manner. Any resemblance to actual persons, living or dead, or actual events is purely coincidental.

For Crusty, my first ever reader.

PROLOGUE: Antithesis

Minjae's Point of View

Not that I was great at sleeping in general…but it was completely pointless to even try that night.

There was a small dance studio downstairs in our new dorm, at the end of a short hallway, next to an even smaller home recording studio. The code to the lock was deeply imprinted in my muscle memory—my fingers typed it practically on their own. The lock clicked, and I opened the door to a room that had quickly become my safe haven. I hadn't been back from the army for more than two weeks, yet I had been here countless nights already.

The sound of my footsteps echoed around the otherwise silent space. The bold 23:04 on the big digital clock on the wall cast a red hue. It was all the light I needed as I pulled the door closed behind me.

It was too quiet, especially for tonight.

I resorted to my old survival tactics, which included connecting my phone to the speakers via Bluetooth before putting on my favorite playlist. A slight smile made its way to my lips as I cranked the volume up until the bass vibrated through my whole body, effectively erasing all negative thoughts. I didn't even have to worry about the noise; the room was soundproofed to near perfection.

Above all else, I managed to forget that *he* was due to arrive shortly.

My body started moving to the beat on its own. Closing my eyes, I let loose; there wasn't better therapy than dancing. The piece I danced to, was an instrumental version of a personal favorite. In an instant, I was in my happy place. Music always had the ability to make my mind go totally blank. All my senses focused on the story and mood of the music, instead of my own demons.

Unfortunately, the song was over all too soon, and another song started playing through the speakers—one I recognized from the first two beats, even. At once, my whole being channeled an entirely different image. Something forbidden…something hidden. Which was, after all, the song's message.

It was one of the oldest duets I had recorded with *him*—my friend, my bandmate…and also my pretend-partner for fanservice. Despite the fact that the track was one of my personal favorite songs out of our whole arsenal, I wasn't very into performing it live. It was just…too much. Too many real feelings were involved. I had managed to erase it from our actual concert setlists ages ago. Most of the fans had likely forgotten it even existed.

Called "Antithesis," the song was about *us*.

Or rather, the fairytale that was supposed to be us.

The steps from the choreo appeared in my head upon hearing the beat, as if they had never left. They were insanely difficult, even for me, but more importantly it was straight up contemporary (aka: right up my alley). I had trained for it from a very young age. It had become hard to resist the urge to dance to it—even though the whole thing was made purely for fanservice purposes.

"Whatever," I muttered to myself as I gave up and let myself dance.

For old times' sake.

It was almost too easy to recall the whole choreography—and the countless memories I thought I had buried deep long time ago. Starting slowly, I made my way across the room, not even counting the steps as they came straight from my spine. My heartbeat matched with the tempo, my muscles tensed and relaxed as if they were specifically designed to move to the beat of this one particular song.

By the second chorus, I was already so immersed in it, I could almost sense him right next to me, dancing his part of the choreo. Too bad the daydream was to meet a sudden end, as during the bridge he was supposed to lift me up by my waist.

Imagine my surprise when a pair of hands grabbed my waist, and my feet actually did lift off the ground. My heart skipped a beat or two, and I flashed my eyes wide open—only to find my best friend grinning at me straight in the eyes in the mirror.

"Hey Min," he mouthed.

I was too startled to reply.

My body refused to stop and take distance from him, which was what it should've done to spare me the heartbreak later. Instead, it automatically continued the choreo, as that's what it was trained to do. No matter what, the show had to continue. Always.

I slid down until the tips of my toes landed between his feet. With my full weight I still leaned against him, my other leg raised and curled around his hip—the ending pose. Our faces were a mere two centimeters apart; I could feel his rushed breath on my face, and my heart no longer beat in rhythm with the music. Rather, it beat double the speed.

The song ended, shattering the magic sizzling in the air.

Finally, I gained back the control of my body—thank all the gods there are—and took some distance. Once I put at least a meter between us, I could finally breathe. Damn, the choreo was demanding.

"I'm surprised you still remember," he said.

Evading his eyes, I replied, "Ditto."

"It has been a while."

"Yeah."

"I missed you."

I missed you, too.

Sold Out

"Phenomenally popular group GRiD–" Click.

"...surprise comeback this Friday–" Click.

"Fans all around the world anticipate..." Click.

"Tickets SOLD OUT in seven minutes–" Click.

"...at Gocheok Sky Dome after a three year long–" Click.

"Will they live up to their legacy–"

The random news anchors' and TV hosts' voices echoed around meeting room four—our usual—as I flipped through the channels of the 65-inch flat-screen mounted on the back wall. Our final meeting before the comeback concert in three days was about to start. We were only waiting for our manager to appear.

What a privileged country we lived in, as we and the comeback we were about to make were the top news of the week. I hadn't thought it would be *this* big of a deal. But ever since we held a press conference about our surprise return, the press had been all over the story—and us—like hyenas. Not that I'd complain. The whole purpose of us being hush-hush over the past years was to make an explosive return to the music scene of the great Republic of Korea.

That's right; almost three years ago, we disappeared from the top of the local music industry. Literally. We'd fallen off the face of the earth, as far as our fans and peers were concerned. They'd been speculating all kinds of crazy things over our absence. Seriously, one tabloid even claimed that we had all died in some kind of terrible airplane accident.

Drama hungry bastards.

The truth, however, was way simpler…and somewhat boring. We had merely dealt with the mandatory military service, which we would've had to go through at some point anyway, a little ahead of our time. Tae, as the oldest, was about to be called up anyway, and the rest of us decided to get it over with.

That wasn't the usual way it was handled. Due to the fact that one would have to be away from the spotlight for a minimum of 21 months, idols normally would go one by one, while the rest of the group continued to perform. We never did anything the normal way. That's us. GRiD: "the special snowflakes," as the industry insiders had joked back in the day. Too bad for them we had sold well, even during our break.

"Minjae, *please*, turn it off," Do-hyun pleaded, cutting off my absent minded channel-surfing.

"In a minute. Hyung, don't you see they're at the *best* part?" I replied and snickered, as they were showing a photo of him.

He threw the pen he was toying with at me.

I dodged it with ease, still laughing. It was just like Do to get annoyed over the smallest things.

On the TV, they were going through some kind of an introduction of us all. There were five of us: Tae, Joonie, Do-hyun, me, and Chris—if you were to put us in order from oldest to youngest, as they usually did. Currently, it was Do's turn to get thoroughly analyzed. The female host didn't seem to have a problem with it; after all, Do was something they liked to call a "visual."

I didn't exactly disagree with that description. With his sharp jawline, messily styled black hair, deep-set, seductive eyes, and just enough of the right kind of bad-boy attitude, he made every girl (and some boys) squeal and lose their collective breath within a kilometer's radius. Well, every lady (or gentleman), these days. At least according to the polls our label LBR Entertainment had run through the years; it seemed like our fan base had grown up with us.

Heck, even I couldn't keep my eyes off his face.

But Do-hyun was so much more than a visual. He was a vital part of our group. Not only was he an acclaimed rapper, but he'd also written and produced almost all our tracks together with Tae. Another unusual GRiD-way—it was not common for kpop groups to make their own music.

This particular TV host wasn't interested in that at all, though. When she was done with drooling over the looks of Do-hyun, she moved straight into the introduction of me.

An age-old clip of me dancing at one of our past concerts started to roll and I shuddered. Looks-wise, me and Do couldn't be any further apart. While technically we were almost the exact same height, and both somewhat fit, that's where our similarities ended. He had sharp eyes, squared shoulders, strong jawline…whereas I had always been a bit soft on the edges. Do's body was the kind one would achieve by going to the gym, while I never bothered. I chose to stay fit by dancing.

Seeing the baby-faced, black-haired me from three years back irked me. Now, I was as blond as one could be and hopefully a bit less…err…round-faced. Hopefully. In any case, I couldn't help but smash the power button on the remote before tossing it in the middle of the table.

Do-hyun rolled his eyes. "*Now* he turns it off."

Thankfully I didn't have to come up with a good response to my friend's teasing as Jiwoo, our manager, waltzed through the door right then, banging it against the wall to earn our attention. Not that she needed to do that; she always had our attention. What? Noona was a gorgeous woman. She had the most perfect, heart-shaped face, paired with sharp, intense eyes, and a body with curves for days. Lately, she had been coloring her hair flaming red, and to say it suited her personality would've been an understatement. Honestly, she would've made a great idol if she could sing or dance to save her life.

"Afternoon, boys! Let's get this rolling," she said, still as hyped about the comeback as she had been months ago. Dropping her case on the table, she added, "Today's agenda: if any of you mess up the setlist once, I'm gonna drill it into your head all night long. Plus, you bunch of drunks can kiss your little party tomorrow night a bittersweet goodbye."

"Hey!" Tae objected. He didn't really drink, but that didn't change Jiwoo's point, since the rest of us certainly wouldn't turn down an opportunity to let loose.

But Jiwoo couldn't quite defend herself, as Joonie cut her off.

"More importantly, how did you find out about the party–" he started with his perfectly lined eyes squinting at Jiwoo. She had been trying to keep our alcohol consumption to a minimum in preparation.

She just waved her beautifully manicured set of claws dismissively at Joonie, saying, "Oh, I have my ways. You seem to have forgotten that I do know you all."

Joonie opened and closed his pouty lips a couple of times, then huffed out a sigh while crossing his arms over his chest. "Fine."

"Good," she said and continued with a bit more of a mysterious tone. "And now that we got that out of the way, we still have one more thing to go through before we even get to today's agenda."

"Which is…?" Joonie asked, raising his eyebrows.

Jiwoo trained her eyes directly at me, her face unreadable. "Fanservice."

My heart flipped inside my chest. It wasn't one of the good kinds of heart flips either. I had some history with fanservice, and let's just say it wasn't my favorite topic.

"Darling," Tae said, pulling his flirtiest face while walking over to Jiwoo. Lacking any shame whatsoever, he leaned his face barely two centimeters from hers and tucked a stray strand of hair that had escaped her loose curly loose bun, behind her ear. "I think we've got that covered."

Jiwoo blinked, seemingly a bit breathless even. A rare sight, to be honest. I didn't blame her. Tae could be pretty charming when he wanted to. It took Jiwoo by surprise because, well, he rarely wanted to.

"Oh, I'm sure you do," she replied with a warm smile after collecting herself. "But that wasn't what I had in mind."

I tensed again, right after managing to relax a little during Tae's and Jiwoo's brief word exchange. *Shit.*

Jiwoo turned to look at me again. "I'm talking about a very special kind of fanservice. *DoMino* kind of fanservice."

A heavy silence settled inside the meeting room.

Yes, we knew all about the controversial gay-shipping-thing. We had even used it to our advantage back in the day. For some reason—maybe because even I could acknowledge that there was some unexpected chemistry between our stage personalities—the pairing between me and Do-hyun was by far the most popular. It would've been funny if it didn't make my life a living hell because we both hated the whole concept with passion.

They even called us *the chaotic DoMino pair*. It baffled me. What romance is there in the plain old domino piece that the fans loved to shove our way at every fan meeting?

I glanced at Do-hyun, who looked equally as uncomfortable. My fluttering heart sank at the sight. Good. I was not about to torture myself and repeat my past mistake, which was also my deepest, darkest secret:

I accidentally fell for Do in real life once.

I wasn't about to let that happen again, not in a million years.

"Do we really have to?" Do-hyun asked, running his hand through his hair in a frustrated manner. "I mean...can't we just focus on making good music for once?"

My heart had already sunk, but now it was drowning. Even better. It was good to remind the useless organ right from the start that me and Do acting like we were secretly together, was only just that: acting for the fans. In reality, we were merely close friends. At least that's what I tried to tell myself all over again.

"Look, I know you two aren't very enthusiastic about this. But I have no choice other than to bring this up," Jiwoo said. "The higher ups are expecting it. The publicity team is expecting it. Heck, *the fans* are expecting it."

Do-hyun turned to look at me questioningly with a crease between his eyebrows. Then, he shrugged, which I already had predicted. He always gave up when it came down to doing something that would get our fans excited.

"Up to you, I guess," he said, eyeing me.

I almost gave up right then and there. If Do-hyun was this okay with it—which I had not anticipated, to be honest—then who was I to fight about it? Then I realized that if I didn't speak up about this now, I might never have the chance to do so again.

I ripped my eyes off Do-hyun's face and turned to Jiwoo while taking a deep breath. "Jiwoo…this is exactly the kind of shit I'm not comfortable with. I'm not doing it."

While Jiwoo only nodded, it took the rest of the guys exactly seven seconds to process what I had just said. I know; I counted. I was expecting their reaction. I rarely opposed anything. Back in the day, that is. But I refused to accept everything and anything all over again. I was done being trampled over like I was a goddamn doormat.

They all started speaking their opinions on top of each other.

"Minjae, I'm siding with the label on this," Tae said, his voice oozing that famous leader authority he rarely used, which became even more powerful due to that exact reason. "We can't afford to lose even one fan. May I remind you that we're making a comeback after disappearing for *three years*. It's not going to be easy, and we have to use everything we can to get back on top."

"If Minjae isn't doing it, I'm backing off too," Do-hyun stated.

"I mean, we could just focus on making good music," Chris countered, looking at Tae. "Though this DoMino thing is huge."

Joonie threw his arms up when everyone turned to look at him. "I'm staying out of this one."

"I knew this would happen," Jiwoo said, shaking her head so the curls bounced around. "Let me handle this. Minjae, can I speak to you alone?"

"But—" Tae started but got cut off by Jiwoo raising her hand while looking at me.

I nodded. Was there even any other choice? I wanted to avoid a full-blown fight right before the comeback concert.

"Everyone, take a break," Jiwoo said to the others and stood up.

I didn't bother moving. They all walked out—well, Tae did with some reluctance. Jiwoo walked up and sat on the edge of the table right next to me.

When the door closed behind the others, I immediately said, "I'm not doing this."

"Why are you making this so difficult? I honestly expected this from Do-hyun…but not from you."

Obviously I wasn't disclosing the real reason to her. Instead, I plainly stated, "I find it degrading."

"Fine," she said. "But I'm still afraid I must press you on this. This is a direct request from director Hangyeol-nim. You and I both know the company can make our lives a living hell if they want to. Especially if the director is not on our side."

Well, shit. She was, of course, right. Even still, I was about to say something like *"bring it on,"* when Jiwoo spoke again.

"Look, how about this? We try this thing, and once we get through the comeback and gain back our previous standing within the company, I'll try to convince them that this isn't necessary. I'm sure we can do whatever the hell we want then. Or maybe this time some other ship will sail better than DoMino, who knows."

I gave it a thought. Jiwoo did make a little sense. Maybe…I could endure it for a little while. "And how long do you think I'll have to put up with this?"

She shrugged. "I'm not sure. Maybe a year or so? I'm sure we can prove ourselves within that. Sooner, if you're willing to give it some actual effort."

A year of torture? Dealing with Do-hyun's mood shifts? Trying not to get too caught up in the fairytale? Hell no.

Then again…what was one year more? It's not like I hadn't done it for years *before* the army. Besides, Do-hyun seemed to be okay with it, it felt a little silly to be the difficult one here. "Ugh, *fine*."

Jiwoo smiled and tapped my shoulder while hopping up from the table. "Good. Take five if you need to."

I was up and through the door to the hallway before she could even finish what she was saying. The door slammed shut behind me.

Midnight

It was good to be back home. Yes, we lived together in a dorm, even though we could very much afford to live on our own. It was so much easier this way, logistically speaking. And I loved the place. It felt like home. It *was* home. More than the barracks where I had spent almost two years of my life. Let's just say I did *not* miss the stench of sweaty camo pants and wet socks.

If only it wasn't for the damn fanservice part of our profession, I would've loved every second of it, and everything that came with the lifestyle.

I mean, I didn't even have to ask, and my glass seemed to fill itself.

As if on cue, Do-hyun held the bottle up and tilted towards me again.

"More wine?" he asked.

To be honest, I never cared that much for wine, but it was an okay drink with food, so I nodded. Like the good hyung he was, he topped off my glass. Unfortunately, I didn't get to take a sip in peace.

"Well, if we are still doing this DoMino thing, why don't we start feeding the fans right away?" Chris asked from across the table, looking at me and Do with narrowed eyes and holding up a phone—the camera aimed straight at us. "They must be *starving* by now."

I nearly choked on the wine. Miraculously, I managed not to, and slowly lowered the glass back on the table while trying to not get irritated. I didn't succeed. "I'd rather not."

"I think Chris is right," Tae said, raising his glass at me. "The sooner we get some new content out there, the better."

"I thought social media was my thing," I said.

"We can share," Chris said, blinking his round, innocent-looking eyes, pleading. Too bad I knew him—that annoying little brat—and *especially* that expression, enough to not fall for it.

"I think I need more soju."

And with that, I stood up, ignoring Do-hyun who was already handing me a shot glass. Instead, I walked over to the shelf by the glass-railing stairs and grabbed a bottle, before heading to the downstairs dance studio.

Once inside, I could finally breathe again.

I walked my way over to the gigantic mirror that spanned all the way from floor to ceiling and let out a long sigh. After cracking open the bottle, I took a sip, welcoming the slight burning sensation of the strong alcohol with open arms.

The dim outline of my reflection in the mirror was colored red due to the clock. It made me look ten times better, to be honest. And reminded me of how envious I was of the image people had of me—or rather my stage persona.

That Minjae was awesome. Confident, sexy…and thanks to the damn fanservice, stage-Minjae got to enjoy what the real me couldn't: being openly romantic with Do-hyun. Well, as much as we could, considering anything really gay was out of the question since…well…it was Korea, after all. The best or worst part though: the feeling was supposed to be mutual.

In reality, it was all acting.

Fanservice. A word that had started to sound like a curse word in my head over the years. Yet, it was a huge part of my life. Yeah, we had that covered, as Tae had so generously put it yesterday at the meeting. In fact, we had been known for it throughout the whole Korean music industry. It was one of the factors that helped us become so huge in the first place.

It wasn't like I hated all of it, though. Sure, I could flirt with the fans. I was used to showing some skin. Mustering up racy choreography was second nature. It was only this one thing people around us liked to do that bothered me: when they'd figuratively smash mine and Do's heads together chanting "kiss" repeatedly.

In a way it was both creepy and bittersweet.

I gulped down some more liquor then screwed the top back on and tossed the bottle towards the couch on my left regretting it instantly. Miraculously enough, it landed right in the middle— good. I wasn't in the mood for cleaning up the mess.

At the same time, Do-hyun marched inside, looking around. I ignored him and a silence ensued. I didn't really know what else to do other than to walk over to the couch, crack open the bottle again and take another sip. Once I realized Do-hyun was still staring at me, I held out the bottle.

"Want some?"

"Sure," he said, already approaching me.

I backed off at first, until I remembered I was supposed to give him the bottle. Grimacing internally, I held it out once more. Do sported a slightly confused face but grabbed the bottle anyway. I slumped on the couch.

The other end of it dipped down not a few seconds after.

"So, what are you doing here alone, dancing in the dark while there's a perfectly good party upstairs?"

I shrugged.

"Don't tell me you're still upset about the whole fanservice thing?"

"Well, aren't you?"

When Do-hyun didn't reply, I glanced at his face. There was a tiny crease between his eyebrows as he pondered for a minute, long enough for me to start freaking out.

I found it hard to believe he wouldn't mind fanservice. Based on the past, at least. He had this habit of shutting me out occasionally. Especially after concerts and stuff like that, when it had been more intense due to the acting being live. Funny how differently we reacted to the whole thing back in the day.

I had fallen in love, and he had become more distant.

I wondered if he'd still distance himself from me after Friday.

"Yeah, I guess…" Do-hyun said eventually, trailing off as if there was more he wanted to say but hesitated. "Though I think my reason is different from yours."

My eyes dropped to my hands. He was right. Surely his reason couldn't be that he had also had real feelings towards me in the past. As far as I knew, he was as straight as an arrow. And even if he was gay, I wouldn't have the slightest chance.

"I guess it is," I said.

"It'll get easier once we get used to it again."

"I surely hope so."

Do-hyun nudged my shoulder with his. "Come on, let's get back to the party. It's not like we can do anything about it now."

One More Thing

Unfortunately, after every great party, a new day is bound to break. Or hammer straight into your skull, reminding you that alcohol was, indeed, a drug…with withdrawal symptoms.

The nice buzz from the night before was all gone and replaced with the sound of a chainsaw revving inside my head. In reality, that sound was my sheets shifting as I curled up underneath the thick comforter, magnified a thousandfold.

I cracked open my right eye the tiniest bit and breathed out in immense relief. At least I had managed to close the thick drapes hanging on my window. It was pitch black. I even managed to open the other eye a bit, feeling somewhat victorious.

Until someone, who I hated from the bottom of my heart in that moment, pulled said curtains apart. He even hollered something about a good morning with a way-too-loud voice as the sunlight poured in. He sounded an awful lot like Do-hyun. Maybe it was my imagination running wild; this absurd behavior wasn't like him at all. He was supposed to be as hungover as I was, and most certainly in his own room.

I regretted not locking the door. I moaned and pulled the duvet over my head, squeezing my eyes back shut. Something heavy dropping on the other side of my king-sized bed wobbling the whole thing—and making me feel a little seasick, I might add.

"Let's go!" the person said, still way too loud. I grew more and more sure it was, in fact, Do-hyun. Whatever he was doing up and about at this hour while he was supposed to be hungover as well, I had no idea.

"What? Where?" My own voice sounding like someone banged boiler lids together, even though I tried to whisper.

"I dunno. Out. To a mall or something."

He had definitely lost his mind.

"But *why*?"

"Well, as this is basically the last day we can escape this place for a bit, we should use it. Everyone else has already left. Tae's at his grandma's, Joonie went to walk on the riverbank...I don't know where Chris is but he's not here. And I'm bored."

I wondered what time it was since everyone else had already left. Probably noon. And I felt a small pang of guilt as well, because Do-hyun couldn't go to visit his family easily; they lived in Daegu, where he was from. As in: a long way from here.

Besides, it wasn't a half-bad idea. It even sounded like it could potentially be a fine, relaxing day where me and Do could both be just *us*. For one day at least—before all the hustle that would undoubtedly make our lives much more complicated after the concert—we could be normal. Not celebrities. Not makeshift lovers. Just plain old Minjae and Do-hyun, the best friends, like in an alternative universe where we weren't famous.

I bet no-one would even recognize us yet. There weren't really any new photos of us except from the press conference.

But at the thought of getting up from bed, a new, powerful wave of nausea crashed straight into the pit of my stomach. I nearly threw up.

"I'm good, thanks," I muttered under the duvet.

He tried to pry the thing off of me. It was a good try, but only from my cold dead hands would he have succeeded.

"I brought water," he said, giving up on trying to yank the blanket off of me and resorting to bribing tactics.

I tightened my hold, just in case. At the same time, I had to admit that the deal started to sound kind of nice. After all, I was so thirsty it felt like I had wandered the desert without water for at least a week.

"And Advil."

Even more tempting. With utmost care, I slid the duvet down only enough to be able to see. Then immediately stiffened, as I was staring straight into the dark brown eyes of Do-hyun. At a very close proximity. I shuddered.

"Keep talking."

He smirked, knowing he was about to win. "Well, you're gonna take the magic pill that'll make the headache go poof. You'll shower, while I figure out my outfit. We'll sneak out."

I narrowed my eyes. "And?"

"As I said, we could go to the mall, do a little shopping, take a walk around the park, eat well."

My stomach grumbled. Admittedly I could've used some food. Preferably something very greasy…

"Imagine the fresh air in your lungs," Do-hyun continued.

I chuckled under my breath. "Yeah, filtered through a mask."

The air pollution could get bad around here. I, for sure, wasn't going out without a mask. I mean come on; I needed my lungs for my job.

"Fine," Do said, rolling his eyes. "How about a tteokbokki stand emitting that wonderful smell all around..."

Now we're talking. "Ugh, okay. Just give me thirty minutes."

His face lit up. "How about twenty?"

"Twenty-five."

"Deal." He hopped off the bed, effectively making it wobble once more. Then he left instantly, not leaving me any time whatsoever to protest.

Thankfully, the wave of nausea that hit me, upon having to deal with the wobbling, wasn't as strong as before. Maybe it was the promise of food that finally got me up from the bed, I wasn't sure. In any case, I forced my stiff muscles to function enough to get me up, but not without a long strand of groans.

Turned out I had been a high functioning drunk last night as well, as I had even managed to put on pajamas before passing out. Granted, a couple of buttons hadn't quite found the right holes to go through. Sighing, I unbuttoned the rest and discarded the whole shirt somewhere across the room on my way to the bathroom.

I must say I loved being allowed to be a bit messy. That hadn't been the case back in the army. Unfortunately, that also meant my room very much looked like I was way too comfortable with being disorganized. Oh well, at least the pants landed somewhere near the laundry bin.

It didn't even take me twenty-five minutes to get ready. Wearing simple light jeans and a light grey sweater, I strolled out of the closet…only to freeze right at the threshold.

Do-hyun was back in my room. He waited for me, standing half-naked beside my bed. It was hard to keep my eyes off his skin and chiseled, toned muscles. Was I dreaming? An almost unbearable urge to run my fingertips along his collarbone nearly drowned me.

I blinked and realized Do-hyun was holding up two hoodies.

"Which one?" he asked.

I didn't see much difference in my hungover, hazed state. They were both plain and black. Both boring and ugly. I think one had a zipper and the other didn't.

"Err, whichever?"

Do-hyun looked at me suspiciously before walking right in front of me and placing his hand on my forehead.

I could feel the rush of a blush creeping on my face. "What are you doing?"

"Checking if you have a fever. Normally you're obsessed about my clothes. Saying shit like I don't have any taste whatsoever."

Well, he wasn't wrong. I just didn't think this was that huge of a deal—we were only going out for a bit. I slapped his hand away. "I'm not your mom and we're not heading to a fashion show or anything."

"Then don't whine about it later," he said, chuckling, and pulled on the one with no zipper. Thank gods—I didn't need to deal with his bare, all too smooth skin any longer. For all I cared, he could have worn a neon green sundress with orange flowers and I would've been happy that he at least had on some clothes.

It was a sunny day, so we were both able to wear a cap and big-ass sunglasses and no-one would bat an eye. I also put on a black mask, insisting that Do-hyun at least bring one with him as well. He refused to wear it but did end up stuffing one in his pocket.

After gathering the necessities—phones, wallets, a water bottle—we headed outside. We didn't even need to speak out loud to decide we weren't taking Do-hyun's bright red Porsche—it was way too attention grabbing. And the others had probably taken the rest of the cars. Still, it was somewhat weird to take the elevator only to the ground level, because normally we would've gone straight into the underground garage. It was almost like we were sneaking out—we didn't even tell our security staff we were leaving, let alone where we were going.

Do-hyun pushed the door open and we hit the street, not that I could see much while partially blinded by the sun despite the heavy sunglasses. What a harsh reminder that I never took the Advil after all.

"Aish," I hissed under my breath, trying to shield my eyes from the harsh sun rays with my arm.

Do-hyun stepped in front of me, holding out the painkiller pack. "I knew you'd forget, so here."

How sweet, though not like Do-hyun at all. I wondered what had changed him in the army, as he was way more considerate than he'd been before. I eyed the box he was holding out to me suspiciously at first—maybe he'd flip at any second and turn to the old Do. But the banging headache made me eventually grab the box and fish out a pill.

I washed it down with water and handed the small box back to Do-hyun. "Now what?"

"I suppose we should walk a couple of blocks before calling a cab."

"Yeah, I guess," I said, nodding. It was a good idea to get some distance from the dorm in the rare case someone—perhaps the cab driver—would recognize us. Besides, we didn't have any guards with us so we had to be extra careful. I even spotted a group of teenagers hanging around a convenience store, but when none of them recognized us, I relaxed. So did Do-hyun, and we started our stroll.

"One more thing," Do-hyun said, abruptly stopping me once we were in a safe distance from other people, planting his hand on my shoulder and looking me straight in the eyes. He was too close again. Way too close. I could hear the pounding of my heart— never a good sign—but my feet were too glued to the ground to take any distance whatsoever. It was like he held me in place with his eyes only.

"What?"

With a blank, totally serious face, he said, "It's a date."

I swear my heart stopped for a millisecond.

"Ugh, stop joking around," I said, quickly turning my eyes to the ground before I blushed epically, then swatted his hand away.

Do-hyun laughed and started strolling ahead on the street as if nothing weird had happened at all.

Non-Date

It was not a date.

After that one little remark, Do-hyun acted as he always did around me. Not that I didn't obsess over it, analyzing his every move like a crazy person for the next hour or so. Because I did. It was all in vain; I knew he was only joking around. It was just my stupid head making things up again.

Which was bad. Really, really bad. At the rate I was obsessing over Do-hyun all over again, I was sure I would catch feelings. I wasn't going to let that happen. We found ourselves at the park right next to the closest mall to our dorm. Except we ended up walking all the way instead of taking a taxi—it was a surprisingly nice day for mid-fall. Seoul was oddly quiet, but then again it was a random Thursday and people would've been at school and work. Seemed like only tourists were wandering this part of the city at this hour.

And yes, we did find a tteokbokki stand at the park. Either the deliciously stir-fried rice cakes were the best I had ever eaten, or I was still seriously hungover. I soon figured it was the latter since Do-hyun wasn't a huge fan of them and he seemed…well, less hungover.

Suddenly, he froze. "Do you hear that?"

Still happily munching my cakes, I muttered, "What?"

"The music! Isn't that one of our songs?"

I furrowed my brow, trying to listen more closely. And yeah, there was a strangely familiar tune coming from somewhere on our right. Though it was played with an acoustic guitar and the singer wasn't any of us. "Yeah…'Echo–'"

""–in the Wind,'" Do-hyun finished for me, while grabbing my wrist and starting to walk me towards the faint music.

It was a street musician, playing our song at the mall's plaza. And it was my turn to grab Do-hyun's wrist when he tried to get even closer.

"Stop! What if he recognizes us?" I hissed, holding him back.

He stopped. "Oh yeah. Didn't think about that."

"Do you ever think about anything," I muttered, letting go of him and continuing to munch down the remaining tteokbokki from the stick.

"It's weird people still remember our music."

"Or they didn't, but got reminded when we announced the comeback. Maybe they'll forget all about us when all the fuss around us dies down."

Clearly I hadn't thought that last part out, as it turned out to be the worst thing to say. At once Do-hyun's smile disappeared and he casted his eyes down. I had forgotten Do-hyun overconfidence didn't reach his music. Shit.

"Yeah, maybe I can't write songs like that anymore."

I nudged him with my shoulder. "Hey, that's not what I meant."

He flashed me a smile that didn't quite reach his eyes and said, "I know," but a startling sound stole my focus.

At first, I thought I imagined it—the all too familiar sound of a camera shutter clicking. But when it happened the second time I couldn't help but glance around. Thankfully there was only this tourist-looking guy on our left sporting a bright blue fanny pack—the ugliest I had ever seen. He was fully immersed in capturing the nearby fountain. I couldn't quite put my finger on what bothered me about the dark-haired guy, though; maybe he seemed a bit familiar somehow. In any case, his demeanor didn't scream paparazzi. I relaxed.

"How about we actually go inside? Didn't we come here to shop?" I suggested, not exactly thrilled to hang around any cameras whatsoever. The last thing I wanted was the first tabloid scoop about me being headlined: "Hungover Minjae spotted shopping with Do-hyun."

"Yeah, you're right," Do-hyun said and we headed inside.

The fanny pack dude seemed to stay behind—of course I had to glance when I discarded my now empty tteokbokki stick in the trash can by the entrance.

I decided to forget all about him.

We hit the shops. Though we didn't buy much since we weren't about to carry a shit-ton of stuff around. Do did end up buying new bracelets for both of us, and I bought some new sunglasses. One could never have enough sunglasses. Especially if they sported huge under eye circles regularly, like I did. Sleep wasn't exactly my friend.

Otherwise we strolled around, trying on the weirdest possible outfits we could find at any given shop. Do-hyun was great at finding the worst pieces of clothing ever, so he aced the game. Only he didn't often realize how hideous whatever he found was until I pointed it out. Like this one time, he paired some murky green camo pants with a bright purple button-up—and seriously thought they went well together. I got a laugh out of that one. I told him it was better that he stayed with all-black clothing after all, like he normally would, as he clearly didn't know how colors worked.

Still, I had a great time.

Until I spotted the damn fanny-pack guy again, hanging by the entrance of one of the shops we had explored. I didn't want to worry Do-hyun, so I discreetly led him elsewhere. Even though I didn't see the guy for another half an hour, I couldn't relax. I started seeing the fanny-pack dude everywhere. I could've sworn I heard the camera's shutter go off a couple of times too, but every time I turned to see, he had the camera down. Either I was being paranoid or losing my mind. He looked harmless enough, why was I obsessed over him?

"Min, don't look...but I think that dude with the blue fanny pack is following us," Do-hyun whispered to me while ordered some ice cream at a cafe.

I guess I wasn't losing my mind after all. Well, that, or Do was also losing his mind. Either way, I nodded. "Yeah, I've noticed, too."

"Let's try to lose him?"

"Okay," I replied, grabbing my ice cream cone from the barista.

Do-hyun waited to get his, and we were off. We hoped we looked like we were only strolling around eating some ice cream, but in reality we were bouncing around the whole place aimlessly, trying to get rid of the creep. It didn't work. It was like he was everywhere at once, and my nerves kept rising higher.

"That guy just doesn't give up, does he?" I asked Do-hyun in a low voice after once again finding the weird fanny-pack creep hanging around.

"Nope, doesn't seem like he will. I'm gonna text Joe."

Joe was his favorite guard and had been with him since our debut. We all kind of had our own preference, except Tae who literally didn't care. Mine was Seong-gi, this middle-aged man who was more like a father figure to me. I did *not* want to text him. He would've scolded me for leaving without telling him.

"Should we try to lose him there?" Do continued, discreetly pointing to a larger shop with three stories full of great hiding spots. "You know, separate and then meet at the men's changing rooms?"

"Okay." It was an old tactic we had used back in the day when encountering creeps, and/or paparazzi. It almost always worked, and then our guards could speak to the salespeople and get them to lead us out through the staff corridors. It only eased my nerves a little. "But Hyung, please keep your phone at hand."

Do-hyun looked at me with an unreadable expression when we entered the shop. He raised his hand towards my face but froze right before he touched it and let it drop to his side instead. "It's gonna be okay, Min. Joe already replied he'll be here in a moment. Let's just lose this fucker real quick and head home."

I nodded and scurried in the opposite way. For a moment I pretended to browse the backpacks hanging at the wall on the right end, but in reality I never let the fanny pack dude out of my sight. He was lost for a moment, then decided to go after Do-hyun. Whew. Do was way better at this game than I was, so I trusted him to shake the creep off.

Still, I took my time exploring the huge store gradually, taking my time heading towards the men's clothing section. Even when I reached it, I made sure like a hundred times I didn't see any bright-blue fanny packs anywhere near me before making my way to the changing cubicles.

I was about to wonder if Do-hyun had made it when he appeared from behind a corner and pushed me inside one of the fitting rooms. When I was about to open my mouth to question him, he downright smashed his hand across my mouth and shushed me, pulling the curtain close with his other hand.

He backed me all the way to the back and pressed me against the wall. Gradually, his grip on my mouth loosened and all what was left was his index finger still held across my lips.

"The creep's close," he mouthed, his voice so silent I barely heard anything.

Not that I could've concentrated anyway. My eyes were wide and my heart was beating a thousand beats per minute—and it wasn't because of the creep that had been following us through the day. To be completely honest, at that moment the creep was the last thing on my mind. Instead, all my body and mind noticed was Do-hyun.

Do-hyun, Do-hyun, Do-hyun.

It was like my heart beat to the sound of his name. For a brief second I thought he would *feel* it beating, since he had his whole upper body pressed against mine. I was technically pinned between his torso and the wall. Even if that had been the case, he was way too preoccupied in keeping us silent and listening to the rest of the shop. He didn't even look at me; he was looking at the curtain for the smallest movements.

Me, on the other hand…I couldn't have ripped my eyes off him even if I tried. And I didn't try. I was too busy studying his handsome face and feeling his body on mine to remember I wasn't supposed to do this to myself anymore.

Dammit. I was still painfully in love with him, and it was time to stop pretending I wasn't. I had lied to myself for two years—enough for me to start partially believing said lie. The army and time away from him had only managed to lull me into some kind of false hope that I had gotten over him. Clearly, I hadn't.

Eventually Do-hyun grinned in victory and turned his deep and dark eyes at me. I was scared stiff that he would somehow find out about my deepest secret—maybe he'd turn into a mind reader or something. My heart was hammering against my ribs faster than ever.

Of course Do-hyun couldn't read minds. But he did freeze stiff upon meeting my eyes. Or time froze. I couldn't be sure.

He moved his finger off my lips so slowly it left them tingling. His expression was unreadable—he didn't even blink. Neither did I. For one brief, fleeting moment, I knew I could've kissed him so easily. Our lips were less than a few centimeters apart.

Someone ripped the curtain open, and at once, the moment was over. We snapped away from each other as if we were zapped by a jolt of electricity.

Both of us turned to the intruder at the same time. I had somehow anticipated it would've been either Joe or the creepo, but instead… It was a middle-aged, huge man with his black hair slicked back and a cord attached to an earpiece, towering over us— one I recognized all too well.

Seong-gi.

For a moment that felt like a year, he studied us with a deep frown between his eyebrows. The only thing he said with a nonchalant, deep voice was, "Follow me."

Natural Flirt

Seong-gi was dead silent when he led us out of the store accompanied by a nice-looking saleswoman. Walking through countless corridors of the "underworld" of the huge mall, we followed them all the way to the underground parking hall. Even when we reached Joe's BMW, Seong-gi didn't let out a single syllable, just opened the back door for us nonchalantly before heading to the front passenger seat himself.

I knew I had screwed up.

The ride home was agonizingly slow. Maybe it was because of Joe driving slower than life, or maybe it was the fact that Seong-gi was unusually quiet. In any case, snails would have reached our home faster.

It'd gotten dark out as well. I hadn't even realized we had literally spent the whole long-ass day at the mall.

I should've told Seong-gi we were going out. Unfortunately my dumb-ass self had chosen not to as it would have ruined the charm of having this one day of being a commoner. Too bad that, in the end, it did end up ruined anyway.

Meanwhile, Do-hyun was totally oblivious to all that. He was grinning like a maniac. How was he possibly in a great mood? Or maybe he had lost his mind. Then again, Joe in the driver's seat didn't seem even nearly as upset as Seong-gi. Maybe he was used to Do-hyun's shenanigans by now. No, scratch that—he was *definitely* used it by now. Plus, they were friends, unlike Seong-gi and me.

I let out a long, relieved sigh once the BMW dove into our underground garage. Finally, we were home.

Unfortunately I didn't get to escape Seong-gi to our living quarters upstairs. Not that I didn't try to, but he stopped me by grabbing my arm before I could set one foot inside the lift.

"You two can go ahead," he said to Joe and Do-hyun.

Joe nodded, while Do-hyun cringed and mouthed 'sorry,' right before the doors closed.

It was dead silent. I couldn't quite reach the eyes of Seong-gi, but I did muster up enough courage to say, "I'm sorry."

"I'm not gonna lecture you," Seong-gi said, pushing the button to call the lift again and letting go of my arm. "You're an adult now. Gone through the army and all."

I raised an eyebrow. "Then why did you keep me here?"

He placed his hand on my shoulder, turning me to look him in the eyes. "Look, I've been working for you for what? Seven years now? All the way from the debut, anyway."

I nodded.

"So I'm only gonna say this once, and with respect. You know that right?"

I nodded again.

He sighed, sounding a little exhausted. "I think that you should…spend a little less time with Do-hyun. You know, keep a little distance outside work hours."

Well, he wasn't wrong. Today, just now actually, I had come to the same conclusion. Only Seong-gi's reasons were most likely different from mine. While he was most likely worried that Do-hyun would get me into more trouble, my reason was more of the personal kind, meaning my heart's health. Seong-gi didn't need to know all that though. Thus, I only nodded once again.

"I know."

"Good," he said, at the same time the lift arrived, and we stepped in.

He exited the lift with a simple wave on floor two where the guards' quarters were while I continued all the way to the top floor.

I walked over to my room, dropped the single plastic bag containing my day's shopping haul on the armchair and planted myself face first on my bed. I was exhausted to the core.

Navigating this whole fanservice thing while acting only friendly towards Do-hyun, who had started to flirt with me uncontrollably even outside work, was proving to be even more difficult than I had originally anticipated after the army.

The worst part was that I had known it would be hard. Only…I hadn't realized it would be *this* hard. Then again, I didn't know when I agreed to this that I was still in love with him.

I didn't get to wallow in those thoughts for long, though. Because of course when seeing Do-hyun was the last thing I wanted, he entered my room and hopped on my bed beside me.

"Did Seong-gi give you a hard time?" he asked.

"Nope," I mumbled against the pillow. "Just the usual."

Do-hyun didn't need to know that Seong-gi didn't want me to spend time with him. But I needed a reminder it seemed. I turned to look at Do, saw that he was already scrolling his phone as if it was his own bed he was laying in.

"Hyung, you know you have your own room too, right?" I asked, whining. It seemed like Do-hyun was well on his way to develop a highly annoying habit of invading my room. I wasn't sure if I could take it for long.

"Yeah, but you're not there," he said, flashing me a smile wide enough to show his perfect row of pearly white teeth, before focusing back on his phone.

See, this was my problem. I could deal with the chemistry between us on stage because I knew it was all acting on his part. But this—these side comments in real life—were driving me absolutely insane and made me imagine things I most definitely shouldn't have been imagining.

I guess he had sort of always been like this—hence me falling in love with him in the first place—but it was now more intense. More fresh. He did it more often.

It was like there were two sides of me. One which was painfully in love with him and whose heart thumped like crazy every single time something like this happened. And then there was the other part of me who realized it was a natural consequence to the fact that we were close friends and Do-hyun was a natural flirt.

It *was* flirting, right? Or had I imagined all of it? Suddenly I started questioning my whole ability to read people at all.

One thing was for sure though: overthinking this wasn't going to make any difference. So I gave up on that and went to my walk-in closet instead. I grabbed a random pair of sweatpants and changed into them; it was like I died and entered heaven when I could wiggle my way out of the extremely tight skinny jeans. I tossed them carelessly to the floor and hopped back on the bed beside Do-hyun who had barely moved while I was occupied. I started browsing my phone as well, too tired to try to get rid of Do.

This close to our comeback, I was too scared to go to social media, which was my normal obsession. I only played this game I had been addicted to lately. It was simple: you had to circle around trying to gain as much of the playing area as you possibly could before someone killed you by crossing paths. I'd almost gained the top spot when I felt Do-hyun's eyes on me.

A tingle went up my spine—a thing that happened every time he gave me one of his intense stares to gain my attention.

Dropping the phone, I turned to face my distraction. There was a slight, almost unnoticeable wrinkle of worry between Do-hyun's eyebrows. Honestly, I think no one else would've even noticed it. To me—who had been staring at his face in secret for years—that tiny change in his complexion was a tell-tale sign that something was bothering him, big time.

"Hyung, what's wrong?"

There was a barely audible sigh before he spoke. "What if they don't like the new song?"

"Of course they'll like it. What are you talking about?" I said, even though I kind of got why he was worried. After all, he was the producer and a co-writer of the song. Aish, even I worried about the reception and I had barely sung my parts and made the choreography.

That, however, wasn't something he needed to hear. What he did need to hear, was encouragement from his best friend. Good thing I had become an excellent actor in that area of life during the past seven-or-so years following our debut.

"It's gonna be fine."

"Yeah, well… it's too late to back off now anyway," he stated with a plain, boring tone. Probably trying to sound indifferent about it but failing completely.

As if to prove my point the frown still lingered on his forehead. I couldn't help but to poke it with my index finger. As predicted, it was just enough to annoy him so much he would stop worrying. Instead, he attacked me, tickling the living hell out of me.

Heart pounding, laughing so hard I couldn't breathe properly, I didn't really pay attention to my surroundings. Due to that, we were in a very compromising position on my bed and I didn't even notice Chris barging in with his phone's camera aimed directly at us.

He turned right back around when we did notice. "Whoops, dear Crew. There's nothing to see here. Seems like DoMino's at it again."

Do-hyun jumped up, tackled Chris and snatched the phone from his hands. I stood up as well, brushing my clothes straight, some blush creeping to warm up my cheeks.

"What are you doing?" he asked Chris.

Then Tae appeared at the door. "What's going on?"

"I was bored and trying to film a tour of our new dorms for the GRiD Crew, when this *hyung* attacked me out of nowhere," the maknae explained while eyeing Tae with those famous wide and innocent eyes of his. That little shit…

Tae was immune to our maknae's powerful persuasion though. He only held out his hand towards Do-hyun, who handed over Chris's phone with a defeated look on his face. Tae played the recorded video from not even a minute ago, his eyes trained on the screen, focused. I could hear my own laughter and instantly felt even more heat rise up my cheeks.

When it ended—thank gods—Tae only tossed the phone back to Chris carelessly. "You can keep it."

"What?!" Do asked, now furious.

Truth to be told, I didn't like it either. But in this household, what Tae says, goes. So obviously I stayed quiet.

"Come on, it wasn't anything serious," Tae replied to Do-hyun. "Didn't we come to the conclusion yesterday that the more content we give the fans, the better?"

Chris flashed a wicked grin towards Tae and scurried off. I stared at the remaining two men in awe—they were shooting each other glances that could've frozen someone not as thick skinned as them to death.

Now this was the Do-hyun I remembered: quick to lose his temper. Not at all like the careful and considerate one from earlier today.

"What's with your obsession with all this extra bullshit? Isn't making good music enough for anyone these days?" Do asked, his eyes ablaze.

Oh, I was with Do-hyun on this one, but I wouldn't have dared to go against Tae, who, by the way, narrowed his eyes and leaned closer to Do with a just as intense–if not *more* intense—glare.

"What's the problem, Do? You're not up to it? Fine," Tae started, spitting the words on Do-hyun's face. "I can do it with Minjae then. Even our ship name would be so…*cool*."

Now that was pure kryptonite to Do. A vein in his forehead was pulsing so hard I was afraid it would pop any minute now. As for me…I started to warm up to Tae's idea.

To be honest, it seemed like a perfect solution to all my problems. I could take some distance from Do. And I certainly wouldn't need to do that much fanservice with Tae compared to what I had to go through with Do. I could focus one hundred percent on hiding my crush on Do, as I wouldn't have to do as much fanservice with him either. My life would become so much easier.

"Ship name?" I asked quietly, not wanting to end up in the middle of the argument between the two angry men. I tried to make it in my head instead. *TaeMin? MinTae? TMin?*

"Mint," Tae said, showing me a wide smile.

"Not a fucking chance," Do-hyun spat through his teeth and proceeded to push the now smirking Tae out of my door to the hallway.

He slammed the door shut behind him and locked it.

Meanwhile my blood started to boil. I crossed my arms over my chest and squinted at my best friend.

Do-hyun groaned at the sight, frustrated. "Now what's your problem?"

"No, what's *your* problem?" I asked, getting more and more annoyed by the second. "This is my room if you haven't noticed, so if you feel like throwing people out, feel free to follow them."

He blinked a couple of times, dumbfounded. I guess it was rare that I spoke to him this way—he was my hyung, after all. I had to respect people older than me, it was the way around here. But he had gone too damn far this time.

"*Fine,*" he huffed, stomped through the door and banged it shut behind him.

I flinched at the sound of the door rattling against the frame. Seriously, a simple apology would've been fine, but instead Do decided to get mad at me. I reminded myself that this was Do we were talking about and however nice he had been to me today, I should get used to this sooner rather than later. His moods had always gone from one end to the other; this was no news to me. I should've remembered that.

Still slightly annoyed, I jumped on the bed again. Then instantly regretted it since the bed seemed all kinds of empty and cold without Do in it. Funny how I had wanted to get rid of him earlier…and now all I wanted was for him to get back right away.

He didn't. It was also getting fairly late, so I reluctantly got up and headed to my bathroom to wash my face and brush my teeth.

When I got back, I noticed my phone on top of the bed was flashing a small light. Intrigued, I snuggled under the sheets and curled up, before turning the screen on.

It was a text from Do-hyun. *I'm sorry,* it said, plain and simple.

Such a wide smile it hurt my cheeks spread to my face—I couldn't stop it. Of course I also couldn't stay mad at Do-hyun—I had always been too soft for staying mad at him for long. Ever.

I hit him with a text too.

It's okay. Good night.

Dancing in the Dark

Too bad I couldn't get any sleep. Which wasn't any news for me either. I was somewhat used to tossing and turning in bed. It was my overthinking brain that I blamed most nights, but today I also blamed Do-hyun. I couldn't stop thinking about him and all that had happened earlier in the day.

Thank gods I wasn't hungover anymore. That would've sucked big time. Seemed like the hangovers had gotten worse over the years, too. I guess I wasn't twenty anymore.

On top of that, the nerves started to creep up on me, as tomorrow—*the comeback day*—was only hours away. For the most parts, I was very excited to get back on stage, back in the spotlight. I had longed to meet some members of the GRiD Crew for well over two years, almost three.

If it wasn't for the damn fanservice…

I cut that thought short and jumped up from the bed. After grabbing my phone and the wireless headphones from the side table, I yanked on the same sweatpants from earlier and a huge sweater, then stomped out the door and headed to the dance studio.

It was a habit—my one coping method.

Not wanting to wake anyone else up, I sneaked past the others' bedrooms, across the dark living room, and all the way downstairs.

I left the door to the studio cracked open to get some light from the hallway inside the room, to brighten it up a little more. Of course that also meant I couldn't blast the music from the speakers, but I could do with my wireless headphones. I didn't want to turn on the harsh white and bright lights on the ceiling of the dancing studio. It would've made me even more awake than what I already was. The goal was the exact opposite tonight: get me to sleep.

Besides, I knew the place inside out by now, so I didn't need that much light. While browsing my music library on my phone, I walked over to the side table. Once I settled for "Contrast"—the single we were to release tomorrow morning—I smiled. No harm in practicing a little. Practice makes perfect. Or, better at least.

I connected the headphones to the phone via Bluetooth and laid the phone down on the table. I had some time before the choreo would start—the song had a long intro—so I stretched briefly while walking my way to the dead center of the room.

Closing my eyes, I let my mind go blank and the music vibrated through my body to immerse me completely. It was almost as all my senses were cut off except hearing, and I floated a little above the surface of the floor. Every muscle, every bone and fiber worked harmoniously together, to create something pleasing, sensual, and beautiful.

To be honest, I loved the song.

The dance, however, was by far the sexiest we had ever had. Compared to the one I had danced with Do-hyun yesterday—one of our first duets—this one took it up several notches. And this was a song for our whole group.

I hadn't exactly meant for the choreograph to be this…racy. It had happened on its own. As if the music had demanded me to shape it in such a way. And I always lost whenever trying to battle against the music. Body roll after body roll I danced to the beat pounding to my ear. With my eyes closed, I fully concentrated on the complicated choreograph, yet still let my mind wander.

I was at the part that I should've done with Do-hyun, when something felt slightly wrong, as if someone was in the room with me. The someone was most likely Do with his habit of invading my spaces. I shrugged the feeling off, though, and continued dancing. For once, I refused to make it my problem.

But when I reached the part where the beat dropped and Do-hyun was supposed to run his hand on my thigh, I could almost feel it. Then I could *really* feel his hand sliding higher, past my hips and on to my side… He even lifted my shirt to expose my abs as he was supposed to in the choreo, but I didn't feel the usual warmness in my heart that Do-hyun's presence normally inflicted.

I was immensely relieved. Maybe I hadn't caught feelings after all. I smiled widely to myself, not even bothering to open my eyes. It wasn't unheard of that Do-hyun would join me in these late-night practice sessions, as the other night had proved. Plus, he wasn't a bad company most of the time when my heart wasn't obsessing over him.

When the song ended, we were both gasping for air. The choreography was by no means easy; in fact, it took a lot of stamina. I didn't want the magical moment to end, so I kept my eyes shut and continued to dance to the next random song that started blasting through my headphones.

"I gotta give it to you, your part of the choreo ain't easy," a voice said very near me, but it wasn't Do's.

The unexpected voice startled me, and I opened my eyes...only to stare straight into Tae's.

The realization that it wasn't Do who I was dancing with after all sent me stumbling back against the dark tiled wall opposite the mirror. I pulled the earphones off with somewhat shaky hands.

"Hyung! You nearly gave me a heart attack!"

"I know. Thought I was someone else?" Tae asked, his eyes gleaming with something…mischievous?

I slid down against the wall, clutching the front of my hoodie in my fist until my ass hit the floor.

Tae sat next to me. "I'm sorry, I didn't mean to startle you."

I glanced at him in total disbelief.

"Yeah, well, okay, I did. And it was hilarious."

"Oof," I huffed, waiting for my wildly pounding heart to decrease its tempo to a normal level.

We were silent for a long while. Tae was probably letting me collect myself. At least at first. And for that, I was immensely grateful.

However, as the silence continued, other types of fears and questions popped up in my head. Like…was he still mad at Do, and would scold me as well? What if he'd guessed my feelings towards Do? He wouldn't kick me out of the group for being in love with my bandmate, would he? What was he even doing here? I didn't exactly hang out a lot with Tae-hyung on a regular basis—and because of that I freaked out.

I couldn't take the silence for much longer, so I blurted out something to end it, "So, umm, what are you doing here?"

He didn't reply right away. Instead, he ran his hand through his hair and took a couple of deep breaths. A frown made its way between his eyebrows. I grew even more worried.

"I've been meaning to ask this for a long time now…" he started, looking me straight in the eyes.

"Yeah?"

"Umm, don't take this the wrong way, because I don't really care either way but… Are you by any chance, err, gay?"

I blinked. I thought that much was obvious by now. I mean, I never did go after ladies like Tae did. Not that I had ever said it out loud in my entire life either. In these parts of the world, it could mean a lot of things. The end of my career for example.

Then again, I didn't see Tae as the homophobic kind. And I wasn't even the most obviously gay in this particular boyband—that award went to Joonie, for sure. Not that he had said that out loud either, so I couldn't be sure…but let's just say I suspected it a lot.

Tae had at least said he didn't care either way, and that tipped the scale in favor of telling the truth.

"Well, yeah."

Tae nodded. "And are you in love with our Do-hyun, by any chance?"

Now that was a harder question to answer. Obviously I tried to evade it. Who wouldn't? Plus, Tae had insisted on the fanservice thing a lot himself.

"Aren't I supposed to be?" I asked, the corners of my mouth turning up to a stiff, unnatural smile.

"Yes, for fanservice, sure. But I meant like, are you in love with him...for real?"

I downright refused to answer, turning my eyes to the floor.

After a while of silence, Tae apparently came to a conclusion that he was on the right track. "Figured."

"How long have you known?" My voice was a mere whisper.

"I started noticing it before the army. And then I kinda hoped it would pass during the break..."

"Yeah, so did I." At this point, there was no use denying it.

There was another long and nervous silence before he answered me. "Must be hard..."

"Kinda," I started before giving in completely and admitting, "Yeah."

Tae looked me in the eyes for a long while. I didn't have the courage or strength to look away. The panic set in again. What was he thinking? Considering kicking me out? I mean, being gay wasn't *actually* accepted around these parts of the world, even though it was a popular fanservice trope.

Then an even more terrifying realization hit me. What if he was about to tell Do-hyun about it?

It was my deepest, darkest secret. No one was supposed to know it. Especially not Do-hyun. Now Tae knew. It was already hard to keep secrets by yourself by living together with five guys, but this was some next level shit I was about to deal with.

But instead of any of those options, he suggested something else entirely.

"What if we really made Mint happen?" he asked suddenly, referring to our newly discovered ship name. "For the fans, obviously. I mean, it would be a win-win situation—you'd get a breather from Do and the fans would get something fresh out of this comeback."

I blinked, surprised. Now that wasn't a turn I had anticipated this conversation to take. I gave it a short thought, but honestly I didn't need to ponder it for long. I still thought it was an answer to all my problems.

"Deal."

Tae smiled at me widely. "Deal."

A strong relief took over me. Tae wasn't going to kick me out of GRiD. I felt silly for even considering he might. We all had been a pack forever by now if we were counting the training time before our debut. I smiled back at him, genuinely this time.

"Though I'm afraid we'll have to keep *some* of the DoMino - elements too," Tae said, apologizing with his gaze. "The fans are all waiting for it to happen. And there isn't enough time to change tomorrow's plans anymore."

"Hey, it's not like I can't handle one more day."

"I know. But still, I'm going to think of something. The sooner we start this the better, right? Just go along with it, whatever happens on stage."

"Of course, Tae-hyung."

Tae got up and headed to the door then. "Sleep tight," he said and winked right before heading out, leaving me there at the dimly lit dance studio to collect myself.

I guess Tae was the leader of this group for a reason. He was observant, intuitive, and always had solutions to our problems, if we just shared them with him. He had clever ways to keep this chaotic group of people somewhat getting along. And he always seemed to have a way with words that made me rest easy.

This time he also did leave me a lot of things to think through. But I was hopeful—maybe this would actually work. Confident that I'd finally get some sleep instead of overthinking, I pulled myself up from the floor and danced to one more random song before heading to bed.

News

"Minjae!" Joonie shouted. Straight in my ear so loud I was momentarily afraid I'd gone deaf. "Min! Come on, *please* wake up. Where's your phone?"

He could've as well shouted to the walls since I only turned over and pulled the pillow over my head. I didn't even know what time it was, but for sure it was too early to wake up. Way, *way* too early. At least considering I had stayed up half the night.

"Ugh, it's the *comeback* day. You better," someone else, possibly Chris, said. I didn't hear that well from under the pillow. Not that it mattered for long, since that said someone hopped on top of me, crushing me under his weight.

Finally, I woke up somewhat, while struggling to toss the annoying maknae out of my bed. I guess he let me, as I surprisingly managed to do that with only a little resistance from his part. Chris was insanely obsessed with martial arts and thus much stronger than me in reality. His cute looks were deceiving. I might or might not have learned that the hard way a couple of times.

For a moment I gathered my sleepy self, trying to pry my slightly swollen eyes open. It seemed like the whole gang of GRiD had decided to take over my room. Do was casually lying right beside me on the bed, fully clothed—thank gods. Tae sat on my armchair over at the corner and with his arms crossed over his chest and an amused expression plastered on his face. Joonie was still hovering on my left, searching for my phone.

While they all stared at me, I grew a little more annoyed. "What's with you all today? Can't a guy sleep around here?"

"Just gimme your damn phone, and I'll leave you alone," Joonie pestered on.

I sighed. I knew it was this sort of ritual of ours, that we would lock our phones up and refuse to go anywhere near the internet before any major gigs. The purpose was to erase all distractions to give our best performance on stage. Back in the day, that is. I hadn't thought they would still insist on said tradition. I wasn't very fond of it.

Look, I needed my social media.

"I'll get bored without it…" I mumbled to myself, before trying to change the topic. "Anyway, what time is it?"

"Almost twelve," Joonie said, now holding out his hand, still expecting me to hand over my phone. Seemed like he didn't plan on giving up anytime soon. I gave up.

"Aish, whatever. Where is it anyway?"

That question wasn't really directed to anyone, yet Do-hyun still replied by nonchalantly fishing it out from under the pillow he was using. Then he handed it straight to Joonie.

"Ugh, if you knew where it was, why didn't you hand it out in the first place?" Joonie asked with a deep frown between his perfectly styled eyebrows.

Meanwhile Do shrugged. "I wanted Min to wake up but couldn't bother with that myself. It was hard enough yesterday."

"Haha, good point, I'll give you that one, hyung," Chris laughed, proceeding to give Do-hyun a high-five. I was genuinely surprised—Chris rarely used honorifics. I couldn't quite tell if he was being sarcastic or not. The little brat.

They all continued chatting as if I wasn't even there. In my damn room. I rolled my eyes.

"Now that you've all had your fun and Joonie has successfully robbed my phone, can't you get lost and let me sleep?

Tae nodded. "Yeah, I guess. Let's go."

And with that, they finally put me out of my misery and exited the room—with the exception of Do-hyun, of course. He continued staring at me with those deep brown eyes of his, his thick black hair styled in that not-messy-messy -look. Despite the fact that my heart was picking up the pace, I decided to ignore him and try to get some more sleep.

I wasn't successful by any standard. It annoyed and baffled me why they bothered in time and time again to try to wake me up if I didn't need to yet. They all knew damn well that whenever I finally *could* sleep, I slept like I was dead and definitely needed those precious hours of rest. I didn't get enough sleep often in the first place so why was it so hard to just let me when I did actually sleep some.

But I got over that irritation quite fast because another annoyance started taking more and more headspace: Do-hyun. He still stared at me, laying casually on *my* freaking bed. Even though I wasn't facing him, I could feel his gaze burning a hole to the back of my head.

I tossed and turned, wrinkling the sheets in the process, but wasn't quite able to fall back asleep.

Eventually, I turned to face Do and threw my pillow towards his face. Hard.

"Why are you here again, hyung?"

"I'm bored," he stated and hit me back with the same pillow.

Blinking, I glared at him in wonder.

"Aish, fine!" I eventually growled, running a hand through my shaggy, damaged-beyond-repair hair while getting up. My fingers got stuck—a rude reminder that I had bleached it one too many times already.

Do-hyun found it funny, though. I saw the reason why when I glanced at the mirror. The hair literally pointed at every possible direction. Trying to tame it with my hands did exactly nothing, so I stomped to the shower.

Fifteen to twenty minutes later, when I walked out of the shower with a towel hanging low on my waist, Hyung was still lying at my bed with his hands tucked behind his head, which still rested on the pillow. His eyes trained directly towards my naked torso. A great need to cover up took over me, but resisted the urge—I mean, it wasn't like Do hadn't seen me half naked before. We couldn't really fuss about privacy while changing clothes between songs backstage.

"Took you long enough," he stated, a hint of annoyance dripping through to his voice.

I shrugged and headed to my walk-in wardrobe only a tiny bit faster than intended. For a short minute I stood there, door closed behind my back and heart pounding like crazy inside my chest. How the hell was I supposed to pull this off? Being in love with him in secret while my heart performed crazy cartwheels every time shit like this happened? All while juggling acting for fanservice and being his good friend as well?

I couldn't wait to focus more on Mint. Fanservice had got to be easier with Tae—I had no feelings towards him whatsoever. Plus, as far as I knew, Tae was as straight as an arrow, so he wouldn't develop any towards me either. No need to make things complicated.

Luckily wiggling my way into some super tight-fitted jeans worked wonders for being frustrated, and I was able to calm down a bit. Though I wasn't sure about what to wear as a top. There was a possibility we would make a brief appearance in front of the fans when reaching the venue for tonight, so it had to be something sexy. Yet it also had to be comfortable, since I'd be in it through soundcheck and all that. I tried on one sleeveless shirt, but quickly tossed it straight into the trash bin—it showed too much of the ugly scar I had on my shoulder. There wasn't really a point in keeping clothes I would never wear.

I settled on a fairly loose, black satin button-up. Leaving the top and bottom two buttons unbuttoned, as well as the cuffs, I decided I was good to go.

Stepping back to the main room, I headed straight to my accessory drawer—trying my best to not notice Do-hyun while I was at it. I hunted down a bunch of rings, a necklace, bracelets and proceeded to put them all on. It took some time to get used to the weight and feel of them again as I hadn't had to wear that much stuff on me for a great while. Then again that's how we were supposed to dress in public from now on—wearing too many accessories—so maybe it was about time to get used to it. I had to get used to it.

Meanwhile Do had appeared behind my back out of thin air. He surprised me stiff as he reached over and grabbed a pair of earrings off the jewellery stand on top of the drawer. I could feel his breath on my neck—that's how close he was. It made me shiver. It was damn hard to focus, but I tried anyway, sucking in a breath through my teeth.

The earrings he chose were one of the fan gifts from back in the day—long silver chains with teeny-tiny domino pieces attached to the ends. A rush of nostalgia washed over me.

"Put this on," Do-hyun hummed into my ear softly, causing another shiver to run from my neck all the way to my tailbone. He handed me one of the two earrings while placing the other on his own ear.

For a hot second I wondered if I should. I knew if they were caught in even one photo, the GRiD Crew would analyze the living hell out of them, and we'd already be the couple of YouTube in our first week back at it. Although, that was kind of the goal now, wasn't it?

I ended up grabbing the earring and putting it on. But feeling a bit mischievous, I also added a bright mint colored, braided faux-leather bracelet on my right hand. It made Do glance at me questioningly, but he didn't say anything.

Finally ready, I turned to face him, opening my arms open wide to ask his opinion.

"It's alright, I guess," he said, giving my mint green bracelet a final side glance. "Now let's get me presentable." He grabbed my wrist and dragging me out of my room.

"But hyung, I'm hungry," I pouted, not quite sure that seeing Do-hyun half naked again was a bright idea. Yesterday had been quite enough for my mental health already.

Do-hyun ignored me and led me straight to his room. It was meticulously clean, almost as if he didn't even live in it. Even his bed was so precisely made there wasn't a single wrinkle. Of course, he nearly didn't live in it—it seemed like he had grown more attached to my room. I still wasn't sure if I was okay with that or not. I sighed at the sight and headed to his closet.

It was as clean and organized, if not more clean and organized, as his main room. Shelf after shelf were filled with neatly folded clothes in mostly dark colors. I was sure I could've never lived like this. I couldn't even begin to imagine the hours he must've put into organizing all of it. Careful to not make a mess, I started digging through his clothes.

This exact scene had been a pretty common occurrence in the past, considering the fact that Do couldn't style himself for shit. It took me a while to get familiar with his new closet, though. The previous one had been a lot…less. Less everything.

Eventually, I threw him a pair of simple black jeans and a white tank top paired with an equally white oversized t-shirt. Hyung complained that he would get the white shirt dirty in no time, but I tuned the whining out before heading to his accessories.

If possible, Do-hyun had even more jewellery and accessories than I did. Plus they were very different than mine. Where mine were *light* both in terms of color and weight, his were more of the statement kind. Another thing that proved we were the polar opposites whatever came to style. I picked him a long pendant, a studded belt with chains, and few black studded bracelets. But when I reached for the glass showcase where he had his rings on display, he stopped me.

"I'll pick those myself," he said, dismissively.

Oh well, I guess he was still obsessed with rings to this day. It had totally slipped my mind, though it did make sense. He had always been like that. I sat on his bed to wait for him to be ready. It didn't take him long.

"Hot-damn, you both look *fine,*" Tae hollered as we entered the living room.

Do shrugged. "I know."

I, on the other hand, blushed a bit and ignored them, walking over to the kitchen part of the open-concept space. I hunted down some ingredients, hoping to stuff my face with some sandwiches—only to end up losing one to Chris, who snatched it from my hand as soon as I had it ready.

I was only able to barely chomp down one piece of bread when Jiwoo stormed in, her red hair styled into bouncy curls and looking overly energetic, I might add. And somehow too cheery. None of us were able to do much else other than blink at her blindingly bright appearance.

She crossed her arms and squinted at us upon noticing us staring her like she had lost her mind. "Don't tell me you haven't seen the news!"

Tae shook his head in disbelief. "We never do before big gigs. You of all people should know that."

"Right," she said, now pinching the bridge of her nose with the tips of the fake nails she was sporting. They were so long they sort of freaked me out a little. "I forgot."

Getting slightly annoyed, I opened my own mouth. "Noona, just spit it out. You already started anyway."

She sighed, gathering herself. ""Contrast" MV hit 10 million views on YouTube."

We became dead silent.

"Already," she added, trying to make the point come across.

None of us still muttered out a word. I guess we all somehow froze.

"The sales are going good as well. At this rate, we might hit Billboard Hot100! Aren't you excited?"

It was Chris who recovered first. "Well, *damn*."

Well, *damn* indeed.

Countdown

Chris's words finally broke our trance-y state and we all attacked Do-hyun who was still frozen in the middle of the room at the same time. I was the first to reach him and grabbed him to a tight hug and whispered three simple words into his ear: "Good job, hyung."

That apparently loosened him up. A wide grin spread to his lips. He only had time to flash me that quick smile before the rest of them reached us and pulled us both into a tight group hug. I didn't mind—that little gesture Do showed me and me only, had already started to mean the world.

Gosh, I was whipped.

Luckily today I would be able to show it at little. Later in the evening, but still. Not that I wouldn't regret everything after— seriously if I remembered correctly, the hangover following a big live concert was much greater than any hangover caused by alcohol.

But I had to save the agonizing until later, since we were supposed to get going fairly soon. When everyone else finally realized it too, it was basically a big hassle. Everyone yelled on top of each other; Tae yelling instructions, Joonie about the schedule and stage outfits, Jiwoo shouting something about calming down. None of us listened.

It took us a long while to chill out.

"I shouldn't have told you anything," Noona said, now rubbing her temple in a tired manner. "I forgot how chaotic you are."

"Oh please, you brought this on yourself," Joonie said, walking over to our liquor shelf with his hips swaying a bit more than usual. "Now, how about some celebratory champagne?" He grabbed a bottle off said shelf.

"Why not?" Chris shrugged, already scurrying off to the kitchen part of the open space to grab us glasses.

"Absolutely not!" Tae said, eyeing us all in turns disappointed. "We have one of our most important gigs tonight!"

Joonie rolled his eyes. "Oh come on, it's not like we're gonna get drunk from one little glass."

I turned my eyes to Tae while grabbing a glass from Chris. I did want to have a drink to celebrate, but I certainly wasn't going to go against Tae. I had to be on his good side. He was my way out of the difficult situation with Do-hyun, after all.

Thankfully Tae could never say no to Joonie if he insisted on something. Thus, he nodded stiffly, giving up.

"Yuss, it's settled then," Jiwoo cheered and grabbed a glass from Chris as well.

Joonie started to fill up the glasses and surprisingly enough, Tae took a glass, too. Hypocrite. Then again, he rarely ever consumed alcohol, so I decided to let it slide. So did everyone else, and we raised our glasses.

"To a successful comeback!" Jiwoo said, while the rest of us replied almost on top of her with, "Geonbae!"

After that, Tae decided we should go over the whole evening one more time. Not that we didn't remember it, but it was supposed to be calming. We all agreed and gathered around the kitchen's bar table. It didn't take us long, and soon noona ushered us to get moving.

A white, luxurious limo waited for us downstairs.

Somehow, I ended up sitting between Tae and Do-hyun. Aish, it was almost like I was sitting between my ex and the new guy— if the fanservice pairings would've been real, that is.

To make matters even worse, Tae noticed my mint-colored bracelet.

"Nice touch," he said, nodding towards my wrist, winking. "You don't happen to have another? We'd match."

"Well, it's braided, so I could undo it and give one strand to you," I said, shrugging.

"Really?" Tae said, almost too enthusiastically. "Then what are you waiting for?"

I narrowed my eyes at him. Was he serious?

Do-hyun also reached over me to glance at Tae. "Wait, you two aren't serious with this Mint thing, are you?"

"Why not?" Chris hollered from the back, laughing. "Let's change things up a bit. You be the lonely guy for once, I'll be with Joonie…" he continued, circling his arm around a giggling Joonie. "…and Tae gets Minjae."

"Oh really, well how about the ship between Joonie and Tae then?" Do-hyun countered.

"We're good," Joonie replied, laughing. "Ain't we, honey?" He then boldly proceeded to send a flying kiss towards Tae.

Tae caught the kiss with a wide grin plastered on his face. They had always been more comfortable with the whole fanservice thing than me and Do had ever been. The fans had declared them to be the "eomma and appa" of GRiD, even. For a brief moment I felt like a homewrecker, before reminding myself of the fact that for the rest of them, all the ships were totally fake.

I rolled my eyes. "Calm down, everyone. It's a damn bracelet."

"Minjae's right, let's not get ahead of ourselves," Tae said.

"Ugh, I don't like any of this," Do-hyun muttered but calmed down nonetheless.

I, however, was so annoyed at Do at that point that I started to unbraid the bracelet. Who was he getting pissed at everyone over just some fanservice, acting as if it was way bigger of a deal? That shit was dangerous to my heart.

Wordlessly, I proceeded to tie the detached cord on Tae's hand.

No one dared to say anything—well, Tae did wink at me. I smiled back.

The rest of the way to the venue was spent in total silence.

When we arrived in a mere minute after that, there was already a massive crowd waiting for the doors to open. And they weren't even going to open for a few more hours. Some of the people closest to the road noticed the limo and pure chaos erupted.

Much to our disappointment, the safety team who were following us with our regular SUV decided that it wouldn't be safe for us or the fans if we'd suddenly appear there, forcing us to ignore them all. Our driver sneaked to the back entrance area with the limo.

The next few hours were a whole mess, really. We were pushed to one room after another, to meet the stagehands and then back up dancers, then the other staff members, etc. Everyone was busy and nervous, and we all had met them before countless times, but there wasn't denying Jiwoo when she insisted on something. I should know. I had first-hand experience.

Right before the final soundcheck, we escaped from the staff and made an appearance to the crowd waiting outside. They went wild, which brought a huge grin to my face. This was why we did this. This was why I started dancing in the first place. After three years, it was a nice reminder. And it somehow made all the fanservice and the lack of privacy totally worth it. I guess you could say I'd do anything for our fans.

Unfortunately, the staff and security caught us in no time, so we were hauled back after only a few finger hearts pointed towards the crowd.

Once we got inside, we were handed our stage gear—earpieces, mics—and the soundcheck began. Even though we had checked it all earlier, it still took a bit over an hour, we still had to make sure everything worked like it was supposed to. That meant checking we all had the channels we wanted to hear during the gig connected to our earpieces and the stage monitor system worked—all that boring stuff.

At the end of the soundcheck, the staff turned the lights off and put on a looped video to all the huge screens showing random geometric figures moving slowly, as well as the text "PLEASE STAND BY" flashing here and there. We did a group hug in the middle of the enormous stage, before the others headed backstage.

I stayed behind to get a good glance around the place. When we first debuted, our grand dream had been to perform on this very stage, in this very stadium, Gocheok Sky Dome, someday. Back then, it had all been a distant dream and we had to prove ourselves about a thousand times over before we finally got to perform here the first time. I remembered that it had been so surreal, to actually have your dreams to come true. And this wasn't even the biggest venue we'd played before the army.

I reminded myself that although we were now somehow starting from here the second time over, I shouldn't ever take it for granted.

And with that, I made my way backstage, to the room where our hair and make-up would get done. Now it was time for us to relax, open up our voices, let the noonas make us presentable…all while nearly 30,000 members of the GRiD Crew made their way inside the venue.

My nerves started to creep up on me again, much like last night but now stronger than ever. I wasn't that confident singing live anymore since it had been a while. And by "a while," I meant three freaking long years. I knew that I had rehearsed like crazy, but I still couldn't help but feel a bit sick in my stomach. The absolute last thing I wanted was to let the Crew down. The second to last thing I wanted was to let the other members of GRiD down. They were all my best and truest friends, the only ones that knew exactly what we went through to get where we were now.

I sneaked a glance at each of the members. All were getting a bit restless in the backstage room reserved for us. Tae stared ahead, sitting on the couch, seemingly the calmest of us all, but I could see he didn't exactly know where to put his hands. Chris paced around the room, in his own little bubble. Joon-seok sat down next to Tae and then got up again, only to sit back down the next second. Do-hyun sat right beside me on the other couch and took a sip from his water bottle from time to time, staring ahead much like Tae. The staff were making themselves busy around us, almost as if they were in a collective panicked state.

Basically, everyone was eager to make this a successful evening. I wished for only two things: one, that I wouldn't mess up too bad, and two, that our message—our performance—would touch and move each and every one of the people in the audience. If we would be able to make their day even one percent more awesome, fun, or happy, it would make everything I'd have to go through totally worth it.

Then Jiwoo glanced at her wristwatch for the hundredth time.

"It's time," she said, earning our attention at once.

"Alright, gather around," Tae said, standing up.

The rest of us stood up and followed him to the hallway. We formed a half circle of some sort, joining hands together in the middle—it was our collective pre-stage routine.

"Now, let's get through this smoothly. We've got this. Everything goes by the original plan," Tae said, although briefly glancing at me discreetly around the last part, winking.

"And have fun," he concluded, and we did one final group hug.

Do-hyun grabbed my hand and started leading me towards our starting spot under the stage. We were the only ones who would come up from the same spot to the stage as it went well with the lyrics of the first song—the rest of GRiD had their own places to be.

I braced myself, staring at our joined hands as we navigated through the under stage maze. I knew it was time for our very own, very personal pre-stage routine. Do-hyun had always said it was his way to get into character. Despite having done it a million times before, I was scared shitless this time for some reason. Maybe because of the break?

But when we crouched down on the stage lift's platform and Do-hyun cupped my cheek, my mind went totally blank. Neither of us muttered a single word, we only stared each other in the eyes.

Not that I needed anything else to get my heart beating for this way too handsome, stubborn and hot-headed man in front of me.

In fact, it was all I needed to forget all about Tae and whatever he had planned for tonight. At that moment, there was only me and Do-hyun. His warm hand placed on my cheek, his dark eyes studying mine.

Jiwoo started counting the seconds leading up to the moment the stage lift would go up, her voice loud and clear on our earpieces. Do-hyun circled his hand behind my neck and pulled me closer, until our foreheads touched together. I was sure my heart was about to burst.

"Five," Jiwoo said. "Good luck boys!"

This was it. There was no turning back now. It was time to let myself *feel*. For the first time in nearly three years.

"Four."

At once as I undid all my mental restrictions, all my feelings towards Do-hyun washed over me like a tidal wave; steady yet strong and powerful.

"Three."

I realized that however much I'd try to evade it…this…there was no way I would ever get over my attraction to him.

"Two."

The best part of performing though, was that Do-hyun had to at least pretend to have some feelings for me too.

"One."

We turned our handheld mics on. Do-hyun winked at me. I closed my eyes and prepared for impact.

"Zero."

No More Surprises

There was no way to put into words how impactful it was to have a collective crowd of *thirty thousand people* chanting your name from the top of their lungs at the same time. I heard it even through the earpieces that were supposed to cancel out all unwanted noise.

Sure, I had been there before, but it hit me as hard as it had the first time. I was convinced no one could ever get used to it. The stage was like a warzone—five men against an entire army—the GRiD Crew, who had been waiting and preparing for this particular battle for a long, *long* time. They were certainly ready for it.

Or rather…thirsty for blood, hungry for drama, demanding to be entertained.

The adrenaline rush that hit my veins was incredible—no rollercoaster or bungee jump could ever match it. No wonder the stage made some people go crazy; I could very well imagine getting addicted to this. So much that any regular moment would start to feel mundane.

"Have you missed us?" Tae boasted after the first song: an ego boosting rap piece with lyrics designed for pure fanservice.

"We definitely missed you," Joonie—going by his stage name Sweet for the next two plus hours—added.

I smiled so wide it hurt. I couldn't even begin to describe how good it felt to be back at it. I was about to burst from pure energy overload.

The first two thirds of the two-hour concert went by in a blur. It was constant racing around backstage, cramped in odd places only to try to appear perfect on stage. Plus, the stage was absolutely enormous, meaning we had to run around it constantly to be able to use it in its full glory.

Before our debut I used to wonder why people were always so sweaty on stage. Now I certainly knew why. On top of the stamina-eating choreographies, we had to sing, change clothes about a million times, run to the next spot, and still look like it was nothing.

Still, it felt like I was born to do just that—exhaust myself to the point of almost collapsing yet continuing as if it didn't affect me at all. It wasn't so bad, to be honest. Plus, we did have some resting time whenever someone performed a solo or stayed behind to entertain the audience.

One of those times, I too had to stay behind while the rest of GRiD were supposed to take a little break, get themselves freshened up and all that. I had prepared to do some waves with the fans, to get them moving a bit before we'd hit the last third of the concert. Look, it was a long concert—the fans also needed some breaks here and there.

Now, I didn't actually get to do any of that because for some weird reason, Do-hyun stayed behind with me. I was about to shoo him off, but he completely ignored me.

"I wonder…" he started, giving me all kinds of side eyes before turning to face the audience. "...does anyone remember this one song called 'Antithesis?'"

The crowd went wild, and shouted to their heart's content instantly, causing a huge grin to spread on Do-hyun's face. Me, however, I froze totally, my mind shouting only one thing inwardly: *No.*

"Yes," Jiwoo said through the feedback system, as if she had read my mind. I guess she had stolen the control of the system from the stage handler again. "Minjae, please, play along. Remember our deal. One more year of this."

I ignored her totally and yanked my earpieces off. I even tried to shake my head discreetly, hoping to gain Do-hyun's attention. He did glance at me, but either ignored me like I had ignored Jiwoo or genuinely didn't notice. Instead, he let out a laugh at the audience's reaction and continued to interact with them.

"Okay, okay, I hear you. You remember, alright…" he started, trailing off to wait for the crowd to calm down. "Now, what if I told you I found out the other day that Minjae *still* remembers the choreo?"

The fans went absolutely nuts over Do-hyun's statement. Meanwhile, I was a panicking mess inside, trying my damn hardest to not show it to the fans even though my smile was probably stiff. I could see there was no way out of doing it, and I very much wanted to disappear the second I realized it.

I hated Do-hyun's guts at that moment. Best friend or not, the love of my life or not, I fucking hated him. Yet, my body betrayed me. My hand grabbed the earpieces and shoved them back in while my lips sported a smile I couldn't stop from spreading on my face, lighting it up.

"That's the spirit," Jiwoo said to my ear. "Starting 'Antithesis' at ten, nine…"

"Will you dance with me?" Do-hyun asked me, speaking to his handheld mic while offering his other hand for me to take.

Not knowing what exactly had possessed my body, I took it while nodding. We both handed our microphones to a stagehand that appeared out of nowhere and faced each other.

The all too familiar melody started playing both for the audience and in my earphones. For a brief moment, maybe a second tops, I wondered how they had managed to prepare the song that wasn't on our setlist in such a short time. It was the live instrumental version, yet I was thankful that we wouldn't need to sing it while dancing to it—the music was enough on its own.

The piece enchanted me, and the story of the song made my body move on its own. I could no longer think about anything.

Though I could certainly feel.

I could feel the bass vibrating through me even more so than in our little practice room back at home. I could feel the stage resonating with the noise. I could feel the fans responding and living it with us—a lot of them even singing along, somehow even remembering the lyrics of the old song.

But above all else, I could feel Do-hyun.

I could feel his fingertips brushing the bare skin on my arm while passing me according to the choreo. His breath on my neck when he circled behind me and grabbed my waist with his hands. And finally his heartbeat, as loud as mine was when I leaned against his chest with my full weight for the closing image.

Our ragged breaths mixed between us as we stared at each other even after the spotlight was turned off, both frozen in the moment. A tight knot appeared to the pit of my stomach when Do-hyun's eyes travelled down from my eyes, before settling on my lips. I could've sworn he even leaned closer, his breath tingling my lips...

In the last possible millisecond, I pulled myself together. The moment was over. At once, we let go of each other and took a couple of steps back. I couldn't help but shiver at the loss of his body heat.

All that happened in the span of a few seconds, then Tae's hand was on my shoulder, almost making me jump half a meter up in the air.

"I'll take over, take a five," he mouthed to me.

Then he turned his eyes on Do, squinting. "And no more surprises."

Do-hyun barely shook his head a bit, grabbed my hand and yanked me forward. He was grinning, apparently still thinking it had been a good idea.

Good. That made one of us at least.

I'd have preferred to forget the whole incident.

Backstage Pass

Towards the end of the concert, I stayed behind to watch Joonie's solo. I had missed his performances. In a way, he was my idol. Behind the scenes, he was this hovering parent to our whole group, constantly reminding people to eat and keeping our crazy schedule on point.

On stage, however, he became this entirely different person: Sweet. It was his stage name, but I thought he had totally owned that name and given it a whole other meaning. Joonie was our lead singer, a sexy dancing demon with an unbelievably wide vocal range. Some considered me to be our group's lead dancer, but in all honesty, I was just hard-working. What Joonie had was pure talent.

I could've stayed there, watching him perform forever. But unfortunately I didn't have time for that. So right before his solo was about to end, I scurried backstage to get my headset mic. I would need it for 'Contrast,' the next song on the setlist. The choreograph of the new song was way too complicated to deal with a handheld mic.

Tae, Chris, and Do-hyun all patted my back when I walked past them, securing the mic in place. I barely noticed the others—I was in the zone. I knew this one had to start perfectly, as we hadn't performed it live ever before. And I was the opening act.

For Do-hyun, I'd give the song my absolute best.

When I entered back on stage, right from the middle entrance, Joonie was still interacting with the audience.

"So tell me, was it a good surprise we gave you this morning?" he asked, and the crowd replied with the loudest response I had ever heard.

That still wasn't enough for Joonie. "I can't hear you!"

While the audience shouted even louder, I cracked my neck. Then took a deep breath and walked to the dead center of the stage. After giving the nearby stagehand my sign, I closed my eyes.

"Minjae, ready, starting 'Contrast' in ten," was said through the feedback system. Good, everything still worked perfectly.

"That's better," Joonie hollered for the crowd. "Do you want to hear it live?!"

"'Contrast' in five," the voice in my ears said.

I showed the left earpiece in place, and most of the noise from the audience was immediately cancelled. Joonie said something else which I couldn't hear clearly since I only had the music, my own voice and stage handler's channels coming through the earpieces.

Filling my lungs with air, I took my starting position. A lot of things happened at once; Joonie's spotlight went off while mine lit up, the cue music started, and the audience went stiff with anticipation.

The air was electric all around me. A new wave of adrenaline coursed through me. It felt like I exploded from within when I let out the first words, pouring my whole being to it. The choreo kicked in, and I couldn't have stopped moving even if I'd wanted to. The beat went through my body like an electric current. I didn't sing and dance anymore; the music moved me, and I merely tried to hold on for dear life.

Somewhere around the end of the opening of my part, the others had made their way to the stage. They became one with me and the music. We were a team. Or rather one piece of art compiled from five individuals fitting together like puzzle pieces.

The chorus hit us like a lightning bolt.

It's nothing but trouble (will you fight or flight?)

We're running in circles (is it wrong or right?)
Our thing is starting to crumble (are you dark or light?)
Making me gamble (pick your poison; black or white?)

The beat dropped and I threw my head back, totally in some kind of trance. Do-hyun's fingertips ran up on my thigh—only this time, I was one hundred percent sure it was him. His mere touch scorched my skin, leaving behind a burning trail.

But when Do was about to reach my waist and lift my loose shirt for a little fanservice moment, Tae beat him to it from my left. Startled and surprised, I nearly missed the next part of the choreo. Not that it mattered—the whole love-triangle thing Tae was clearly aiming for, drove the GRiD Crew absolutely wild. Seriously, I could hear them even through the in-ear monitors blasting the background music in full volume.

I flashed a brief grin towards Tae, thoroughly amused. He winked back at me, making the crowd grow even wilder.

After "Contrast", we ran backstage as soon as the spotlights turned off. It was time for a video about our comeback and some flashbacks from the past to start playing on the larger than life screens on each side of the stage. It was time for us to catch our breaths for full ten minutes—and, boy, were we in need of that.

Time had flown by, and we were already closing in on the end of the concert. I had totally forgotten how draining having a live concert was—my body was basically screaming for help already at this point. I wanted nothing more than to crash on a couch for the whole ten minutes.

Too bad I didn't get to.

I was the last one to reach backstage and was immediately met with a very odd sight. For some reason, Do was furious and had cornered a very amused-looking Tae against the wall. Bewildered, I blinked. To be honest, I had already all but forgotten the whole thing Tae did on stage. In my mind, it was such a small thing that it was practically nothing.

Do-hyun clearly hadn't forgotten anything about it.

"...the hell did you do that for?!" Do-hyun asked, raging on. He even grabbed Tae's collar and pushed him roughly against the wall.

Meanwhile Tae only chuckled, sporting an amused expression. He threw his hands in the air in a sign of surrender though.

"Relax, it's just some fanservice," he said, a full smirk playing on his lips. "As Joonie said earlier, let's keep it interesting."

"Enough with this 'Mint' bullshit!" he snarled under his breath, so angry I was almost expecting him to hit Tae. "Min's mine!"

My eyes widened and I even had my mouth hanging slightly open. What the fuck was going on here? Was Do too immersed in his stage persona or what?

"Is he now? Then you should take better care of him, or I'm gonna take him from you," Tae countered. Was he suicidal? Surely seemed like he was, or at least he was seriously lacking in the survival instinct department, at least based on the murderous look Do was giving him.

I lost my patience with both of them. *"Enough."*

As if caught like a deer in the headlights, they both turned their eyes to me. Looked like neither of them had noticed my appearance in the first place. Slowly, Do let go of Tae's collar, his fingers unclenching one by one while Tae's smirk melted off and was replaced with a worried frown.

It wasn't like I didn't want Do-hyun to be a bit possessive—quite the contrary. The problem was, I knew it was a mere fantasy. Do-hyun didn't really care about me that much—he was in character. I knew from experience he'd turn a cold shoulder on me to counterbalance it for a couple of days after a concert. That was just who he was. It had happened after every damn gig, big and small. This particular one wasn't going to be the exception, now was it?

My chest clenched painfully as I tried to swallow back the angry tears that were right about to break free. I blinked rapidly, desperate to not let them see how much the whole thing actually affected me.

Do opened his mouth to say something, but when Joonie and Chris came over to see where we had gotten stuck, he fled. Darting off like a bullet, he ran somewhere, and I lost sight of him in seconds. I rubbed my temples. The whole thing was starting to give me a severe headache.

"Minjae, I'm sorry…but I think you should go after him so we can continue this show," Joonie stated softly, reminding me that we did not, in fact, have time for this.

After a brief nod, I darted after Do. In the end, I was the only one who could get him back onstage whenever he lost his shit while in character. That, too, I knew from experience. There was no other option than to bury my own feelings about the whole thing deep and try to get him hauled back on stage. This was, after all, one of the most important concerts we'd ever have to deliver.

I found Do-hyun in one of the other backstage rooms.

He was sitting on the couch, hanging his head low and playing with one of his rings. The staff hovered around him, worried, but he ignored them. In fact, he didn't even seem to notice them, trapped in his own little world.

Sighing, I channeled whatever I could muster together of my stage persona, this polished, shiny, confident character called Minjae. If Do-hyun was too immersed in his character, the only way to bring him back was to give the character what it wanted: me. Or rather, the stage-Minjae. Besides, I had to take some drastic measures because time was running out. There was no time to think things through. This would either work or backfire epically, but I had to take my chances.

So, I took a deep breath and walked straight to him, before making my way onto his lap, facing him. Do-hyun froze, but ultimately let me do it. I circled my arms around his neck, purring his name to his ear.

"Do-hyun…hyung… I think we should head back."

"I know," he said, still not making any effort to get going.

"The others are waiting," I said, burying my face to the nook of his neck, trying to hide the fact that I certainly wasn't the person I was playing. My facade was cracking, fast. As fast as my heart drummed, reminding me that my body did, in fact, react to his closeness more than it should.

The staff members started disappearing around us.

Do-hyun took in a shaky breath through his still clenched teeth. "I can't...I can't face Tae," he said, his tone sounding somehow hurt, angry, and apologetic at the same time. "I can't stand him. I can't deal with his hands on you. I want to chop them off and feed them to the wolves."

I lifted his face up with my hand on his chin, trying to force him to look me in the eyes. I wasn't very successful—he kept evading me. Once again, I reminded myself that we didn't have time for this shit and shouted, "Look at me!"

Finally his eyes found mine.

"It doesn't matter," I said with a bit of a softer tone. "Whatever happens it's just *fanservice*. It's *all* just fanservice."

Somehow, Do-hyun seemed even more hurt. Fuck. I wondered if I should've cleared it up that I meant Tae, but I wasn't sure if I could handle that level of honesty—even while channeling stage-Minjae.

But somehow, eventually, Do-hyun came around after staring me in the eyes the longest time. He wrapped his arms around me and pulled me tightly against his chest to my ultimate relief. I glanced at the clock on the back wall and a relief washed over me—we still had two minutes left.

My heart, on the other hand, was secretly shattering into million tiny pieces for the hundredth time. As sweet as Do-hyun could be in these rare moments, it wasn't going to last for long. I knew that this...thing...we had on stage, would come to its rightful end. Once the cheer died down and the spotlights no longer burned my skin, Do would want nothing to do with me for a day or two.

I pushed that though to the back of my mind. This night was way too important. I wasn't going to jeopardize it.

Someone cleared his throat behind me. I jumped up from the couch and Do-hyun's arms immediately.

The said someone turned out to be Chris, smiling at us somehow mischievously, as if he was up to something. I narrowed my eyes at him, trying to figure it out.

"Let's go?" he asked, his eyebrows raised.

Both Do-hyun and I nodded back at him, realizing we were too busy to question him. In fact, we had to run to make it before the video ended. When we reached Joonie and Tae, they both eyed us with worry at first, but as Chris shook his head, they relaxed and smiled. It was almost like they were having an inaudible conversation. It freaked me out a bit, to be honest. Nevertheless, we passed them all and took our spots in the middle of the stage.

The video ended right then, the spotlight lit up and Tae started to speak.

"Crew, are you enjoying tonight?!" he boomed into the microphone, and we watched the enormous stadium light up with endless amounts of glow sticks being lit up at once, in addition to cell phones and flashlights. The audience even started to chant our names again.

I was actually taken aback, practically forgetting the incident with Do backstage. In fact, we all got a bit emotional at the sight of it. The fans were obviously very important to us—without them, we couldn't do this. Without them, we were nothing. Without them, we couldn't make music, and even earn something from it. Without them, we wouldn't be able to do something we all loved doing as a profession.

Seeing and hearing that we mattered to them too was a feeling I couldn't describe. Even Tae, who was the most unaffected of us all, had to compose himself a bit before continuing.

"Look, I know it has been a while..." he started, and the crowd went silent at once. Seriously, you could probably hear a pin drop. They were all that eager to hear what we had to say.

"I believe I can speak with all of our voices combined when I give you a big, enormous, gigantic thank you for sticking with us, despite our agonizingly long break."

Do-hyun got himself composed and continued where Tae left off. "I know we have some explaining to do..." The audience went wild again, not agreeing with him, but silenced again when he continued. "Well, we didn't exactly go on a vacation, but I can honestly say we all missed you."

Tears burned behind my eyes when it was my turn to speak. I had the hardest part, as if tonight wasn't hard enough already... Unconsciously I took Do's hand in mine; guess I just needed him to get through this. He didn't mind though, he just squeezed my hand reassuringly, and I finally got myself pulled together.

"Truth be told, this night was so close to never happening..." I started, referring to our short discussions about disbanding after the army. "Because we seriously considered if we would even make it again. But thankfully, our label supported us one hundred percent, and we were given this amazing and enormous second chance."

Joonie continued. "We just want to apologize for being away for far too long. I hope you will all forgive us..." he said and nearly broke down when he ended his part.

"But we're back now, and we're going to make it bigger than ever. And WE LOVE YOU, CREW!" Chris ended and we all crossed our thumb and index fingers to make a heart sign and had a short moment of silence. Listening to our fans cheer like there was no tomorrow was enough noise already.

In that precious moment, we all believed we could actually pull the whole comeback thing off. I wished it would continue forever.

Party, Anyone?

I can't remember much of the rest of the concert. I guess I did wade through the thing somehow, but my mind was definitely somewhere else. Mostly it lingered on the moment I shared with Do-hyun during the surprise performance of "Antithesis." Then the moment we shared backstage. And the speech.

The adrenaline rush kept us all going for a long while after the encore. Way too hyperactive, we all bounced around backstage—you know, opening a bottle or two of champagne with Jiwoo, thanking the staff, hugging everyone... It was a whole mess, to be honest.

I was the first one out of us five that collapsed. I knew it was happening sooner rather than later, which was why I was already heading towards our personal backstage room when my legs almost failed me. My intention was to lean against the wall for a brief moment before continuing my trek towards our break room, but a still way-too-energetic Do-hyun appeared in front of me.

"Tired?" he asked.

"Yeah," I replied, almost unable to keep my eyes open. "Just give me a minute."

Do-hyun smiled and turned around before crouching. "Come on, I'll give you a ride."

"A piggy-back ride?" I asked, my eyebrows shooting up. "We're not ten."

"Oh, come on, you're tired, and I can get you to a couch much faster this way."

What a tempting offer. But I knew it would get me into trouble once Do-hyun snapped out of his stage character. Being too close to him when he would eventually snap was dangerous business.

"I don't kno–" I started, but an unknown force hit me to the back, cutting me off. I collapsed, colliding with Do-hyun's back.

All air left my lungs upon the impact. And I was too tired to move, though Do-hyun's close proximity made my heart do some more of those weird flips. After the stars which had momentarily taken over my vision subsided, I noticed a laughing maknae running away from us.

"You evil little shit–" I hissed, pissed off. Clearly, he had pushed me.

"You're welcome!" Chris hollered, before disappearing around the corner.

I cursed under my breath yet Do-hyun only laughed.

"Hold on tight," he said.

Then he grabbed my legs and pushed us both up. Sure, I would most definitely fall, I couldn't help but take a sharp breath and wrap my arms around his shoulders. "Aish, are you sure about this?!"

Do-hyun staggered a couple of steps forward, laughing, before regaining his balance. My heart was beating crazy fast and my head felt light, but right then I wasn't sure if it was because of Do-hyun or the fact that I was still sure we would collapse and meet the hard floor sooner rather than later. Either way, I couldn't do much else than hold on with my dear life.

"Well, you are a little heavier than on stage, I think," Do-hyun muttered under his ragged breath.

I hit his head, but instantly regretted it as Do staggered a little towards the left wall upon losing his balance again. I tightened my hold even more to not fall. "Then let me down."

"I'm kidding," he said between his laughing fits, before tightening his hold on me. "And nope, we're doing this."

"Hmph," I muttered, but didn't dare to protest anymore.

Instead, I settled for trying to hold on until we'd reach our private backstage room. It was right around the corner, yet it felt like it was kilometers away. Not that I didn't exactly want to be this close to Do, but I must admit…feeling his every back muscle flex and relax upon every step and feeling his hands on the backs of my thighs was driving me absolutely nuts. Not to even mention the stunning, sweaty, after-gig scent of his that mixed with mine. It probably should've made me feel disgusted, yet I found it absolutely perfect.

I leaned my chin against his shoulder, too tired to resist the urge. It was hard to even start bracing myself for the looming, famous snap of Do's that was going to happen any minute now. I wished he was always that nice to me.

Eventually we staggered through the door to our break room. Do-hyun carried me straight to the nearest couch and laid me on it carefully, as if I was somehow fragile. A bit reluctantly, I let go of him and slumped further down on the soft couch.

"Thanks."

"No problem," he replied, crashing down right beside me. "I don't remember going live being this exhausting. I'm beat to death."

Yawning, I mumbled, "Yeah, me too."

In fact, I could've killed for a little shut-eye while waiting for the others to drop, so I tried to move to the other ends of the couch in order to lie down. Do-hyun didn't let me go, though.

"And where do you think you're going?" he asked, grabbing my waist, and pulling me back to his side.

"Hyung," I whined. "Just let me close my eyes for a second, please."

"You can do it right here," he said with the softest tone ever and pulled me further down against him so I basically ended up lying on his lap. I would've protested, knowing he could flip any second now, but it was too damn comfortable.

I couldn't move a muscle. My eyes fluttered shut even though I tried to resist the drowsiness. Everything around us was still in full-chaos mode; the staff still ran around, as well as the rest of

GRiD, but I was in my own peaceful little bubble with Do-hyun. I barely paid any attention to our surroundings.

In a short while, I felt Do-hyun's hand running through my tangled hair, sending all kinds of shivers and tingles down my spine whenever even a square millimeter of his skin touched my scalp. It was like torture, but the kind I could've gotten used to.

"How can your hair be so soft and shaggy at the same time?" he wondered so quietly I wasn't sure if I was supposed to even hear it.

I replied anyway. "It's been bleached a lot lately," I said, forcing my eyes to open, at least halfway.

Instantly, I met Do-hyun's gaze as he looked down on me with an unreadable yet somehow so soft expression. The slightest smile played on his lips as he continued brushing through my hair with his fingers, his eyes studying my face as if he had never seen it before. It was like my heart stopped beating altogether, yet the blood in my veins was rushing so fast it made me light-headed.

The door banged open hard enough to hit the wall, and both of us twitched a bit, startled.

It was Tae, standing in the doorway. Not batting an eye on us, he crashed to the armchair next to our couch. "Fuck, I'm tired."

Just when I was planning on closing my eyes again, Joonie collapsed on the couch opposite us. Even Chris lost his stamina eventually and landed next to Joonie. Not one of them seemed to notice Do and me. I wondered why. It wasn't like we hung around this close to each other after concerts. For my own mental health, I used to avoid him at all costs in these moments.

For what must've been at least ten minutes, we all were just there, looking in the distance while trying to stay alive. We caught our breaths while marveling at the fact that we had, in fact, pulled the concert off. Apart from going a little off script by Do-hyun hijacking my time with the Crew and his meltdown after "Contrast," there hadn't been many, if any, mishaps.

Then Jiwoo dashed through the door, her eyes blazing fire as she held out a champagne bottle.

"Party, anyone?" she asked, already opening the bottle. When no-one moved a centimeter, let alone replied, she added with a defeated face, "No? You all know everyone's waiting for you to show up to the after party, as well."

Ugh. All I wanted was to shower and sleep. In fact, I had forgotten all about the after party at our label's headquarters.

Tae sighed. "Jiwoo's right," he started. "We should at least show our faces. Let's clean up and go."

None of us felt like partying all the way to the small hours, oddly enough. But we did stay for a while to not seem rude. Tae even gave a small speech, thanking the staff for making our concert a success. Soon enough, we all excused ourselves and headed back home.

On the way, I let my mind wander while looking out the heavily tinted window of our SUV.

Waiting for Do-hyun to snap and give me the usual cold-shoulder that had always followed a live concert through the whole thing had been exhausting…but it never happened, much to my surprise. And much to everyone else's surprise, as well—I caught Tae, Joonie, Chris, and even Jiwoo all side-eyeing us a couple of times during the party.

"What are you thinking about so hard?" Do-hyun asked, snapping me out of my thoughts and back to reality. "The frown lines on your forehead are gonna become permanent at this rate."

"Nothing, I'm just tired."

"Then sleep," he said, circling his hand behind my back before pulling me closer. "I'll wake you up when we're at home."

Screw it. Screw it all, I thought, as I let my head drop on his shoulder. If he was going to be this sweet to me, then fine, I was better off enjoying it while it lasted. Besides, who was I even kidding, thinking I could ever resist?

I guess I did drift off momentarily, as we reached home in such a short time it felt like a second, tops. Do-hyun shook my shoulder lightly when the car stopped.

"I'm already awake," I said, reluctantly straightening myself, already missing the warmth of Do-hyun's body as we separated. I even shivered. It was so cold. Or maybe I was just tired. Either way, I stretched and hopped off the car.

We all crammed on the same lift, none of us wanting to stay behind. The ride was a living hell for me though, as I was pinned between the back wall and Do-hyun. As if today hadn't been too much already.

Once the lift stopped, we all scurried off to our own rooms. Just as I was opening my door, Do-hyun grabbed my wrist to stop me.

"Min…" he started, his eyes trained to the floor.

I blinked and wondered what he could possibly have in mind. His expression was unusually nervous. Unconfident. He even fiddled with his hands.

I broke the silence. "What?"

"Umm, nevermind," he said and dashed to his room so fast I was left frozen on my threshold, my jaw hanging slightly open.

What on earth was that? I shook my head to clear it up and opened my door. I seriously needed a shower.

I took a longer, more thorough rinse, compared to the little freshening I had done at the arena after the concert. I turned the water temperature to scorching hot and let it ease up the muscles on my back.

Once I was in my black satin pajamas—my favorites—I walked back to the main room and crashed on the bed. I preferred to sleep naked, to be honest, but when you're not living alone, you just had to be considerate towards others. Yes, I could have locked the door, but I didn't. Mostly because I never woke up to my alarms, if I got any sleep in the first place.

At that point I was so tired, I contemplated if I could've lived without my phone until the morning. But then again, I wondered if the fans had noticed the smaller things…the bracelet, the earrings. How did they take the whole comeback? Did they have fun? What did they think of Contrast? Antithesis? Surely it would've been nostalgic. I needed to check Twitter.

Instead, I was planning on hunting Joonie and the phone-stash down when I opened my door.

Surprisingly enough, Joonie was already there right behind my door, having his fist up as if he was about to knock. I guess he was exhausted as well, as he merely dropped his hand without even flinching.

"Good, you're up. Here," he said, handing me mine as well as Do's phones. "Give it to him, will you?" he asked, yawning all the while.

I nodded, and Joonie strutted off to the other side of the hallway and straight into his room. I couldn't blame him for leaving this up to me, since no-one knew what mood Do would be in now that he had been alone for some time. I went directly to Do's door—better get this over and done with sooner rather than later.

Wrong Bed

My usual style with Do was to barge in at any given moment, but this time I hesitated at the door. I mean, he might've been changing, or showering, or something. Or maybe I was stalling. Huffing out another breath and gathering my willpower, I knocked on the door.

I was immediately answered by a muted, "Come in."

As I had no idea of Do's mood anymore, I turned the handle carefully and walked in slowly. Back in the day, he had always been a mess after going live. It was basically one of two options: either he would keep his distance or he would be extremely cold towards me. I truly hoped it wasn't the last option since he had been surprisingly nice today.

He was sat on the edge of his carefully made bed in his pajamas, toying with one of his rings again. I didn't really understand his obsession about his rings, but I wasn't going to tease him about it now. It wasn't worth the risk. I had already gotten this far without having to deal with his temper tantrums.

"Here, your phone," I said, handing over said device.

I was ready to flee if he showed any signs of snapping. Trust me—I had learned to see them ahead of time over the years. But he was as calm as ever. He merely took his phone off my hands and continued staring ahead into the distance.

I nervously ran my hand through my ashen hair, not knowing what else to say. Eventually, I mumbled a good night, turned around, and headed towards the door.

"I'm sorry," Do-hyun said out of the blue, making me stop on my tracks before I could take a step.

I frowned. "For what?"

"I don't know. Everything." He let out a frustrated sigh. "Lashing out after 'Contrast' today, for example. You didn't deserve that and…maybe Tae didn't deserve that either."

Well, that was surprising. "It's okay, I just don't understand you sometimes. You know it's only fanservice."

I was way too tired to deal with this now. Yet, I was curious. Why was Do being so nice?

"Well, yeah, but I'm so used to it being just us…I don't know. Forget I said anything."

I nodded, taking a second attempt at leaving. I didn't get very far though, as Do grabbed the sleeve of my pajama shirt.

"Stay," he said, so quietly I nearly didn't catch it.

I froze and studied his face for a long time, looking for signs of…well, anything that wasn't supposed to be there. Anger, humor, whatnot. There wasn't anything; he wouldn't take his eye off the floor, much like when he had stopped me at my threshold earlier. It also looked like he really meant it.

And that right there weirded me even more out. Sure, we had slept together a couple of times in the past, but that had been when touring or traveling with the group. Especially when we had been only starting out and didn't have the resources for extravagant hotel rooms for all of us separately. Never, ever had he asked me to stay with him like this. I was basically tearing in two—one half of me just wanted to take advantage of the situation, all the while knowing I would get my heart broken into tiny pieces all over again. Then there was the other part of me, who wanted to leave as soon as possible to protect whatever was left of my heart.

What became my ultimate downfall was Do-hyun looking me straight in the eyes with his incredibly beautiful and sexy, dark brown ones, pleading to me. Needless to say, I picked the first option and let him pull me in his arms. We hugged like that for a moment before he tucked me gently under the blankets and followed right after.

My heart bounced like crazy and blood rushed to my face, making me blush. Thus the relief was quite extreme when he turned the lights off right away. No need to show him how much this whole thing affected me.

I couldn't face him, so I rolled around, facing the opposite way, and tucked my phone under the pillow. Do wasn't affected in the slightest, he just casually snuggled right beside me, wrapped his arm around my waist, and pressed his warm body against my back.

I stiffened. I mean, Do-hyun had this habit of hugging practically anything whenever he slept—but he wasn't asleep yet. I swear my heart was about to hammer its way out of my chest at this rate. This man was going to be the death of me. He was so unpredictable he was giving me whiplashes left and right—it couldn't have been very healthy.

Do-hyun must've noticed my sudden stiffness.

"Is this okay?" he asked softly while his breath tingled on my neck, making me shiver uncontrollably.

I couldn't do much else than nod silently, as my brain basically shut itself off. Actually, this whole thing was pretty much not okay for my mental or emotional health, but at that moment I couldn't remember how to say no. I was sure I wouldn't be able to sleep one blink. Shockingly though, Do-hyun's steady breathing and the warmness of his body pressed against my back made me drift off in no time.

When I did wake up in the middle of the night—as predicted— it took me a while to realize that I wasn't in my room or in my own bed. But when it did hit me, it hit like a crashing wave. I damn near started hyperventilating. Or I would've, if I wasn't still too tired for any physical activity whatsoever.

Plus, it was getting pretty warm, with Do-hyun still pressed against my back. I tried to close my eyes and have some more sleep, regardless of my sudden awareness of him behind me— wrapped around me, actually, as he also had one of his legs on top of mine. I could feel the tickle of his breath on my neck, his hand laid casually on my waist, his chest pressed against my back… Soon enough, I was losing my mind on top of the almost hyperventilating.

I tried to take some distance which only made it worse. Because when I so much as stirred, Do-hyun only tightened his hold on me, mumbling something incoherent in his deep slumber. What was even more disturbing about Do-hyun pulling me even closer, was that I suddenly felt something…rather hard…pressing against my behind.

A boner.

It was one of the most natural things to happen while one slept, yet feeling it grow and harden against my butt was driving me mad in no time.

Never in my life had I blushed that deep or as fast as I did right then. My imagination started running wild, my brain mustering up scenes that would most certainly never happen in real life. And Do-hyun would most likely kill me if he'd ever find out what I was thinking about at that exact moment.

Hint—everything was X-rated.

Still, I couldn't stop the thoughts once they appeared in my brain, as vivid as if it was really happening. I imagined he would wake up horny, then slip his hand under my shirt, still half-asleep. I imagined turning around to question him, but he would silence me with his hungry lips on mine.

But when I started imagining what his skin would feel like under my fingertips if I ran my hand over his chiseled tummy and broad muscular chest, I realized I should flee. As fast as possible. Before I accidentally did something really, really stupid. Something that I wouldn't be able to take back in a million years. Like wake Do-hyun up and kiss him.

My heart trembled, pounding a million beats per minute. I carefully slid off the bed, afraid I would wake Do-hyun up and have to explain where I was going and why I was sporting a massive tent in my pants. Thankfully he was fast asleep, and only turned around to hug his comforter instead of me. Good.

After fishing my phone from under the pillow, I proceeded to tiptoe as fast as I possibly could out of Do's room. Then, I nearly ran inside my own room once I was in the clear. Tossing my phone to my nightstand, I slid under my blanket and pulled it all the way up, over my head and all.

I was afraid to think.

But thoughts are impossible to control. It almost felt like I was violating Do-hyun's privacy somehow, but I absolutely couldn't help but imagine I was still in his bed…his boner pressing against my behind…his warm breath tickling my neck…his hand on my waist, then the same hand slipping under my shirt…his voice, coarse and low, murmuring my name in my ear…

I could almost feel his touch leaving a burning trail on my skin when I ran my own hand across my chest, then my stomach… I almost couldn't muffle the moan that escaped my lips as I imagined his on my skin, his tongue flicking on the most delicate spot at the base of my neck.

I bit the back of my hand as my hand went further down south on its own—I had lost the control ages ago. For a while, I fondled the length of my member from the top of my pants while my other hand was still busy playing Do's part on my abdomen. Of course, that wasn't even nearly enough for my greedy, horny mind, so my hand found its way under the pants soon enough. My brain, my imagination pulled even more lewd images out of thin air and displayed them without any mercy for my wildly beating heart, which was already having a hard time keeping up.

It didn't take my body long at all to start building up pressure in the pit of my stomach. It took me even less time to release said built up pressure. Toes curling, every muscle in my legs tensed, I reached the peak. Muffling a wild, loud, and desperate cry against my pillow, my whole body twitched and turned uncontrollably at the same time the warm seed poured into my hand.

For a moment, I lay there, my whole body as relaxed as it could ever be. On cloud nine, drunk on endorphins and exhausted, I was finally freed from all possible thoughts.

Then the regret hit me.

What the hell I was thinking? Had I just seriously masturbated at the mere thought of Do-hyun? Inflicted by a very natural night wood he had had in his sleep?

Gross. I felt so damn gross. I was repulsed by my own thoughts and more ashamed than I had ever been before. Not that I hadn't…err…played with myself before while thinking about Do-hyun, but this time it felt as if I had done something wrong and forbidden. Yet I couldn't exactly deny it—my release on my hand, turning sticky, was a fairly good reminder.

I groaned under my breath and scrambled out of bed, heading straight to my bathroom. Grateful that we had a housekeeper, I tossed the stained pajamas and underwear into the laundry bin before hopping to the shower for the second time for the night, glad our rooms were fairly well soundproofed so I wouldn't wake up the others.

I turned the water to ice cold and let it beat my back for a good while. Then I stayed for a minute longer still, until my teeth clattered and my whole body shivered. Deciding I had punished myself enough, I wrapped myself in a warm, fluffy towel and dragged my exhausted body back to bed, hoping the comforter would swallow me whole, and I would disappear.

After all, it's impossible to control thoughts. Unfortunately.

Just the Two of Us

I wasn't able to sleep for a long time. Instead, I woke up a million times, tossed and turned so much my sheets wrinkled and started to press on my back. Still, I tried my hardest to fall back asleep, time and time again.

After not being very successful, I finally gave up and fished my phone from under the pillow; it was only 5:30 in the morning. Aish, these nights could go on forever.

I sighed and passed the time by browsing Twitter. Based on the tweets and trending list, our comeback had been more than successful. The trending list was basically just us with various hashtags.

Somehow #mint had made its way to the trending list too, which of course made me curious. Could that one tiny thing on stage really cause that much interest amongst our fans? I had to click it...and yes, it was pretty much just gifs, photos, and videos from last night. Again, I couldn't help but open one of the videos—which turned out to be a huge mistake.

A deep blush crept up on my cheeks when I tried to watch a very focused, high-quality video of me, Do, and Tae on stage, but it was just...too much. Do had a mischievous look on his face while his fingers brushed my thigh, heading up... And when Tae had lifted my shirt—well, let's just say he wasn't looking that innocent either.

And me...I looked, for lack of a better word, promiscuous. Somehow, my surprised look seemed to translate to a very lewd one on camera. The whole thing honestly made me wonder how I was even capable of looking like that in the first place. I couldn't take the embarrassment anymore—instead, I locked the screen, carried the phone to the furthest corner of my room, laid it on top of a drawer, and darted right back to bed.

My face hit the pillow, and I tried to sleep again. Despite how tired I was, after a while tossing and turning, still feeling uneasy while remembering the video from last night and my other not-so-innocent activities, I decided to get up and find out something else to keep my mind busy.

I grabbed some comfy stonewashed jeans from my closet and a plain white oversized t-shirt, put those on, and headed to the kitchen. The clock had finally dragged itself to the morning instead of night, and I was getting hungry.

As soon as I arrived in the kitchen, I noticed that Tae was up already. He was frying some eggs in the kitchen and asked if I wanted some. I nodded and went ahead to brew some coffee, wishing I wouldn't have converse before getting some caffeine in my system. It was sort of like our morning routine: Tae would make us all some breakfast and I would be in charge of the coffee making. When I didn't get too much sleep, that is.

Tae was always up early. Me, not that often. For me, it was either sleeping till noon if no one woke me up or not getting much sleep at all. I yawned when I finally got my cup of the life elixir called coffee in front of me and sat at the table.

"Morning, hyung."

"Couldn't sleep again?" Tae asked with a slight frown. He was always worried about everything and anything. Sometimes, it was a bit annoying. But honestly, the worst worrywart of us was Joonie, so it could've been worse.

I shrugged. "I did sleep some, but I woke up early."

Tae nodded. To my relief, it seemed like he was satisfied with my answer and didn't try to pry. We both proceeded to eat the breakfast in a comfortable silence. Tae never felt the need to fill the silence with nonsense blabbering and neither did I.

"So, what's happening today?" I asked Tae, with my belly now satisfyingly stuffed.

"Nothing much, we have a day off. Better enjoy it since it's the last one for a while," Tae answered, with a half-smile plastered on his face.

"Good, I was getting bored anyway," I said while smiling back at him. "I guess I'll head to the dance studio for the day then."

Honestly, I didn't take dancing as work, even though it was part of it. I just loved it so much that I spent most of my free time doing it. Or planning choreographs. Or watching other dancers on YouTube for inspiration. Or maybe I was really a workaholic, like Joonie and Chris seemed to think.

"Not so fast," Tae said, cutting my escape short. "Jiwoo texted and asked if we could do a short vlive. You up for it?"

"Yeah, whatever. But why?" I replied, raising my eyebrows. Wasn't this supposed to be a day off?

"You know, just to thank the fans for supporting us even after the long break..." he said, trailing off.

"Okay, I'll go wake up the others."

"Well, um...it can be just the two of us."

Tae messed nervously with his hair and dragged me towards the couch. My eyebrows knitted together, but sat next to Tae nevertheless.

As it turned out, Tae had already set up everything. As soon as I got myself comfortable, he started the vlive with his tablet propped up on a tripod in front of us. At first, we chatted about various topics and when the questions started to roll in we tried to answer as many as we could. Soon, there were too many to keep up with, so I leaned closer to try to read the comments and questions.

Apparently, I annoyed Tae by shifting around too much. He casually pulled me on his lap and continued talking like he didn't do anything weird. I was confused for a short moment but decided to go with it—at least now I could see better. It seemed like the fans were excited already to see us this close anyway. The hearts and kissing emojis kept flowing in.

I almost missed Do-hyun walking in on us, rubbing his eyes sleepily.

"Do-hyun! Come say hi to the Crew, we're having a vlive," I said, waving at him, suddenly energetic. High from last night or something.

I couldn't help but get excited that he was finally awake.

I realized my enthusiasm of seeing him was a mistake, as I noticed something cold flashing in his eyes as he saw us. It was too late to take it back though, and Do-hyun joined us on the couch, only narrowing his eyes once when he met my gaze. Shit. He was clearly pissed about something. Maybe it was the famous after-concert snap, only delayed? I didn't exactly want to find out.

He gathered himself pretty quickly and was soon chatting with the fans as nicely as me and Tae had been. But he sat oddly far away from us, all the way on the other end of the couch, barely even fitting on the screen.

I decided to shrug the weird feeling off and continue to focus on our fans. Besides, they were a way better company than a sulking Do-hyun anyway.

Eventually, Tae ended the vlive, promising that we were really back now, so our followers could expect to see more live broadcasts in the future. Once I was positive the streaming was totally off, I turned to face Do-hyun, somehow wary of what expression I would find from his face.

It was a slightly sour one, and he didn't say a word when he hopped up and walked briskly back to his room and slammed the door shut so loud the bang echoed around our dorm for quite a while. Tae sighed and gestured for me to follow Do, so I did.

The whole thing worried me since I could already see that Do was in a foul mood for some reason. I didn't care to knock or anything, I just dashed right through his door and further inside his room. Do had his back towards the door, and I was met with a pretty hostile attitude right off the bat.

"Get lost," was his greeting for me.

I sighed and tried to see his face, but he avoided me altogether, spinning to the other direction every time, or just evaded my eyes. After a while of that, I finally gave up on trying to figure things out by myself and opened my mouth.

"What's with you now?" I asked. "I mean, I'm getting pretty tired of these sudden mood shifts. Just yesterday you snuggled with me on your damn bed"—*having a boner I might add*—"and now you're pissed at me?!"

"Nothing."

"Oh, really," I said, sarcasm dripping from my voice.

It clearly pissed him off, and he finally turned around to face me. "Well, what's up with you and Tae then?!"

Now that took me by a surprise. It didn't make any sense. What did Tae have to do with any of this? My brain hurt from even trying to figure it out.

"Tae?" I asked, frowning.

"Yes, Tae! Seemed pretty close just now on the cou—" he started but changed his mind in the middle of the sentence and stared me right in the eyes, anger searing through his irises, but something else was there too. Something cold. Something I couldn't quite place.

He continued. "You know what? I don't even care. Just go play with your new toy... You're always in the way anyways, and it's getting annoying. Leave me the hell alone!"

Although the words sunk in with a delay, they effectively left me speechless and breathless. They were like daggers of pure ice, stabbed through my heart. They left me frozen solid. All I wanted was to dart away right away, but Do's death stare kept my feet glued tightly to the floor.

This was it, the snap I had been waiting for.

If I knew it was coming, why was it so incredibly hard to even breathe, let alone move? Maybe it was the delay, last night, or the fact that I hadn't been used to this, after being away for so long. But the whole thing hit me harder than ever before. My heart crunched in my chest so painfully I was about to faint. A lone, warm tear rolled down my cheek. I couldn't stop it. I couldn't keep it in like I normally did. And there were more of them burning right behind my eyelids. A lot more.

Do-hyun spotted the escaped tear, too, as his eyes lingered in that direction and his features softened, jaw became unclenched. He even touched my arm and took a step closer, but his touch was like an electric shock; I flinched away. That also finally made me wake up from the trance and realize I could, after all, move.

I darted right out of his bedroom, dashed into my own room, slammed the door shut, and locked it before completely falling apart. The silent tears soaked up my face as I leaned against the door and rested the back of my head on the cold surface.

Do-hyun was right behind me, apologizing through the door. My knees gave out when I heard his now softer voice, and I sunk to the floor. Hugging my knees, I tried to tune him out. I wasn't very successful though—I could still hear his apologies a tad too clearly. But I didn't want him to see me like this.

Vaguely, I heard someone else walk beside Do in front of my room's door.

"Were you an idiot again, Do?" Joonie asked with a disapproving tone.

I didn't hear Do reply to him, but apparently, he gestured something to Joonie, since he just sighed before speaking again.

"Give him time, he'll come around. He always does," Joonie said, but oh, how I wished he wasn't telling the truth. "Although, I can't understand why, because you're always a complete ass towards him," Joonie added before I heard his steps receding.

Do knocked on the door one more time.

"I'm sorry," he said once more, before I heard his steps fading into the distance, as well.

I sat right there on the floor, hugging my knees for a long while. An hour, maybe even two, passed before I finally collected myself, cursing my sensitivity to this stuff to hell.

It wasn't like Do hadn't been a douche before, and I seriously thought that I had gotten used to it by now. I guess I hadn't, especially after the whole army thing.

Either way, what a shitty way to start a rare day off. Rinsing my face with cold water, I tried desperately to get rid of the evidence that I had just basically bawled my eyes out. Unfortunately, it didn't erase all the puffiness in my eyes, so I made a mental note to try to avoid Chris and his obsession with sneakily taking videos and photos of us and tossing them all online.

I changed into some sweatpants and a grey oversized t-shirt before heading to the dance studio. On the way, I stopped in front of Do's door and pondered for a moment if I should go in or not. Ultimately, I skipped it and walked straight to the studio down-stairs. If Do still wanted to make up, he could as well find me himself.

The studio was my happy place. Nothing cheered me up like good music and some dancing. This time, I switched all the lights on, closed the door, and walked straight over to the PA system. I already started to relax when the first beats of my playlist, con-sisting of random danceable songs, filled the room.

After an hour or so, I had worked myself out to the point of exhaustion. I lay on the floor, in the middle of the room, staring at the ceiling and listening to more music. I loved the feeling of the bass vibrating through my body, erasing all stiffness on its way to the core of my existence.

The door opened, startling me a bit. It was Do-hyun, looking quite guilty, I might add. Still, I was a little wary as I sat up and crossed my legs. He approached me silently I didn't quite know what else to do or say other than wave hello. He did end up right in front of me and sat down, flashing me an uneasy smile. I'm sure the smile I showed him back was just as uneasy.

Do-hyun scratched the back of his head. "Err, look…" he started. "I'm sorry, okay? I guess seeing you and Tae so close all of a sudden took me by a surprise."

I sighed. "Hyung, you of all people should know that it's just fanservice. It almost seems like you're actually jealous. Which is obviously good for work, but..."

He evaded my eyes and muttered something I couldn't quite catch.

"What?"

"Nothing. Can't we just forget the whole thing? I promise I'll behave."

I had a hard time not to sigh again. "I've heard that before. Seriously, these weird mood shifts of yours are giving me a whiplash."

"I know and it wasn't supposed to happen this time. I—I tried. I'm sorry. I'm really, really sorry."

"It's okay," I said, punching his shoulder lightly. "Just try a little harder next time, eh?"

Do-hyun smiled, this time genuinely. "So, are we good?"

"Yeah, we're good."

Was there even another choice?

Mad Love

Everything went back to normal after that. We hung around the dance studio, rehearsed some of our choreographies whenever one of our songs blasted from the speakers, and talked. The topics varied from music to our comeback concert, what shows we were supposed to visit in the next few weeks to promote our comeback, and the soon-to-be finished new album. The only matters we both avoided were fanservice…and especially Tae.

Do's mom, Sun-hee, called at one point and they spoke on the phone while I scribbled down some notes about choreography for the newer songs we hadn't had the chance to perform live yet. I felt a faint stab of jealousy like I always did when she called, but it wore off when she wanted to talk with me, too. I didn't know my own parents; I had been abandoned when I was a baby and spent my whole childhood at different foster homes. Somehow, though, Do's family had taken me in as their own after I joined GRiD, so it wasn't that bad I guess.

I smiled warmly when Sun-hee asked me about our comeback concert. She was sorry that she hadn't had the chance to come watch it live—though I didn't mind one bit, since I've always been a bit shy about the whole fanservice thing around her. Even if I was positive she was okay with it, since she never mentioned it. I ended the call in a much brighter mood and Do and I went back to whatever we were doing before.

Maybe it wasn't good for us to be working on our day off. But we didn't really get into it, so for us, it didn't count. When we were seriously working, we would be at the recording studio, or on our way somewhere to promote or something. For us, just dancing and talking were considered free-time activities. To be honest, most of our teenage and adult lives had consisted of only music, so we practically didn't know what else to do or discuss. Well, excluding the time spent in the army of course, but not one of us liked to talk about that.

By the evening, we ended up lying on the couch, my head resting on Do's lap much like we had after the concert. I had no clue how, but it wasn't like I was about to complain. I mean, Do-hyun was being nice again, which was all that really mattered.

The guide track for my next solo song—which was supposed to be published with the upcoming album—began to play through the speakers. The melody my heartstrings, moody yet still beautiful. I loved it. That melody was played by Do-hyun on piano since as a rapper he didn't really care that much about singing. He composed the song himself, but I was supposed to come up with the lyrics.

The only problem was that I had never been very good with lyrics.

"Have you figured out the lyrics yet?" Do asked, still stroking my hair gently. It was almost like he had read my mind.

I shook my head, a bit embarrassed. I knew they were waiting for me to complete this, since it was basically the only one still missing from the new album. Well, Joonie's solo was a work in progress as well, but at least it had lyrics already.

"It's okay. If you want, I can write them for you, as well," Do said, trying to reassure me.

"You could…but then it wouldn't feel like mine at all," I said. "I mean you already did everything else."

"True."

We became silent, running out of words. It was nice, although my heart started to have some silly ideas all over again. I tried my best to mute it. It didn't do any good to have any ideas about us romantically together, since obviously it wasn't going to happen. Ever.

"Wanna dance to it?" Do asked then.

We both got up.

Now, what I did have for this song was choreography—yes, I know, wrong order. And because Do and I were almost always together, he knew it too.

I started the guide track from the start, and we both started to move with the music. Do didn't really have a part in it, though, so he either mimicked me or freestyled through.

I let the song wash over me and immerse me. It was a good track. Why I hadn't I been able to come up with the lyrics yet? At this rate, the beautiful motif would go to waste.

While lost in thought, Do had made his way much, much closer. I took a few steps away, trying to get some distance between us, but he moved with me like there was a magnet between us, pulling us together. Soon enough, he had pinned me against the brick wall with haze-filled eyes and leaned closer.

I gulped and closed my eyes—he was just way too close all over again. He even ran his fingertips from my wrist all the way to my elbow and back. The touch felt like it was burning my skin. With his other hand, he grabbed my neck, and then I couldn't move even if I wanted to. I opened my eyes, meeting his hungry gaze— it made me bite my lip before parting them. Do let out a deep sigh before leaning closer…and closer, until our lips were barely a centimeter apart.

Just then, the song ended, thank all that's good in the world. It woke us both up. Do practically jumped away from me and snapped his gaze away from mine. I shivered at the loss of his body heat.

"I-... I need some, err, distance. Sorry," he said, and hastily darted off.

Just like that, I was left alone in the room with weak knees and a spinning head. I crashed to the couch and rubbed my temples, trying to make my head stop spinning before I would throw up.

What...just...happened?

It was almost...almost like Do was going to kiss me. No, I was about damn sure he was going to kiss me before he came back into his right mind. I touched my lips slightly with my index finger and let my mind dream for a moment. I even played the song again...and again.

Slowly, my mind started to form some lyrics to the guide track, and I quickly wrote them in my phone's notes. It was just some words and short sentences for now, but they seemed to fit the desperate and moody, yet still beautiful, tune.

I even started to hum the random words and thoughts to the melody of the chorus part...

I'm going mad...
It's not real...
Bittersweet...
Is this real?

I played with the order for a while before I was somewhat satisfied. The lyrics still weren't perfect, and I only had something for the chorus, but it was a start, at the very least. I smiled to myself and decided to forget the moment earlier with Do. After all, I wasn't even sure what had happened.

Maybe it was nothing.

Movie Night

By the end of next week, I came to the conclusion that for Do, our moment last Sunday at the dance studio definitely wasn't nothing. And how I knew that? Well, he avoided me like a plague for the whole week. Sure, we had been extremely busy, but normally he made time to tease me, at least. Or invading my privacy in my room.

He definitely hadn't been kidding when he said he wanted some distance from me. Damn, he didn't even make me dress him up anymore. I barely even saw him outside of work settings. There was no fanservice whatsoever during the countless interviews we attended that week, which sort of started freaking me out. In fact, I was certain he had *never* avoided me this long, even counting all his past snaps after live shows back in the day.

It was getting on my nerves. And I became seriously bored without the company of my best friend—which he still was, even considering I had developed feelings way past friendship level in my own heart.

Naturally, like the good little idol I was, I decided to fill my unwanted free time with a little solo vlive chat with my fans. I had the time. I was bored. I might've as well worked.

Soon, I had my tablet propped up on my nightstand as I leaned comfortably against the headboard of my bed. At first, I chatted about various work related things with the fans, but of course the Crew was always hungry for drama—they asked where Do-hyun was, since we usually streamed our vlives together. Obviously I tried to avoid the topic as much as I could, but when every other comment was about that, I couldn't avoid it for long or it would've seemed very rude.

And once I started, I ended up ranting about the whole Do-is-avoiding-me-like-the-plague thing in full.

"...so basically, I'm not sure what's happening here. Maybe he's just busy? I kinda miss him though. You know how to help me, right?" I ranted away to the front facing camera of my tablet.

The comments went so crazy, I really couldn't keep up anymore.

"Whoa, how sweet of you that you are all concerned. But I'm sure it's nothing, it's just some phase of his and we'll be back at it in no time," I said, paired with a wink towards the cam.

Smiling, I tried to read the comments for a while. It was interrupted soon enough, since there was a sudden flood of comments which were mostly just one hashtag: #savedomino. It piqued my interest, but then Tae decided to interrupt my vlive by dashing through the door and hopping on my bed beside me.

"What's up, Crew?" he asked.

I rolled my eyes at him.

"Go have your own vlive," I said, although jokingly. I was closing up anyway, so it didn't really matter.

"Nah, I'll just crash yours," he replied and relaxed, leaning against the headboard right next to me. He even grinned towards the front cam of my tablet.

Guessing I didn't really have a choice, I shrugged and we continued chatting away with the GRiD Crew for another short while. Soon enough, we said our goodbyes and ended the live broadcast with some promises to be back live soon. Tae left after it ended without much of a word, which seemed kind of odd to me. It reminded me of the weird hashtag which had been flooding at one point during my live stream…

After opening Twitter, I hastily typed in #savedomino. At first, it was just random photos from back in the day of me and Do with some disturbing captions, but one fairly recent photo caught my eye.

Oddly enough, it was taken from our comeback concert—even further, it was taken from the backstage room. Somehow, someone had managed to take a picture of me sitting on Do's lap on the couch. I shuddered—it was way too creepy for my liking.

It was posted by someone whose handle was @crewinsidr. I was just about to check out their profile when I was interrupted by a text. From Do-hyun. So, yeah, of course it distracted me.

So you and Tae are best friends now? the text said.

I hmphed. *Well, I guess I have no other choice as my original best friend has been avoiding me like I'm some contagious disease.*

Been missing me? ;) his next text said.

I couldn't help but grin widely when typing my response. *Well, a little. But I'm good now, seems like you're at least alive and kicking.*

It took about .2 seconds for him to reply. *Just been busy, you know how it is.*

Busy my ass. Still had time to watch my 24 min long live...

Just for like 4 seconds. Been working on your track... How's the lyrics?

Well, that hit me below the belt. *Only have some for the chorus.*

Then drag your ass down here and we'll work on it.

I sighed. Okay, I did miss Do, a lot. But that didn't mean I wanted to work on my solo. But I knew I had to, so I nevertheless crawled out of the bed, if not a bit reluctantly. With my notebook in tow, which held some scribbles for the lyrics I had worked on the past week, I made my way downstairs.

We had the smallest, tiny recording studio there, right next to the dancing studio. It wasn't anything like the one at our label's HQ, but it was good enough for testing things out and messing around. Apparently, it was Do's new favorite place; he had been hanging there all the time when he'd been avoiding me. Not that I'd stalked him or anything. It just seemed like a similar place for Do as the dancing studio was for me.

The recording studio door was slightly open, so I sneaked through as silently as I could. Do was focused hard on something on his laptop, so he didn't notice me at all. Good.

"Hyung, I'm here," I whispered in his ear, making him jump up from his chair.

"Min! Fuck, I was scared shitless..." he said and tried to grab my wrist.

I dodged his attack. Do-hyun didn't give up though, and soon enough I was pinned on his lap in his chair, not able to move at all despite my great efforts.

"Weren't we supposed to work on my song?" I deadpanned, making him forget his attempt at making me regret my sneakiness.

"Yeah! Now let me see the lyrics," he said, overly enthusiastic all of a sudden.

He still didn't let me go, though.

After a while of struggling, I gave up. Do just simply wrapped his arm around my waist when he was sure I wouldn't wiggle my way out of his grip. Ignoring my now racing heart, I decided to focus on the task at hand and handed him my phone where my notes for the chorus part were written. He took it and proceeded to read the lyrics on both my phone and the notebook a few times.

"It's actually not that bad...and goes with the mood of the track."

I nodded, not knowing what to say.

"You'll just have to think about what you want to say that fits the theme for the verses and the bridge, no need to overthink it," he continued, while still reviewing the words.

"Remember the melody?" he asked after a while.

"Of course," I shrugged.

"Wanna try to sing it on tape? You know, to see if it fits?"

Yeah, well basically anything to get me away from you, you're way too close, I thought. What I said out loud was, "Whatever."

Finally, Do-hyun let me go and led me to the smaller, heavily soundproofed room inside the small studio that was separated from the main room by a large window. I dragged the bar stool from the corner in front of the heavy-duty microphone and sat down. I didn't bother to open my voice—this was just about seeing how it could go.

Do had already made his way back to the other room and spoke to me through the speaker system.

"Starting…two bars prior chorus?" he asked.

I nodded, put on the headphones, gave him a thumbs up, and inhaled deep. The music started, but I missed the start of the chorus by a millisecond, so I gestured to Do-hyun to cut it. The music stopped, and I raised four fingers up to sign him that I wanted the music to start four bars prior chorus after all. He nodded and the music started again.

This time I was prepared.

I didn't really give it much thought, just sang, channeling the same feelings I had had while writing the lyrics last Sunday. Do-hyun had always told me to not hide anything while singing, so I held nothing back. It was by no means perfect, but I really enjoyed singing it in some weird, bittersweet way.

After I had sung the chorus once, I was anticipating that Do would cut it and given me some thoughts…but that never happened. Instead, the guide track kept playing the second verse, for which I had nothing. I stayed silent, trying to signal him that I was done, but Do didn't even seem to notice me. He stared ahead, deep in thought, and let the tape play. I was confused as hell but ended up singing the chorus again when the second verse ended. And then again right after it since it seemed to fit.

Eventually the music came to halt and Do-hyun emerged from the booth.

"It's good," he said and cleared his throat. Looking somewhat out of it, he headed straight to the keyboard and played a few notes.

Do couldn't sing for shit, even if his life depended on it, so he showed me how he wanted to change the melody by playing it. I nodded, he went back on the other side, and I tried to sing it like he had shown me. We continued that way for at least an hour, both focusing on work. It made things considerably easier for me since Do didn't tease me as much as he usually did.

At one point, we started to argue over the melody. Do didn't seem to hear the difference when I tried to sing it, so I dragged him to the keyboard and played it for him.

"See? It's not the same!" I fumed.

"Then how about changing to a higher key here?"

I rolled my eyes. "I'm not Joonie-hyung, I can't go that high."

Do leaned against my back, rested his chin on my shoulder, and put his hands on top of mine. I had a hard time focusing all of a sudden.

"Then, how about this way?" he asked, and played the tune by moving my fingers on the keys with his own warm hands.

I took in a sharp breath through my teeth. He was—once again—way too close to me, and I could feel my stomach clench. I had to turn my head away from him as the blood rushed to my face. He finally noticed how close he actually was and retreated, giving me room to breathe.

"Umm...so yeah. Maybe we should wrap it for today?" he asked while running his hand through his hair.

The gesture drew my gaze towards his hair, and I couldn't focus for shit on his words. Only then did I noticed that he had gotten a haircut while avoiding me, and the strongest urge to run my hand through it swallowed me whole. It was still longer on top and had that too sexy messiness going on, but the sides were shaved short.

My hand was already twitching, aching to touch him, when I realized I was staring. I nodded as a reply to Do's earlier question, and he walked over to the next room to save his work. I shook my head discreetly to try to clear it.

Whew, that had been close. I wasn't exactly thrilled to screw everything up now that it seemed like I had gotten my best friend back.

We headed upstairs together. As it turned out, the rest of the guys were watching TV. It was an action flick that seemed somewhat interesting, so we joined them. Even though we had this enormous couch in our living room, it was still a bit crowded when all of us used it at the same time. Do took up a lot of space, basically taking over the whole divan part of the couch. Needless to say, I had a hard time finding a comfortable position.

After a while, Do grew annoyed with my constant moving and basically dragged me to sit in between his legs and wrapped his hands around my waist. I struggled for a while, trying to escape, until Chris shot me an annoyed glance. I gave up and leaned my back against Do's warm body. He started to trace the skin on my arms with his fingertips, which made me oddly relax.

Eventually, my eyes started to droop. I fell asleep, right there in the warm embrace of Do.

Talking Pillow

"Wake up! We're gonna be late at this rate," someone, probably Chris, shouted. Straight in my ear.

Somehow, I was feeling quite cozy. And extremely sleepy. In fact, I couldn't bring myself to move at all. Besides, it was warm. My pillow was warm, my comforter was warm, the bed was warm… everything was warm. It was like I was wrapped in a heated blanket that was designed for me and me only.

The outside world was cold, and I didn't want to freeze. Besides, I had surely dreamed about something nice, and had Chris rudely interrupted my sweet dreams.

So, I went ahead and ignored him completely. However, my huge and warm pillow started to move on its own, making me frown. I still didn't want to wake up completely, so I shrugged the weird feeling off and moved to an even more comfortable position.

Then, my pillow started talking.

"Umm...Minjae? I think we need to get up. Like, seriously."

The thing sounded an awful lot like Do. At once, I came to the conclusion that I was having a very weird but pleasant dream. Curling into an even tighter ball against the soft and warm pillow, I squeezed my eyes shut even tighter than before. Now I most definitely didn't want to wake up.

"Do-hyun, you're not helping," Chris's sarcastic voice dripped through the dreamy haze to my consciousness.

My pillow sighed. "I guess there's no other choice then."

I still tried to ignore the rest of the world, but a very sharp pain on my earlobe made it impossible. Fluttering my eyes open in a flash, I finally woke up completely and hopped up.

"Ow! What the hell?!" I yelled, my head spinning from the sudden movement.

When my mind finally wrapped around reality, I noticed three things at once: One, my pillow was, in fact, Do. Two, judging by the huge smirk on Do's face, he had bitten my ear. Which, by the way, was still aching. Three, Chris was filming this whole thing with his phone.

Apparently, I had slept the whole night on the couch with Do. My head started to spin again—along with my poor heart picking up the pace. But just when I was starting to wonder which one of the two idiots I was going to murder first, Joonie started talking from across the room.

"You have exactly 21.5 minutes to get yourself ready to go. We have a photoshoot to attend to, remember?"

"Aish! Forgot it actually..." I said while darting towards my bedroom and, more importantly, my shower.

After fifteen minutes or so, I was positive that I had made a new record on getting myself ready to go. Granted, I didn't have to do anything for my face or hair since they were going to slap an enormous layer of make-up on me anyway and style my hair before the photoshoot. I only had to shower and brush my teeth super-fast and put on some random clothes.

Still, even after my extreme speed, Joonie was already ushering everyone out the door the instant I exited my room. I hadn't even had time for breakfast. Oh well. Maybe that'd actually be good for the photoshoot, since I wouldn't be bloated. And I didn't get to wallow in that thought for long, because we were rushed straight into the downstairs garage.

We took Tae's—or *our*, as he liked to say—plain SUV once again, since it didn't draw any unnecessary attention. I knew the reasons, but it didn't stop me wondering why the hell we had this much money if we still could only rarely use the more, um, *beautiful*, cars. Like Do's fiery red Porsche, which I'd had the pleasure to ride in like two whole times.

On the way to the studio, I finally had some time to try to wrap my head around the morning's events. I sneaked a glance towards Do, who looked like nothing out of the ordinary had happened. In fact, he was just casually staring out of the heavily tinted window of our SUV, sitting right next to me. For some reason, the fact that he didn't seem the slightest bit affected started to get on my nerves. Why was I the only one who always got caught up in the moments? Why was I the only one who got flustered?

I opened Twitter to get something else on my mind...only to bump right into Chris's video of us from this morning.

"Chris, you posted this on our Twitter page?!" I yelled from the back seat, making everyone jump.

"Of course. You were way too cute together to pass up the opportunity," he replied from the front seat like it wasn't a big deal.

"Let me see," Do asked.

Afraid he'd flip out again, I hesitated. What if the photoshoot would end up awkward? But in the end, I couldn't stop him from seeing it sooner or later, even if I wanted to, as it was, indeed, on our very public Twitter page. I reluctantly handed him the phone.

Preparing for the worst, I watched his reaction carefully. But Do surprised me yet again; he only grinned through the whole video. After it ended, he handed my phone back and leaned forward, closer to Chris.

"Good job, Chris! Now send it to me, too," he ordered to Chris with a smirk.

"Of course, hyung!" Chris sounded way too enthusiastic and somehow sarcastic at the same time.

"What? Who are you and where's Do?" I muttered, basically to myself. Though Do-hyun definitely heard it.

"I'm right here, babe," he replied, still grinning as if he had lost his mind once and for all.

I crossed my arms over my chest. What in the world was happening? It was almost as if Do-hyun didn't really mind the fanservice that much after all…rather, it looked a lot like all the lashing out on me had happened out of jealousy. Chris publishing the pic of us sleeping together on our couch online was clearly fanservice—yet Do-hyun didn't seem to mind at all.

And right then, in that car ride, he wasn't even in his stage character. Yet, he still wasn't thrown off by it.

For the remainder of the ride, I was thoroughly baffled by this new reaction. Meanwhile, Chris and Do continued babbling on and on about the video. Even Joonie joined the conversation happily, making me feel extremely outnumbered. Only Tae looked like he was slightly annoyed about the topic at hand...yet it was probably only out of sympathy towards me. He did know about my difficult situation after all.

To my relief, we soon arrived at the studio and I could focus on work.

"We're here," Tae announced from the driver's seat, and we all hopped out and headed inside before someone recognized us. Our security staff had followed us, but as it was fairly quiet. They didn't even bother to get out of their car.

Once safely inside, we were greeted by an army of stylists, make-up artists, the photographer, and his crew. It was a hassle for about an hour after that, but as soon as I saw the studio, I got chills..

The whole gigantic room had been turned into some kind of futuristic, enormous, black and white chessboard. Seriously, the king was taller than me. I was impressed, the setting fit so well with the theme of the album now titled "Contrast," after our very successful single. A brief flash of guilt also flowed through me because only mine and Joonie's solos were still missing. I shook the guilt off for now, though I did make a mental note to seriously try and finish mine soon.

My solo shoot was after Chris's, and it was over in a blink. It was good to know I still had the touch for it. To be honest, being a dancer helped, as it was also fairly easy for me to follow the photographer's instructions. After all, dancing was posing in its own way. Joonie was after me and handled it just as well. He was also done in no time.

The difficulties began when our rap-line, meaning Tae and Do, had to pose. And let me tell you, they hadn't improved at all since our last photoshoot. If possible, they were even worse than they had been before the army. Tae's shoot took forever because he clearly overdid his facial expressions; the photographer had to ask him to tone it down several times.

Do was the complete opposite of Tae: expressionless. He looked like he was made of plastic, unnatural and stiff. I snuck closer, worrying about the outcome. He noticed me and smiled genuinely for the first time, and the photographer finally got one good photo. Unfortunately for me, the photographer's assistant noticed our silent exchange and made me help them get through the shoot.

We ended up continuing straight away with the smaller unit photos, as the staff seemed to like the mood between Do and I for some reason. There was supposed to be a concept of me, Do, and Tae all together, but the photographer didn't like it, so it didn't happen. They had a brief—and somewhat heated—argument with Jiwoo about it, but she ultimately gave up. Apparently, she had finally met her match. Tae was paired with Joonie instead and Chris would join them. Which left only the two of us standing awkwardly in the middle of the giant chessboard.

The photographer decided that there were too many distractions and drove the others away, all the while muttering something about ruining the mood.

Apparently Do and I had absolutely no attention span whatsoever, because we started playing chess. It wasn't easy to move the giant pieces, but we managed. They were actually made of papier-mâché, although they looked like wood, making them lighter than they appeared. We had our fun for a while, and I didn't even notice that the photographer had started taking pictures again.

Even though I wasn't super good at the game, at least I was better than Do. I checkmated him, which naturally pissed him off to no end. He even ended up kicking his black king over. I laughed my lungs out at the sight. I swear sometimes he was so damn childish.

"Sore loser, I see," I said after calming down a bit, although I still chuckled under my breath.

A glint of mischief flashed in Do-hyun's eyes.

"Just stay still for a bit, and we'll see," he said and darted after me.

Laughing at full volume again, I ran around the board, hopping over the fallen pawns and pushing the larger pieces towards Do to distract him. He was way quicker than me though and had good reflexes, so he closed in on me rapidly.

As a last desperate attempt to get away, I made a full 180-degree turn and planned to make a surprise attack, but unfortunately I stumbled over a smaller pawn I hadn't seen.

"Watch out!" I heard Do yell, but it was too late.

I fell toward the floor with incredible speed.

With one swift movement, Do was right there and tried to catch me, but somehow I ended up pulling him to the floor with me. He did manage to slow us down a bit, so when I hit the floor, it didn't hurt as much as I had prepared for. The only problem was that he fell right on top of me, nearly knocking the breath out of my lungs.

"You alright?" he asked, propping himself up with his hands.

I could only manage a nod, as I was suddenly lost in his deep brown eyes. My heart thumped so loud; I was afraid he'd hear it. I was already preparing some explanations for that—adrenaline, shock, whatever... but I ended up not needing them since his eyes hazed up like they had the last time we were at the dance studio.

Lost in our world, I couldn't help but stare him in the eyes when he leaned closer to my face. I could already feel his breath on my face when I finally came to my senses and blinked. I gulped and turned my head to the side, preparing to push him off me…

The photographer had other ideas though.

"Don't move!" he ordered, suddenly right beside us and startling us out of the spell.

Do-hyun's eyes cleared up, yet he still didn't make a move to stand. At the same time, Tae darted inside the studio, but stopped on the edge of the board to stare at us, completely at a loss for words. I pushed Do off and sat up. My head spun, and I wasn't even sure if it was because of Do or the fact that I hit my head slightly.

Tae cleared his throat then. "Ahem...we still have other pics to take and you two have taken a while here," he started and grinned. "And I think...now I know why."

I shot the darkest glance I could possibly manage towards Tae, trying to silence him with my eyes before he exposed my feelings to Do. "It's nothing. You're seeing things."

"Oh, am I?" he asked with a mischievous smile.

"Shut up, both of you," Do said, pulling me up from the floor.

Well, if my earlier realization about Do-hyun being jealous over my stage persona was correct, I was in for another wild ride.

Maybe it was my turn to take some distance.

Escape Methods

After the incident at the photoshoot, I realized I needed some time off from it all. And by "all," I meant Do-hyun and everything related to fanservice. The way he seemed to be just *too close* all the time lately gave me headaches and made me imagine things I shouldn't imagine. It was honestly getting too much for me to handle.

In short, I was tired. Exhausted. Going insane.

Still, instead of facing my problems head-on, I ended up avoiding Do at all costs. Yes, I was a coward. No, Do didn't deserve this treatment. Yes, I was being extremely childish. Yes, I was doing the exact same thing he did to me last week. And most importantly—I couldn't care less anymore. I was done with the whole thing; being in love with Do, fanservice, his weird behavior, acting as if I was only his close friend and wanted nothing more while in reality, I wanted *way* more. Too much more.

To my ultimate relief, we were all extremely busy all the time for the next few days, making it somewhat easy to avoid him. Our days started before it was even humane to wake up, and we worked so late into the evening that we practically passed out as soon as we got back home. The short breaks we had in between, I spent with Tae. He understood me and kept me busy enough to not have time to spend with Do.

Today, however, was a bit different. We had been scheduled to work on our own projects for the day, which basically meant that I was supposed to be with Do at the studio. Yes, still working on my solo piece. Do had bombarded my phone with calls and texts the whole morning while chasing me around our dorm, but I just couldn't bring myself to answer him, let alone face him.

Seriously what the fuck is going on, Min? read another text.

Annoyed out of my mind, I stuffed my phone back in my pocket and walked across the hallway of our dorm to the door on the other side. Glancing around, hoping to not see Do-hyun, I raised my fist and knocked on Joonie's door.

He answered instantly, blinking, and looking a bit startled upon seeing me at his door.

"Minjae? Good, coincidentally I was just about to come get you."

Hmm. Last I recalled, there weren't anything scheduled for us. "Get me?"

"Yeah!" he exclaimed, his eyes lighting up with excitement. "There's this new Seoul-based designer brand offering us a collaboration opportunity for the tour outfits. Wanna come with me to visit them to see if we like their ideas?"

Typical Joonie. If I was somewhat following the trends, Joonie was a true fashion enthusiast. Still, this was a way better idea for avoiding Do-hyun—who wanted nothing to do with fashion whatsoever—than my idea of trying to force Joonie to work on some choreography with me. I didn't even have to think about it one second and only blinked before replying, "Sure."

"Great! Let's go." Joonie grabbed a jacket from the coat rack and pushed me towards the lift.

I took a quick look at my outfit: dress shoes, light grey ripped and stone washed skinny jeans paired with a white oversized t-shirt. Good enough. Except I was missing something important. "Wait, I need a jacket."

Joonie nodded and stopped at my door.

I dashed in, rummaging through my closet to find the one dark green faux-leather jacket I knew would go well with the outfit, grabbed some random silver bracelets, and dashed right back out while still tinkering them in place.

"What do you think?" I asked Joonie.

He barely even glanced at me.

"Good enough, let's go," he took my wrist and yanking me towards the lift again. "I'm so excited! I've seen some of their collections and they're so talented! The way they play with colors..."

I chuckled at Joonie's babbling, yet tuned out for the time being. I was just relieved to have something else to do other than work on my single with Do-hyun. Smiling to myself on the elevator while Joonie still blabbered on and on about the designer, I pulled out my phone and texted Do-hyun.

Sorry, the phone was on silent and something came up. I'm heading out with Joonie. TTYL?

The reply was instant. *Seriously?! We were supposed to work on your solo today!*

Yeah, I know. Maybe later.

I stuffed the phone back in my pocket, just before hopping into our SUV.

Joonie had stopped talking and was eyeing me weirdly when I sat down beside him in the middle row of seats in the back of the car.

"What?"

"I just remembered, weren't you supposed to work with Do-hyun today?" Joonie asked.

Oops. "Err...yeah, but it can wait until later."

Joonie squinted his eyes at me but let it drop. His regular guard, Mr. Choi, hopped on the driver's seat, and we were off.

We ended up spending a good two hours at the brand's showcase studio. I admit—all their ideas were great, in my opinion. And Joonie was even more impressed. We only needed the label's stylists' approval, but I doubted they would go against us.

It was a good escape from all my problems. A nice break. Especially from the one big problem named Do-hyun. Unfortunately, on the way back to our dorm, the dread of having to face him sooner or later started to creep up on me all over again.

Whether it was luck, fate, or a pure coincidence, my phone beeped just as Mr. Choi parked the SUV in our dorm's underground garage. It was the vlive app, notifying me that Chris had started a broadcast. A wide grin spread on my lips—I couldn't have figured a better escape myself. Crashing his vlive would be a perfect excuse.

Surprisingly enough, Chris even welcomed me with open arms, and we chatted with the fans for a good 45 minutes. What did flatten my mood a bit was that I noticed another #savedomino flood at the end of our stream. The photo posted by that @crewinsidr popped into my head at the sight of the hashtag.

A deep discomfort followed the memory, and I knew I had to mention the whole creepy ordeal to Chris—he was the biggest nerd amongst us after all. Thus, once he was finishing up and shutting down the live, I pulled up the account on my phone and handed it to him.

"So, have you seen this?" I asked.

"What about it?" Chris asked, raising his eyebrows while shrugging. "Looks like a normal fan account to me."

Was he serious? "Well yeah but look closely at the photos."

He scrunched his eyebrows together while scrolling yet didn't seem to get it. Something was off, but I couldn't quite put my finger on it. I squinted at him.

"I mean…some of them are from backstage and other places where the general public shouldn't be allowed in. Which leads me to suspect it's someone from the staff."

Chris rolled his eyes. "Geez, chill. Besides, it's great fanservice anyway."

"Still, can't you look into it?"

He shrugged again. "Whatever. If it makes you feel better then fine."

"Thanks." I grabbed back my phone.

Maybe it was nothing. Maybe it was something. But for sure I wanted to get to the bottom of it. If being careful made me paranoid, so be it.

Didn't matter for long, though, because my phone vibrated again, and I had to run. If there was something to be said about Do-hyun, he was damn persistent.

My last lifeline was Tae.

Unfortunately, I knew he was working on polishing the new album, so I wasn't too keen on bothering him. For a short moment, I contemplated if I could get away with hiding in my own room and pretending to sleep to avoid Do, but my decision was made for me when my phone beeped in my pocket again.

It was a text from Do.

That's it, you can't hide forever, it said.

Without thinking things through, I darted into Tae's room, sans knock. He was indeed working, fully focused on something on his computer, headphones on and all. He didn't even notice me when I walked in.

In my full panic mode, I wasn't exactly thinking like a fully functional adult. Thus, I bluntly yanked Tae's earphone's off and whispered rather harshly: "Hide me somewhere, quick!"

Weirdly enough, Tae didn't even blink, only glanced at the door upon hearing a knock and pointed towards the underside of his bed. I dashed there in a heartbeat, ignoring the stab of ultimate shame that hit me in the chest like a dagger—yes, I very much knew how childish I was acting.

Tae walked to his door and opened it.

"Hey, have you seen Min?" I heard Do-hyun ask at the same instant.

"No. Go away. I have work to do," Tae replied, sounding surprisingly nonchalant and calm about it.

Unfortunately, Do didn't give up. Instead, he walked right past Tae and straight to his walk-in closet and yanked the door open. I nearly snorted. Of course, he'd go to the closet first...oh, the irony.

"Look, I know he's hiding here somewhere. He already used up Joonie and Chris," Do said after he had inspected the closet long enough to make sure I wasn't there.

"I don't know what you're talking about. Go fix your own problems. I'm sure you just pissed him off again," Tae said, and from what I could see under the bed, he seemed to push Do right out of his room.

There was a long silence after that. The dust under the bed started to creep up on my face, trying its best to make me sneeze. It took practically all my willpower to hold it in.

"I think you can get up now," Tae finally said with a strained voice. He was clearly holding in a good laugh.

"That's it, I've officially hit the rock bottom of my entire life," I muttered, crawling out from under Tae's bed, sneezing so many times I lost count.

Tae couldn't hold the laughter in anymore when he saw me, all covered in dust and eyes watering. I frowned at him and tried my best to brush off at least some of the dust. When I was somewhat satisfied, I crashed on top of his bed, thoroughly embarrassed and exhausted.

My phone buzzed with another text from Do. He wrote that he'd wait in his room, and I could go there when I was done hiding. I threw the phone on top of the pillow somewhat harshly and sighed. Did he really have nothing else to do but harass me with these endless text and phone calls?! Damn, the one single song couldn't be *that* important.

"What should I do?" I asked Tae pleadingly while propping myself up to a slightly more comfortable position with my elbow. It was a pretty nice time to hear some good advice from our great leader.

"You know you'll have to face him sooner or later?" Tae asked. Though, it sounded more like a statement rather than a question.

"Yeah, I know." I huffed.

"And you'll have to work with the song, too. He's not wrong about that," he continued.

"I know," I huffed again, though I wasn't so sure anymore—for all I cared, they could just cut it from the album entirely.

"Then what's the problem?"

"It's just...he's just...too much. He has been too fucking close all the time lately, and I can't take it anymore. I can't *breathe*."

"Yeah, I've noticed. Look, have you ever thought of telling him the truth?"

"Of course, but what's the point?" I started. Tae opened his mouth to interrupt me, but I didn't let him. "I'm sure he'd understand why he can't do those things then, but I'll lose my best friend in the process...and maybe even a band member."

Tae rolled his eyes. "Exaggerating much? Besides, have you ever even considered that he might like you back?"

I blinked a couple of times before even considering replying. He wasn't serious, was he? Then again, he did look very serious, staring me down with his dark eyes sharp and focused.

"Obviously not," I started and gave it a short thought. "Even if he did, what good would that do? We wouldn't be able to actually be together, at least not publicly."

"Um, yeah, you got a point somewhere in there." He scratched the back of his head. "But you can't keep hiding under beds forever."

I rolled my eyes. "I know."

"Then, you should know what to do."

"I don't know...it's not that easy. I…" I trailed off.

If that was all he had to offer as an advice, I had to admit I was fairly disappointed. I mean, none of it included me keeping my secret, which was still my ultimate goal. Unfortunately I didn't really see many other choices anymore, other than coming clean.

I'd opened my mouth to ask some more when Tae's phone beeped on his nightstand. I reached out to grab it, but he rushed forward to snatch it himself before I could reach it. I only managed to catch a glimpse of the name of the sender: Jiwoo.

"I gotta go," he said, typing something with his phone at the same time. "Some work stuff came up…"

I frowned. "What came up?"

"Just some guys at the marketing department, having some trouble with some stuff," Tae replied, already grabbing his jacket from the armrest of his chair while yanking on some shoes at the same time.

"But I still don't know what to do," I whined.

"Tell you what," he ran his hand through his plain brown hair somewhat nervously, "if you need some time away from Do-hyun, you could hang here at my room with the door locked while I'm away… but you really need to talk with him soon. "

"Yeah, I guess." I shrugged with nothing left to do but give in.

Tae flashed me a wide smile. "Good. See you around later," he said, already strolling to his door.

I knew I couldn't avoid Do forever. But I still hadn't figured my way out of this whole situation. As much as I didn't want to think about it, I had to admit that quitting GRiD might be the only way out of this mess that didn't involve telling Do about my feelings towards him.

But these guys were like my family, and my only one at that. It hurt too damn much to even think about the possibility of quitting. But then again, it might be the best solution for them, if I was casually cut out of the equation.

Surely they'd find someone to replace me. It wasn't like I was the only guy in South Korea who could sing and dance at the same time. Or they could continue with just the four of them. And I was mostly positive that I might be able to pull it off solo. Probably.

Conflicted and deep in thought, I somehow ended up subconsciously walking right to the dance studio I had avoided for days. I wasn't even sure how and when I left Tae's room.

Without giving it any more thought, I yanked the door open and switched the lights on. Still, in my thoughts, I nearly rammed straight into a waiting Do. Apparently, he had been there all along.

He damn near gave me a heart attack too.

"Gotcha," he said while smiling warmly, before grabbing me into one of his warm and way too compelling hugs.

Creeps

My heart started to race like it always did when Do-hyun did something unbearably sweet like that. I couldn't help it. And it had been the number one reason why I'd been avoiding him in the past few days. But that wasn't something I was going to tell him. So, I endured it, stayed still, and let him hug me while I tried to compose myself after the initial surprise of bumping into him here at the dimly lit dance studio.

To be honest, I should have guessed that he'd try to surprise me here. After all, he knew this was the one place I always eventually ended up when I was upset. It was a soothing open space with enough room for dancing and a calming dark brick wall opposite the mirror wall.

It had started to bother me a bit how well Do really knew me. Yes, I knew he only saw me as his best friend, but moments like these didn't help me get rid of my more...romantic feelings. Heart crunching, stomach fluttering, head spinning feelings.

"Why have you been avoiding me?" he asked with a soft, yet clearly hurt, voice.

My heart clenched again. Tae had suggested that I come clean to Do, and this was one of the most perfect moments for that…but I couldn't bring myself to say the things I had been bothered by lately. Not in a million years. Or at least, not today. I considered denying it but Do knew me too well for that.

So instead, I said, "Just reasons. Forget it. You wanted to work on the song?"

Do narrowed his eyes at me and I tried my hardest to keep a straight face. Eventually, he dropped it and let go of me. Good. Being that close to him was dangerous. For both him and me. I could no longer guarantee that I wouldn't do something incredibly stupid.

"If you want, but, honestly, I'm not in the mood anymore. How about we hang like we always do? I've missed you," he said.

I couldn't have been more relieved. I nodded and everything went back to normal. I put on some music and started to practice one of our choreographies while Do blabbered on about work and various other things. Although the whole scene might have seemed weird to anyone else...to us, it was normal. And I could very much work with normal. For now.

The only interruption to our peace was Tae.

"Hey! I brought some fried chicken, anyone interested?" he hollered from the threshold, holding up two plastic bags with containers inside.

I hadn't even noticed I was hungry, but my mouth watered upon noticing the sweet scent the food sent into the air all around us. I nodded enthusiastically to Tae, who smiled and walked across the floor and sat right next to me on the floor.

"Fancy some dinner?" he asked Do-hyun as well.

Do eyed us both with an unreadable expression, but did eventually nod, before ripping the other bag from Tae's hands, physically tearing it with his force. My brows scrunched down at the sound, but I kept my focus on my food and started munching down the noodles and chicken.

Tae leaned back against his arms.

"So, what have you guys been up to? Any progress on Minjae's solo?"

"Err, nope," I admitted, a pang of guilt hitting my chest. "We haven't gotten to it yet."

Do-hyun shot Tae with one of his cold stares. Even I shivered.

"Can't you just relax for a moment? Not everything's gotta be about work," he snarled under his breath. Why Do was this bitter towards Tae? It had grown to levels that made me slightly uncomfortable, even. But at the same time the last thing I wanted to do was to get in the middle of it.

Good thing that Tae was in a good mood—he only laughed.

"Okay, okay, chill. Geez," he said, then threw his hands up in a sign of surrender and stood up. "I guess this *hostile atmosphere* is my cue to leave."

"You can stay," I said, trying to plead him with my eyes. To me, he was a welcome distraction from all things Do-hyun. And I was hoping he wasn't too mad at us. Well, it didn't look like he was, but still.

"Nah, I'm gonna go," he said. "I have some business with Joonie anyway."

"Good," Do-hyun muttered. "Don't bother to come back."

I poked him with my chopsticks. "Shut up already!"

Tae had already made his way to the door. I waved at him as a goodbye, to which he replied with a wink, probably trying to remind me of our earlier conversation about confessing to Do-hyun. I blushed involuntarily, which in turn effectively made Do glare at me suspiciously when the door banged shut.

"Seriously, what's up with you and Tae lately?" Do asked.

I gulped. It was fairly difficult since my throat was suddenly somewhat dry. "What do you mean?"

"I mean…" he started then paused, clearly thinking his words through. When he found them, he shrugged and stuffed his mouth with more food after mumbling, "Nevermind."

I wasn't going to object, so I didn't reply. It wasn't like I was thrilled to explain Do why me and Tae had gotten a little closer lately. Thankfully the mood normalized soon after. My poor heart—it wouldn't be able to withstand much more of his mood changes for one day.

Just when I was about to get up and put the food container in the trash, Do-hyun spoke again.

"Oh yeah, I forgot to mention; Joe identified the fanny pack dude from the other day. Just paparazzi in disguise."

I shuddered. "Still creepy."

"I know."

We fell silent again, listening to music and munching down some of Do-hyun's candy as a dessert. But the whole thing with the creepy guy in the mall made me remember the equally creepy account on twitter, so I fished out my phone from my pocket and pulled up the account @crewinsidr once again.

"Speaking of creepy, have you seen this?" I said, shoving the phone into Do's hand.

He frowned as he scrolled. "Who is this? Must be a staff member, right? I mean, just any random person can't access these places..."

"I know, right? And that's from the comeback concert backstage!" I said when he reached the pic where I was sitting on his lap.

"You should probably show this to Chris."

"Already did..."

"Okay, good, he'll figure this out," He scrolled down some more, before adding with a smirk, "But I must admit, we look kinda hot in these."

In a flash, he tackled me to the floor so fast I couldn't keep up. Just like back in the photoshoot a few days back, I was pinned below him, and he started to lean in, smiling warmly on the way. My heart made some cartwheels all over again and I could barely breathe.

"Now, let's continue where we left off..." he mumbled softly before cupping my face with his hand.

Once again, Do was way, way too close. My panicking body reacted like I was burned by his touch, and I pushed him away harshly. Do's warm smile turned into confusion first and then— hurt. I couldn't face him with the blush creeping up my face again, so I shuffled up from the floor and sat on the couch.

After a moment, he followed me and tried to touch my arm. It was a light, casual touch, but again my body acted on its own, and I jerked my hand away. To be honest, it was beginning to be too hard to even sit on the same couch as him, and I had an urge to dart away from the whole room.

Maybe my body had enough, or my mind, I wasn't sure…but whatever it was, I couldn't hug him, let alone touch him at all.

Do gave up and even moved a bit further away from me, giving me space. I saw from the edge of my vision that he was visibly confused, hurt…and maybe even a little upset? I hugged my knees, trying to keep myself intact. My chest ached because of the sudden distance, and at the same time because he was still way too close. Half my soul was reaching out to Do, half was pulling me towards the door. Another moment of this and I swore I would tear in two.

The silence became more and more torturous with every second that passed.

But it was Do who got fed up with the silence first. "Minjae, please, just talk to me. I'm not sure what I did this time, but I'm sorry I hurt you."

"It's nothing."

Do glanced at me like I had lost my mind. "Don't even try that crap with me anymore, Min. I know something's up."

I took in a sharp breath in my somewhat panicked state. Maybe it was time to open up, just a tiny bit. This whole thing had been going on way too long, and I was tired. Years. Tae may've been right, and we'd both be better off after talking things through. Or everything would turn for the worse after, but right at that moment, I didn't even care one bit. Honestly, any option would be better than continuing in a lie forever.

There wasn't really another way out anymore.

I mustered up some courage and although I still couldn't face him fully, I decided to give the truth a go. Finally, after years of hiding my true feelings, I opened my mouth with the intention of saying what I really felt, for once.

"Do-hyun...I know this sounds cliché, but it's not you, it's me. You did nothing wrong. You never have."

"Whoa, wait. What? Why does this suddenly sound like a breakup talk?" Do's eyed widened.

I smiled to myself, to hide the pain. "Maybe it is..." Sort of. Hopefully not.

Do frowned before replying. "I—I'm confused."

There was another strained silence. I couldn't find the right words, and Do simply waited patiently for me to speak…at least, as long as I held still. When I got up from the couch and started to pace around the room, trying to think, his patience ran out.

"Stop pacing and start talking. Now," he spat. Then seemed to realize he was being too harsh and dropped his formerly stiffened shoulders. "Sorry..." He trailed off and lifted his hand to stroke my cheek. I slapped it away before he could even reach my face, making Do finally back off one step.

Blood boiled in my veins and pounded my skull from the inside out, making my vision blur and head spin. "That's just it! You're always so fucking close. I can't even think!"

Do's eyes widened. But I wasn't having it anymore. I had had enough. I took a step forward and shoved him with both of my hands, hard, making him take a couple of more steps back.

"Stop messing with me!" I pushed him again, one step further. "Stop flirting with me!" I tried to push him again, but my anger started to melt away so I couldn't move him anymore. "And stop being so fucking nice all of a sudden!"

My anger was replaced with hurt and I could feel the tears burning behind my eyes. One even escaped and rolled down my cheek. Do looked like he wanted to hug me because he couldn't figure out where to put his hands.

For once, he didn't do it and only said, "I didn't know it bothered you that mu—"

"I'M GAY!" I shouted in his face, cutting him off, starting to feel furious again. "Of course it bothers me that much! So sorry if I need a fucking breather sometimes. I know it's just fan—"

"I know." Do whispered so softly that, at first, I didn't even notice.

"—service for you, but..." My voice faded when his words registered in my brain. "Huh?"

"I know you're gay," he replied, aloud enough that I could hear the words clearly.

His words felt like a punch right to my gut, making me lose my breath. I stumbled a couple of steps backwards. "What?"

He shrugged. "You're in love with Tae, aren't you? I mean I've seen how you look at him..."

My brows scrunched together. Tae? What did he have to do with any of this?

"...you always push me away when he appears and then you even defend yourself around him, just like the other day at the photoshoot. And all the flirting..." He paused, took in a deep breath, then started to fume again. "Plus, lately, you've been spending time with him way more than before. Then there's the way he looks at you, too... I've been wondering for a while now, are you guys like, together?"

He blabbered on and on about me and Tae, sounding so sure that he had figured it all out.

And he clearly didn't like it. At all.

Yet, he couldn't have been more wrong in his entire life. To me, it sounded absurd... I couldn't help but start laughing like a maniac. When I finally was able to calm myself down a bit, Do was already looking at me like I had lost my mind once and for all.

"Do...Tae has nothing to do with this..." I started and took a deep and shaky breath before continuing: "I'm in love with you."

What If

When those ill-fated words left my lips, the time stopped. There was an almost infinite pause between every heartbeat, and I didn't dare to move a millimeter.

Then several things happened at once.

First, Do-hyun froze stiff; he didn't even blink. His mouth fell agape, and his chest waivered, like he tried to take a breath, but his lungs abandoned him. I had to turn my eyes away from his now widened ones.

He must've been speechless with disgust.

The ultimate realization of what I had done hit me like a fully loaded truck going a hundred kilometers per hour on a speedway before an abrupt stop. My breath stuck to my windpipe, my vision blurred, my chest ached as if there was an elephant trampling over it like it was just a piece of trash, and my head felt light.

I had to get out of there. I needed to be anywhere else but there. Now. No, actually make that yesterday. Maybe even to a time before all this mess happened, this disastrous thing of falling in love with Do in the first place. At the very least, I wished I could've rewinded back to the second *before* I said those words out loud.

Never, ever should I have fallen in love with him, let alone tell that to his face.

Forcing my feet to move by sheer willpower, I sped to the door as fast as possible. Only Do was faster. He recovered from his shock at the same instant I moved and grabbed my wrist, trying to stop me. Desperate and determined to get out of the room that had once been my safe haven, I yanked my arm back and made a second attempt towards the door. Do grabbed my hand again. I squeezed my eyes shut tight, not sure what would happen next.

Nothing happened.

After a while, the curiosity got the better of me and I pried my eyes open just a teeny-tiny bit, just to see whatever his reaction was. To my surprise, he was staring at me with his eyes mellow and soft. It was almost as if he was waiting for me to look at him before saying a thing.

"What did you say?" he finally asked.

I looked at him like he had lost his mind. He didn't really think I was going to say it all over again, right? One time had been too much already. I couldn't face him when I replied, so I turned my gaze away. "You heard me. Not gonna say it again."

Do let go of my wrist to rub the back of his neck in a somewhat nervous manner. "You're not joking with me, are you?"

I rubbed my newly freed wrist as my heart grew heavier the more I pondered my next words. Do-hyun was clearly giving me an easy way out of this whole conversation, but I knew I would've blurted it out sooner or later anyway, so there wasn't really a point in evading this topic any longer.

"Unfortunately, I'm not. But believe me, I wish I was. And just so you know, I am aware that this whole flirting thing is for fanservice only and I know you only see me as a friend. And it's okay, I never expected anything more."

There, I finally said it. Let it all out, so to speak. It was like a huge boulder full of worry dropped from my shoulders all at once.

Do only continued staring at me in total silence, so I took the initiative and added, "I think I need some distance from time to time or it becomes...too much."

I have to admit, saying it all out loud it took a whole lot of weight off my shoulders. Now Do knew what I was struggling with, and it was up to him to decide what he wanted to do with the information. I could only hope and dream it wasn't going to rip this group apart—these guys were my everything. They were the family I'd never had before.

For sure, I knew things would become increasingly awkward between us for a while. Still, I had hope that maybe we could go back to being just friends sometime in the far, far, *far* away future—at least Do-hyun didn't seem like he was disgusted or angry at me. Just surprised.

But when the silence stretched to a long, torturous, and strained one, I grew nervous again. After a while, I took a careful glance at Do-hyun's face. He was still staring at me intensely, again as if waiting for me to face him fully before speaking.

"What if I told you that I'm in love with you, too?"

He'd spoken so quietly his voice was but a mere whisper.

It was like my brain shut itself down completely. Yes, I understood the words technically speaking, but I couldn't figure out what he really meant by them. I tried to look away to think, but I wasn't very successful with that either; Do's gaze was so intense it was impossible to look away or get my body moving. I blinked, hoping it would break the tension, but I couldn't break free from his spell however hard I tried.

After a moment, as he waited for my reply to his question, his eyes darkened and he took a step closer. That broke me free from the trance, and I held my hand up, stopping him before he could come any closer. At the same time, the realization of what must've happened came to me: Do-hyun had either slipped into his stage persona or he was confusing the two.

"If you told me that, I wouldn't believe you," I said, the resolution clear in my mind. There couldn't be any other explanation for Do-hyun's weird words.

He blinked. "What? Why?"

I sighed, pinching the bridge of my nose while trying to figure out how to explain it so it would stick to Do-hyun's impossibly stubborn brain.

"If you really loved me, would you snap at me after every gig? Would you avoid me for days after doing a little fanservice? I don't think so."

"What does that have to do with anything?" he asked, brows furrowed as if it was hard to figure out the meaning of my words.

I was getting frustrated with the whole topic. How could I explain this to him so he would understand—both that he did not, in fact, have any real feelings towards me and that he really needed to keep his distance from me or I'd go insane? I pinched the bridge of my nose while thinking about a response.

"Min, I don't understand," Do continued when I couldn't come up with anything, his hands curling into tight fists.

"I admit that stage-Do could have a…crush, maybe, on stage-Minjae. But you can't confuse that with real life. For you, it's just fanservice—nothing more, nothing less. I already got confused; don't make the same mistake."

Do tried to get closer to me again, but I backed off, so he stopped mid-step.

"But–" he started.

"But nothing!" I yelled. "Look, all I wanted out of this was that you'd keep a little distance from me from now on, because I can't take it. Can you do that much for me or not?"

His lips in a thin, tight line, he backed away a couple of steps. Narrowing his eyes at me while stuffing his hands in his pockets, he nodded.

"Good," I muttered, turning around and yanking the door open. "See you tomorrow," I called over my shoulder and stepped out.

This time, he didn't try to stop me.

Not Fanservice

"Minjae?" Chris called from the other end of the table.

I was way too deep in my thoughts to notice much around me, let alone register Chris's calling. I spelled my name wrong on another limited edition dvd-box I was signing, so I tossed it to the ever growing pile of ruined merchandise in the middle of the table before paying much closer attention to the next one. Thankfully that one didn't fail; I was almost proud of myself when I handed it over to Joonie, sitting next to me, so he could sign his name on the cover as well.

When he didn't, I finally woke up from my daydreams and glanced at him.

"Hello? Earth to Minjae?" Joonie said, raising one of his perfectly shaped and filled in eyebrows. "Are you okay?" He placed his hand on my forehead.

I frowned. "Yeah, I guess. Why?"

"Chris has been calling your name for at least five minutes."

"Oh." I turned my attention on the brat.

"Finally," Chris sighed. "Took you long enough."

"What do you need?"

"Can you fetch more of these vinyls from storage?" he asked, browsing through the freshly signed pile of Contrast vinyl records. "At least four of these are no good."

I had a hard time not rolling my eyes. "Why don't you fetch them yourself?"

"Well, I didn't ruin them in the first place..." he said, trailing off while holding up one of the ruined ones where I had only scribbled a z-shaped...well, shape.

Ouch. I guess I deserved that. I stood up, stretching my stiffened arms and back a little.

Do-hyun, who was seated next to me, flinched away upon noticing my hand, which I had accidentally stretched out too close to him. My heart clenched. It had been like this for a couple of days already, and I was losing my mind. I might've slammed my chair back in its place under the table with a tad too much force before stomping away.

To say things were awkward between Do-hyun and I would've been an understatement. And I hated myself for it. Why on earth did I decide it was a good idea to let him in on the secret that I was in love with him? Clearly, it hadn't worked the way I had wanted it to.

Bitter, tired, and angry, I yanked the storage room's door open—only to come face to face with Do-hyun. Not the real-life Do-hyun, obviously, but a life-sized cardboard version of him. It was this whole huge billboard that was supposed to go to Seoul Station—the railway station at the dead center of the city—yet now it was only waiting here at the storage, resting against the white brick wall at the back. I was in the picture too, right next to Do-hyun, as was the rest of GRiD. However, Do was the only one looking straight into the camera, so it felt like he was staring directly at me.

I stepped aside and let the door close on its own. In some kind of a trance, I grabbed a pile of the vinyls I was supposed to fetch from the shelf...but I wasn't able to keep my eyes off the cardboard Do-hyun.

I stared at the huge picture for a long while, vinyls hugged against my chest. Do-hyun stood out from the rest of us. The lights inside the storage room were so dim that the ray of light coming through the doorway—as the door hadn't shut properly—lit up only his face. In the picture, I was looking at Do-hyun with a dreamy, very fanservice-y look on my face. I remembered the photoshoot as clear as day—it had been a couple of months ago, back when I had been under the impression I had gotten over my first crush on him.

Boy, had I been wrong, naive, and innocent.

The guilt stabbed my heart once again and my stomach clenched so painfully I couldn't help but double over, crouching all the way down to hug my knees after laying the pile of vinyls to the side.

"I'm sorry, hyung, for making things weird between us," I muttered to myself and the cardboard Do-hyun.

"Then why don't we talk things through?" someone with an all too familiar voice said from behind me as the door shut with a bang.

I jumped up, my heart picking up the pace, going from zero to one hundred in a nanosecond. The real-life version of the photo I had been staring at was staring back at me.

"Hyung! Why are you here?"

"Chris asked me to fetch these," Do said, holding out a pile of what looked like limited edition Contrast photobooks. "Apparently, you're not the only one who has been messing up the autographs today."

"Huh…"

"And don't change the subject!"

Shit. "I– err," I tried to figure out a plausible excuse to flee, which was rather hard, being on the spot like this. Noticing the vinyls on the floor, I picked them up swiftly and took a couple of hesitant steps towards the door, which Do-hyun blocked.

"Um, I should go, Chris is probably waiting for these," I said very awkwardly, holding out the pile of records.

Do-hyun took the records from me and placed them back on the shelf. "No. We're gonna have a little chat first," he said, turning to face me again. "I mean, we're both miserable. I think it's time."

"But I have already said what I had in mind and it ruined everything," I admitted, my voice barely louder than a whisper.

"Then I'll talk and you listen until I'm done. Deal?"

Not really seeing a way out of this—or the room—anymore, I nodded.

Do-hyun laid the books he was holding on the shelf before taking a deep breath. "I've really thought through what you said the other day," he started. "And I still stand with what I said: I'm in love with you, too."

I shook my head. He couldn't be in love with me. That part still didn't make any sense. Maybe he was pitying me or something? "Hyung, I don't need your pity. Can't we just go back to the way we were?"

"For fuck's sake, Min!" Do-hyun almost yelled, clearly frustrated. "I keep telling you I love you and you keep brushing it off with every possible excuse your adorable yet dumb little head can come up with!"

My eyebrows shot up at his sudden rage—and I still had my doubts despite the seriousness in his eyes. "And you're sure this isn't just because of fanservice?"

Do let out a long, strained groan and brushed his hair back. "Argh, not again with the fanservice!"

And before I could mutter out another word, he backed me up against the wall and pinned me there. Staring me straight in the eyes, he cupped my cheek, before softly brushing his thumb along with my jawline. I became paralyzed.

"Do you see any fans around here now?" he asked, with the softest, gentlest voice I had ever heard coming from his mouth ever before.

I gulped, shaking my head slightly, my eyes widening at his sudden very close proximity. His touch on my cheek was burning; the trail his thumb brushed on my skin left it tingling. It was hard to form complete thoughts, let alone speak.

I didn't.

He grabbed my waist with his other hand then and pulled me closer. My chest collided with his, and abruptly I felt like it was where I was supposed to be: in his embrace. It was like my body had been missing a piece and just now found it. My body took over my mind and started acting on its own. Before I knew it, I was leaning against him. Maybe my body was now giving up on resisting him altogether.

"Are there any fans, any cameras around us now?" he asked again with a low whisper.

"No," I whispered, or rather only breathed.

It was hard to focus. Do's face was so close to mine that I could feel his breath tickling my lips—so dry in an instant that I had to flick my tongue across them.

He noticed and at once his burning gaze darkened as he stared at me, leaning even closer. Barely a few millimeters separated our lips.

"Then it's obviously not fanservice."

His soft and gentle lips touched mine and something inside me cracked. I was so done resisting the urge to do this, that I finally let all the feelings out that I had bottled up for years and kissed him back with all the force I had in me. At that precious moment, I forgot all my fears and insecurities, and just let go.

Do growled against my lips and pushed me against the wall in the back, right beside the huge cardboard ad of us, pinning me tight between him and the bricks.

There was a spark in my stomach and tears of something I had never experienced before burned behind my eyes. One managed to escape and rolled down my cheek, eventually reaching our joined lips. Salt hit my tongue, and I didn't even care what Do thought about it. This moment was so unbelievable and perfect, that I began to think it was, in fact, a dream.

All my senses went in overdrive. I could feel the sharp edges of the bricks sinking into the skin on my back. I could feel Do's warm body burning me up. I could feel his lips against mine, moving feverishly and sending a whole bunch of the famous butterflies to my stomach. I could smell the faint trace of his cologne, and I could taste the sweetness of the candies we had munched while signing the merchandise. I could hear my fast heartbeat and the sharp, quick breaths he took whenever he could while not letting our lips part once.

When we finally parted, just for a moment to take a proper breather, I opened my eyes slightly. Now that I allowed myself to feel, it was like I saw his face in a whole new way. I could see his flushed cheeks. I could see his lips, which were now slightly swollen from the impatient kisses we shared. When my eyes finally reached his dark brown and warm eyes, my chest exploded with all kinds of feelings...mostly happy ones, since he looked as happy as I felt.

He leaned in and kissed me again as feverishly, if not more so than before. And then again. And again. So many times I started to feel a little lightheaded from the lack of oxygen and all the feels that took over my whole being. Still, I wasn't satisfied—in all honesty, I craved for more.

Unfortunately all too good things were bound to come to an abrupt end—that was my life in a nutshell. This time, it came in the form of a very annoying maknae's voice reaching us through the door.

"Guys! What the fuck is taking you so long?" Chris shouted, right when we also heard the door handle go down.

At once, me and Do-hyun snapped away from each other. In a hurry, we both picked up the respective items we were each supposed to be fetching, just in time. The door opened fully. After being in the dim lighting so long, the corridor's brighter lights blinded me momentarily.

Then I was staring straight at a baffled Chris, who was hanging at the threshold to the storage room.

"Did I...interrupt something?" he asked, squinting at us.

While I gulped down the bile that had risen up in my throat upon the ultimate nervous breakdown, Do-hyun only laughed.

"You know, just the usual," he said. From the corner of my eye, I saw that he even winked at Chris. What in the actual...?

Shaking my head, I gathered my shattered self and then cleared my throat. "Err, here," I said to Chris, handing over the pile of vinyls. "I have to pee," I lied through my teeth and pushed past both.

Thankfully, neither one of them stopped me and I was able to flee to the bathroom. I went straight into a stall, slammed the door shut, leaned my back against the wall, and just…stood there…for a long time, catching my breath. My heart was still beating a million beats per minute and I clutched the front of my shirt in my fist, hoping it would help some.

Newsflash—it didn't.

Did we… Did I just kiss Do-hyun? Had I been enjoying it way too much? Did we really get interrupted by Chris?

Of course I knew the answers: yes, yes, and yes. Yet, my head was still screaming no, and I couldn't blame it. If someone had told the Minjae from two months back, when the picture for the giant advertisement was taken, that this would happen, I would've laughed in their face. There was no way I could've imagined then that in a couple of months, I would be getting hot and heavy with Do-hyun right next to the finished billboard on a random workday afternoon.

Maybe it was a dream after all?

Although, when I touched my lips, I could clearly feel they were swollen. And even my dreams could never do justice to the real thing. I mentally slapped myself. Now was definitely not the time to give myself any more delusions. It had been a hard enough wake-up call to realize I hadn't gotten over Do-hyun in the first place. Plus, I had to get back to work.

With that in mind, I walked over to the sinks and splashed my face with cold water, hoping to calm down the raging blush I was still sporting. I could see in the mirror that it didn't help much, but it did calm me down enough that I could get back to work and face the others.

After taking a deep breath and hyping myself up, I walked back to the main room of our floor in our label's headquarters. Blatantly ignoring my heart, which started thumping loudly against my ribcage as soon as I spotted Do-hyun back by the table, I made my way next to him and sat down.

I guess I managed to hide the storm that was still raging inside me, since no-one lifted their eyes from their respective tasks. I, too, picked up with signing the merchandise—and this time I was even able to focus, miraculously enough. In addition, my lips turned into a smile whether I wanted or not.

From the corner of my eye, I noticed that Do-hyun was also smiling. And he certainly didn't keep any distance from me anymore—at all. In fact, he was so close that our arms brushed against each other from time to time. And every damn time it happened, it sent all kinds of tingles to the pit of my stomach.

My cheeks hurt from how much I smiled. It sort of felt like I was glowing from the inside out. I wasn't sure if I had ever been as happy before in my entire life.

Eventually, Do-hyun reached the last piece of merchandise we were supposed to write our autographs on—a photobook—and tossed it over to me.

"Finally done," he said and yawned, before starting to stretch his back.

I tried my hardest to not screw up the last piece (I didn't) and handed it over to Joonie. He too scribbled his name on the first page and pushed it towards Tae. All three of us watched Tae sign his name on it intensely, and then we stared at Chris when he was doing the same.

There was a collective and loud relieved sigh when Chris finished and tossed the book to the successful pile. We were finally done.

Do-hyun turned to look at me with his eyes somehow sparkling. "Let's go home?"

I cringed. I knew I still had a meeting to go to so I wouldn't be able to go home for a while. To be completely honest, I had never been as reluctant to stay at work as I was now. All I wanted was to go home and finish whatever we started in the storage room—who knew, maybe Do-hyun would come to his senses at any moment and break my heart. He wasn't well-known for his stability.

"About that…" I started hesitantly, knowing I couldn't skip work.

"Yeah, sorry, Do," Joonie said, interrupting me. "Me and Minjae still have a meeting to attend."

Into Thin Air

I couldn't focus for shit. With my mind lingering on the kiss I had shared with Do-hyun in the storage room, I kept zoning out a lot. The meeting was about our stage outfits, and normally I'd have been all over it…but not this time. It must've been at least a thousand times I repeated the conversation leading up to that kiss, still finding it hard to believe that Do-hyun had actually said all that. Then I wondered what would've happened if Chris hadn't interrupted us so rudely.

Joonie, on the other hand, was in ecstasy, and it was entirely because of the fashion. Given my distracted state, I was thankful for him as he kept asking questions, suggesting changes, and hyping up the main designers that were working with us. Which was great, because I didn't have to contribute that much on whatever they were working on.

Still, it felt like ages before they concluded the meeting. They even insisted us to take some accessories as gifts, probably hoping we'd wear them so they could get some recognition. I didn't exactly mind because their accessory collection was right up my alley style wise, but I also just wanted the meeting to be over and done with.

At first, I couldn't have been more thrilled to get back home. Then I realized that I would actually have to face Do, and all the doubts from earlier started taking up more and more space in my head. Everything had been left laid open because of the interruption, and I think that became my downfall. I was fully immersed in my downward spiraling before we even reached the parking hall.

When we hopped inside the label's Mercedes, which we were borrowing since the others had taken the SUV, there wasn't much else on my mind than questions.

How was I supposed to act around him now? What if he had changed his mind about me? And if he hadn't changed his mind, what would the two of us become? A couple? Friends with benefits? Should we tell the rest of GRiD or hide? Hiding would be safer, but then again we lived with them—what if they found out on their own? Well, Tae seemed to be okay with how this would turn out, but how about the rest of them?

I glanced over at Joonie, who was sitting next to me on the backseat. He was looking outside through the tinted window, drumming his nails quietly on the lid of the gift box the brand had given us.

"Joonie?"

"Hmm?" he hummed, turning his attention from the window to me.

I couldn't stop myself. "Have you ever fallen in love?"

He smiled, yet his eyes looked a little sad at the same time. "As a matter of fact, I have. Twice," he said, his voice soft and wistful. "Why do you ask? Have you?"

I tried to hold down from blushing—I'm not sure if I succeeded. "Err…what if it's a bit…problematic?"

"Honey, look at me," he said, pointing at himself from head to toe before letting out a chiming laugh. "Would my affairs ever be *un*problematic? In this society?"

Well, he had a point. Looking at him, it was blatantly obvious that his demeanor was rather…controversial. At least in these parts of the world. Even now, he had make-up on, even though we weren't on stage. His long pink hair was in a low bun, and he was wearing high fashion. To top it off, at least the blouse was obviously from the women's section with that deep v-neck. Some would have argued he was being original or weird, but the majority of people would undoubtedly file him in the too-gay-to-function category.

"Umm, I guess you have a point."

Joonie replied with a wink.

But what really piqued my interest was the fact that I began wondering…was he coming out to me? I mean, one can't just determine whether or not someone is gay based only on people's looks and a gut feeling—and Joonie had never said to me that he was gay, directly.

My absentminded wondering was cut off by my phone vibrating in my pocket—a text from Do-hyun. At once, my heart picked up the pace as I held the phone in my slightly shaking hand, clicking the message open.

I miss you already, the text said and at once, the tingly, glowy feeling settled in my stomach once again. All the doubts evaporated as if they never even existed in the first place and I smiled.

How much longer till you get off work? He'd written.

We're heading home now, I typed back. On a whim, before I could chicken out, I added, *I miss you, too.*

His reply was almost instant. *Let's meet at the dancing studio after you've settled? Tae ordered take-out, so no dinner tonight.*

Sure, I wrote back, although hovering my thumb over the send button for a while, before finally hitting it and stuffing the phone back in my jeans' pocket.

"Wait a minute…" Joonie said, his eyes sparkling like diamonds. "You're glowing? Why, what happened?"

I bit my lip a little before replying, "Nothing."

"Is this because of Do-hyun?" he insisted. "Have you two made up from whatever was bothering you this past week?"

I glanced at him. He was still smiling though, so I didn't have a full-blown panic attack. Just a minor one. What the hell was I supposed to tell him? That I had fallen in love with Do-hyun? Yeah, right.

"Yeah, we had a little fight. It's all good now," I said vaguely, keeping my eyes on the window.

"Good," Joonie said. "Though now I'm curious. Did you fall for Do-hyun, by any chance?"

I couldn't mutter out a single word, which resulted in long and strenuous silence. Joonie was the first to give up, right when the driver parked at our dorm's underground garage.

"Fine. Don't tell me," he said, sounding a bit bitter. "But if you are planning on seducing anyone, you're gonna need these."

He rummaged through the gift box. Eventually, he picked up a bunch of necklaces and laid them all on my lap.

I picked one up, curious. It was a black, thin lace choker. I raised my eyebrows. How on earth was a necklace supposed to help me "seduce" anyone? In fact, I doubted I'd ever have the confidence to even try—with or without the help of some random jewellery.

As if reading my mind, Joonie winked and said, "Oh, please, I've seen how obsessed Do is with that neck of yours."

Once the car was parked, I darted out as if it was on fire—the conversation was already turning awkward anyway. Besides, I had places to be. Not to mention that the suspense due to not knowing where things stood between Do and I was killing me. I couldn't have made my way upstairs, stuffed the new chokers to my drawer, and chomped down the food Tae had delivered straight to my room faster than I did.

But right when I was about to dash out of my room, I hesitated. The doubts once again flooded my mind, and my hand froze right above the door handle. I still had no clue on how I was supposed to act around Do-hyun. And what if…we got caught? Clearly Joonie was already suspecting something. Tae practically knew if he could put one plus one together. Chris was always sneaking around—the little shit.

Also, what was going to happen tonight? I was certain Do was already waiting for me downstairs. But would we just talk? Or would more kissing be involved? Aish, I shouldn't have eaten any garlic sauce.

I ended up dashing to my bathroom and brushing my teeth real quick. And while I was at it anyway, I brushed my hair as well—not that it helped much, it was too damn damaged and frizzy due to all the bleaching. I really had to stop bleaching it sometime soon.

Then again, what if Do-hyun only liked me as a blond?

I received another text.

What's taking so long? it read.

Shit. I knew I was stalling, and I did want to see him. So why was it so hard to actually walk downstairs? I guess I had lived in a dreamworld for way too long to actually deal with this stuff in real life. Stuffing the phone back in my pocket, not even bothering to reply to Do, I decided to just deal with the situation head on.

After a final glance at the mirror, I strode out of my room before I could hesitate again. Thankfully there was only Tae hanging out in the living room, and he didn't ask any questions when I bolted past him. I waved at him before hopping down the stairs two at a time.

The closer I got to the studio, the more nervous I felt. My palms were sweaty, so I brushed them on my jeans' sides. I didn't let it stop me; I was already too close to turn back.

But when I raised my hand to type the passcode on the lock, the door opened and I nearly collided with Do-hyun, who was rushing out. Music blasted through the speaker, the loud volume of it taking me by a bit of a surprise as I hadn't heard a thing before—damn the room was well soundproofed.

For a hot second, both of us stared at each other, cemented to our spots.

"Good, you're here. I was about to come and get you," Do-hyun said, before grabbing my hand and yanking me inside.

I couldn't do much else than to follow him, staggering through the door. Then I didn't have any more time to panic, or even remember I was nervous, since Do simply spun me around, and I fell right to his embrace.

With eyes gleaming, he smiled at me. "Took you long enough."

The heat rose up my cheeks due to the silly thoughts I had lingered on while stalling. It was time to change the subject. "Mianhae," I apologized simply. "So do you still want to talk, or…?"

"Nah, I'm so done talking," he replied, smirked, and then I felt his lips on mine.

My mind became instantly empty of all thoughts, and my hands wrapped themselves around Do-hyun's waist as I lost the control of them in an instant. Much like last time, I could feel *everything*—Do-hyun's warm hands on my waist, his body against mine, his lips so gentle and careful…yet it was still so different compared to the moment we shared back at the storage room.

There was no rushing, no desperation in my actions. Instead, I took my time exploring Do-hyun's lips. I enjoyed the glow that seemed to only grow within me to the point I was almost exploding. I still put every single thing I felt for Do into that single kiss, not being able to hold anything back, but it was all somehow steadier this time over. But it didn't lack intensity—in fact, I think I loved him more than I had this morning, if that was possible.

Do-hyun took his time, as well. He held me tight against him, as if afraid I'd run away the instant he let go. His tongue flicked across my bottom lip and lingered there for an unnecessary—but at the same time very pleasurable—amount of time.

Somewhere along the way, while our lips still moved in unison, we made our way to the couch. Or rather, Do dragged me towards it and made me sit in his lap once again. I didn't resist, but it felt kind of weird to be with him like this, even though it had happened before...for example, at the backstage of our comeback concert. Which seemed like ages ago, even though it had been only a couple of weeks back.

Tonight, everything felt way more intimate. Do-hyun's lips started exploring even beyond my lips—and when they reached that certain spot on my neck, right below the ear, I couldn't help but shiver uncontrollably. Maybe Joonie was onto something when he declared that Do-was obsessed with my neck because a low grumble left his lips when I threw my head back, and he had better access to it.

I very nearly couldn't believe this was actually happening, yet it felt so real I couldn't have imagined it even if I had tried my hardest.

And apparently, we both had felt the exact same way, without knowing about each other's feelings. That realization made my head spin—how oblivious was I, exactly? I honestly felt like an idiot.

Do's train of thought must've been in line with mine, because he took a breath and said, "I can't believe that you feel the same way as me..." He buried his face in the nook of my neck, finally done devouring it.

I nodded in agreement, before moving to his side from top of him, but he still kept his hand curled around my shoulders, keeping me close. I was so happy, that I could've burst into tiny pieces and vanished into thin air.

Saranghaeyo

We didn't speak for a long, long while. There really wasn't much to talk anyway, and the silence was soothing in some weird way. It was like we were still best friends, who could just be together, comfortably quiet. The difference was that now we were holding each other, touching each other, and sharing some sweet kisses.

The only downside was that I became a bit nervous that it all happened there, right on the dance studio's couch. Literally, anyone who had the door code—like most of the staff, not to mention Chris, Tae, and Joonie—could have accessed the room at any time.

I glanced at my phone for the time, and it startled me a bit. It was already past 10 p.m. "It's getting kind of late..."

"I know...we should head out," Do replied.

But neither one of us made a single effort to get up from the couch for a long while. For me, it felt like the perfect dream would end as soon as we'd face the outside world. It was silly to think that, I knew, but the whole thing still seemed unreal to me.

Do searched my eyes for a long while before eventually standing up. He stretched his arms a bit and then pulled me up as well.

"Let's go," he said and headed to the door, dragging me along.

"Where are we going?" I asked. I had thought we would just go back to our respective rooms for the rest of the night and sleep. Not that I was about to get any sleep either way, considering sleeping really wasn't my forte.

"To your room, obviously..." Do-hyun replied.

Ah, right. His habit of invading my room. I nearly forgot.

He opened the door slowly, and a mischievous smile appeared on his face as he glanced at the corridor, making sure it was empty. I chuckled at his playful sneakiness, but he shushed me and winked. It made my heart melt once again.

Just like that, we tiptoed towards my room in the middle of the night. It was like we were teenagers, sneaking past sleeping parents to make out in my room. And what made it hilarious, was the fact that we both were fully grown, adult men. I was damn nearly losing it again and laughing; only Do's serious expression kept me from cracking up.

He didn't let go of my hand even once on the way, and honestly, for me that tiny but thoughtful gesture was everything. It made this whole thing feel more real in a way—our moment had lasted even though we weren't in the dance studio anymore.

As soon as we made it to my room, Do shut the door slowly and locked it. He dragged me further in my own room which made me chuckle all over again, although I hid it behind a fake cough. This time, he didn't shush me but clashed his lips on mine instead.

That was a very effective way to make me silent.

This time the kiss deepened much more quickly, probably because we were really in a private space now. No one had access to this room, other than me of course. We even fell on my bed, my back hitting the soft duvet.

Soon enough, I let out a small moan as Do-hyun's hand found its way on the bare skin on the side of my stomach under my shirt.

Unfortunately, that sound apparently distracted Do so much that he parted with me hastily. I opened my eyes, surprised by the sudden disappearance of his warm body on top of mine.

Then my eyes met with confused and blushing Do. Yes, the usually confident, arrogant, and handsome Do, of all people, was blushing. A lot. And I noticed that he was sitting oddly far from me considering today's events.

I heaved myself a little more upwards, leaning against my elbows.

"What happened?" I asked, slightly concerned. Was this finally the moment he was coming to his senses and running away or something? "What did I do?"

"I– uh…you didn't do anything wrong. It's just… hard."

"What's hard?" I asked, even more baffled.

Do-hyun shifted, looking a little uncomfortable. "Well, it's hard to resist you. Amongst other things," he said, smirking, as he shifted his hand so I could see the bulge in his pants.

Oh.

"You know, this is all kinda new to me..." I started, but was cut off by Do immediately.

"It's new to me, too," he replied. "We'll take it slow."

I smiled at that. Slow was good. Slow meant that it was going to last. Hopefully. And honestly, we had been circling around each other for years now, as it turned out, so what difference could a few more moments do?

It was reassuring to know we were in the same boat as what came to the…err…sexy things. However, the whole ordeal made me wonder things ahead. The same flood of questions that had circled my mind the whole day starting from the moment we kissed the first time, took over my mind.

Still, I didn't want to ruin the moment, so I only asked one thing: "What happens now?"

"I don't know," Do-hyun said, pulling me closer to him. "But I'm done keeping my distance from you."

Smiling, I circled my hands around his waist as well. "You don't have to. Or actually, please don't."

Do-hyun leaned closer, until our foreheads touched lightly. He was smiling for what I could see, and my chest hurt from all the feels clenching my heart. The poor muscle was so tiny under the pressure.

"Saranghaeyo," he whispered.

And that right there was all I needed to hear to stop worrying about the future. Sure, I knew nothing about tomorrow or the day after that. But right now, this very moment, was beyond perfect.

Distraction

Do-hyun's point of view

Chokers.

Those damned *chokers*. The damn things should most definitely have been illegal. At the very least, not in fashion. I had grown to detest those things more than anything. Those seemingly innocent, tiny little accessory pieces, were downright driving me mad. The way they clung to the neck, subtly drawing your gaze towards one, soft, kissable spot was just...wrong. On so many levels. It was way too much. Unacceptably hot. Sexy beyond words.

To my complete destruction, Minjae—that sneaky little tease of a man—had been addicted to those highly annoying pieces of jewellery lately. It was almost like he was purposefully testing my limits, slowly making me go insane by constantly touching his neck.

Like I wasn't hot and bothered already.

He pretended that he didn't even notice what he did to me, acting all innocent and oblivious...but I knew better. Who in their right mind wouldn't have noticed the effect they had on me? In conclusion, there was no other explanation other than that he did it on purpose.

Every single day, he wore one. It had been going on for two weeks straight. My patience was only barely hanging there by a very thin thread. For two weeks, I had been downright tortured with no end in sight.

The more I thought about it, ever since that one, dreamlike night about a month ago, when we had both *finally* admitted our feelings towards each other, it had been like this. He was always there—close, but just barely out of my reach. And the chokers were one of his many torture devices, albeit the most effective one so far.

Ah, but today...today was that much extra. Today, Minjae had casually decided to wear not one but *two* chokers, as if one wasn't enough already. The one on top was your pretty basic, thin, black ribbon. Totally acceptable. Not that noticeable. Although, still a bit tempting.

But the lower one...fuck. Obviously, it was from the same collection, as it was mostly your basic black ribbon. In addition, this one had this small and shiny, star-shaped pendant. It jiggled from the slightest movements, hypnotizing me. Every time Minjae spoke, the pendant moved, too. Every time he shifted in his seat, the pendant shifted too. Honestly, I had no idea what was going on at this point in our interview.

Yes, I was that distracted.

Apparently, the radio host asked Minjae some pretty challenging questions since he bit his lower lip before answering. Well, that, or he wanted to mess with me even more. He started to play with the star-shaped pendant with his hand, making me nearly growl from frustration.

It took every last drop of the restraint I had in my body to get through the interview without ripping that damned thing off of his neck. By the time the interview finally ended, I was so ready to grab my Min and drag him to the nearest hotel and keep him there for at least a week. Possibly longer if I could. But oh no, of course, I couldn't do that. Because as soon as we were done, our security personnel led us straight to Tae's SUV and we headed to the next interview. After that, we barely had time for a quick take-out lunch at the back seat of the car, and we were off to a meeting at our label's headquarters.

Right off the bat, at our regular meeting room, my mind drifted back to my daydreams. They were mostly talking about the Mnet Asian Music Awards—the MAMAs—with Minjae and Joonie, our dancers. Apparently, the other people at the committee wanted to have more collaboration stages this year. It didn't really concern me since I knew we'd perform "Contrast", and that was it for me. Instead, my mind circled back to thinking about Minjae and what I'd do with him if we were alone...

My only lifeline was that evening, which was supposed to be free. For the whole day, or maybe for the whole week, it was the only thing that kept me sane—the faint hope of maybe, possibly, hopefully getting some alone time with Min. But my dreams have been crushed before. Mostly by Tae, who always seemed to invent some clever ways to ruin my plans; sometimes it was having vlives with the whole group, other times he wanted to work on the new album. If it wasn't Tae that ruined my plans, it was Joonie insisting to have some quality time with the group, having nice dinners, and other such bullshit.

A sharp pain in my ankle ripped me from my thoughts. I searched the culprit with my eyes and was met with grinning Minjae.

"What?" I arched my eyebrows.

Minjae didn't even look at me. Everyone was quiet. They were waiting for me to speak. I turned my eyes to Jiwoo, my face probably resembling a question mark.

Jiwoo literally facepalmed. "Do-hyun, I asked you for like three times, what's going on with the album?"

"It's basically finished. Only Minjae's solo is..." I started, thinking about the correct way to express it without ending up being guilt-tripped to work the whole night. I did conclude eventually, "...a work in progress."

The deadline was looming, yes, but there wasn't a rush. I snuck a glance at Minjae who surprisingly didn't look guilty. Maybe he had finally finished the lyrics?

"May I remind you we need at least three weeks for the production and so you might want to get to it," Jiwoo blabbered on, like I didn't know by now how this works.

"When?!" I snapped. She was the one that had packed our schedule this tight. She didn't exactly have the grounds to tell us to just "get to it".

She sighed. "Alright, point taken..." She scanned her calendar for a moment. "Well, there's just interviews and some meetings for tomorrow and the day after. I think the three of you can handle those by yourselves?" She turned to look at Tae, Joonie, and Chris.

Unfortunately, that bastard Tae opened his mouth to protest—he always wanted to do things with the whole group. To my relief, he agreed to it when Joon-seok shot him a dark glance. Thank gods for Joonie. I could have basically hugged him right at that moment. The only one who could smack some sense in Tae's brain was Joonie.

"It's settled then. By Friday afternoon, I'm expecting a nice, completed, and wrapped up demo in my email. Then Tae can sprinkle some magic over it, and we're done by the end of next week. Now get to it," Jiwoo stated and ended the meeting.

And just like that, I had scheduled myself two whole days with Minjae, just the two of us. I grinned. I had practically forgotten the whole track because of our packed schedule, but right now I was very glad that I had remembered. After all, it wasn't often you could get away from some boring interviews and have time to spend with Min.

And because we hadn't had the chance to talk it through yet, I wasn't even sure what this thing we had was. Me? I wanted him to be mine and mine only. I wanted him to be my boyfriend, obviously. But unfortunately, I couldn't possibly decide that on my own, so basically, nothing much had happened since the day. We were still in the awkward "kind of dating, nothing official" zone. Maybe like one tiny step away from the friend zone.

I could have blamed our extremely tight schedule, or the fact that we were both exhausted to the core after our insanely long workdays, for not being able to spend time with him. To top it off, Minjae was pretty much busy with choreographing, the upcoming MAMAs, and planning our stage performances for the world tour. I was pretty busy with fine-tuning the new album, which we would promote on the world tour. All of us were also promoting our comeback in addition to the upcoming album, so yes...things had been pretty hectic.

But this was getting ridiculous now. I had been able to touch him casually every once in a while, or sneak in a short, barely there half-hug, or share a short kiss or two. But nothing more. We never ever seemed to have the chance to be alone, just the two of us.

Granted, I had promised him that we'd take it slow, but I was already regretting that. Sometimes, I even considered shouting to the world my feelings, just to be able to touch the guy sometimes. But of course, we had to live in this society, where fanservice was okay but nothing more. So our thing was a secret—and a high maintenance one at that, considering we lived with three other guys.

Now, I was going to have to do something about the chokers, because there was no way I could focus on work if he was going to continue wearing those.

Like I predicted, Tae ended up wanting to work through the evening, too, polishing up the album with me. So once again, Minjae was already asleep when I was finally finished with Tae and arrived home. Though this time, I wasn't as pissed as usual, since I knew I'd have tomorrow and the day after with Minjae.

It was only about 10 p.m. so I probably could have woken him up...but I knew sometimes he had a hard time sleeping, so I couldn't bring myself to actually do it. I never could. He always looked like a dead person after having one of those nights, so when he did have the opportunity to sleep, I let him sleep. Simple.

Instead, I booked us an actual, fully equipped recording studio at the HQ for the next day and headed to bed. If I knew Minjae at all, he had "forgotten" to set an alarm, so I set mine for 7 a.m. It would be a true pain in the ass to get him up tomorrow; I'd have to start early. I didn't mind—he was cute when he was grumpy.

Nothing

For reasons I couldn't understand, I didn't get to wake Minjae up the next morning as I had anticipated. Instead, I had to endure an entire hour of him and Tae fooling around in our kitchen. Yes, I knew about their weird morning routine of making breakfast for us all whenever they both got up early. For some reason though, it irritated the hell out of me today.

Like, who wouldn't get irritated with them? For example, the way Minjae called him "hyung" all the time with his husky, sexy morning voice pissed me off to no end. Not to mention the way Tae looked at him fondly whenever their eyes met. I mean, Minjae was supposed to be *mine* now, so what the hell was up with this incredibly domestic atmosphere around them?

Well, technically, Minjae wasn't mine—yet. But shouldn't it count for something that he had said that he loved me? Yes, Minjae had also said, a few times now, that there was nothing going on with him and Tae...but at this point, I pretty much doubted it.

But as my mission for the whole month had been to try to not be a huge jerk towards Minjae anymore, I didn't say or do a thing about it. Despite being internally beyond irritated, I kept my mouth shut and decided to focus on my coffee. Which, by the way, was pretty much as black as my soul. I welcomed the bitterness of the beverage with open arms, as it matched my mood perfectly.

I confronted Min as soon as the door closed after Tae and the others heading to a morning interview.

"Still telling me there's nothing going on with you and Tae?" I took take a sip of my coffee.

Minjae snorted and rolled his eyes. "I think Tae-hyung has his eyes on…someone else."

"Who?"

"I don't know…maybe Joonie?"

I nearly choked on my coffee. "What?! But he has claimed to be straight forever!"

"Maybe he is. But Joonie is different," he replied while messing nervously with his ashen hair, blushing a tiny bit and all. *Aww*.

Reluctantly, I gave the revelation a good thought, absentmindedly toying with my coffee mug. It even started to make sense at some point...they did spend a lot of time together. But that was for work, right?

It wasn't my business. Though there was not use denying that my mood brightened one hundred percent after that little conversation. And more importantly, I realized that we were actually here alone, just the two of us—finally. I glanced at Minjae, who was now nervously sipping his coffee on the opposite side of the table and avoiding my gaze. It was kind of cute to see him this flustered.

I downed my coffee and got up to walk around the table. On my way, I noticed that he blushed a bit more, making him look even more adorable. I grinned when I reached him and wrapped my arms around his tiny waist from behind.

"Missed me?" I asked, nuzzling my face against the nook of his neck, taking in the extremely intoxicating scent of Minjae.

It was probably me who had been missing him more, but I was most definitely not going to tell him that. It was way more entertaining to tease him. I mean, who wouldn't want to when he was wearing yet another one of those chokers. This time, it was a thin lace ribbon.

I was waiting for the usual witty retort, but it never came. Slowly, I came to my senses and noticed Minjae getting

160

uncomfortable, fiddling around with the hem of his shirt. I backed off a little and tried to read his expression. He looked like he had forgotten how to breathe, and he was still avoiding meeting my eyes.

"What's wrong?" I asked, having learned from my past mistakes that trying to figure him out on my own wasn't going to work.

"Nothing," he said, but it was way too rushed.

"Don't give me that, Min, I know something up. I know you, remember?"

A range of expressions passed on his face, as he seemed to struggle to come up with an answer.

"It's really nothing, hyung..." he started, but I sensed there was still more, so I kept quiet. "I just...I don't know how to be around you anymore," he concluded eventually, turning away from me so I couldn't see his face.

I sighed. Of course. Should have known that he would feel shy around me now. I myself still couldn't believe that he had had the courage to tell me about his feelings in the first place. I was just the same, but I couldn't keep resisting him anymore.

"Look, it's the same for me, too," I said. "We'll figure this out together."

He nodded, but still didn't fully face me.

Slowly, trying not to startle him, I turned his chair around. I gently nudged his chin with my finger to make him look me in the eyes. "Minjae, stop stressing. Everything's gonna be fine."

He started to open his mouth to protest, but I didn't let him. Instead, I leaned in. Intoxicated by his closeness, I finally let my body do what it wanted the most. When my lips touched his incredibly soft ones, it felt just like the first time over a month ago. Something warm wrapped close around my heart, clenching it so hard it almost hurt—in a very pleasurable way.

Minjae leaned his body closer and deepened the kiss. I was just as surprised as I had been before, that he could go from zero to one hundred in less than a second. One moment, he could be this most adorable, overly cute creature, melting everyone's heart into a puddle. Including mine. The next second, he'd be the total opposite; the sexiest, rudest man to walk on the face of the earth. He was one of those people who had the ability to casually set your insides on fire, while barely passing by.

When he wrapped his hands around my neck, I lost it completely. I let out a strained growl against his lips and wrapped his legs around me. After lifting him up from the chair, I carried him to the nearest couch. As soon as we both hit the couch, I was all over him. My only excuse was that I couldn't get enough of him now that I finally could touch him like this.

With a hazed mind, I had absolutely no control over my body anymore. My hand practically moved on its own when I tugged his black dress shirt out of his jeans and reached his incredibly soft, bare, and warm skin underneath.

Just then, when I started to trace the side of his abdomen softly and eagerly, Minjae lost it. I was sure I'd lost any even remotely coherent thought completely when he moaned slightly against my lips. Thankfully the voice also made my head clear up a bit, and I was able to put some distance between us.

It took a while for my mind to get back to reality. Meanwhile, I stared at Minjae's flustered and heated face. His lips were slightly swollen, his eyes barely open and filled with haze. His light hair, bleached almost to the point of being translucent, had messily spread to the pillow. The sight almost made me lose myself all over again, I couldn't believe I had this effect on him. Not to even mention how much it made me want even more.

This wasn't the right time for more. For one, we actually had to work today. Secondly, I honestly didn't want us to go too far yet. We had barely admitted that we even had feelings towards each other, and the last thing I wanted was to make him regret this. Us. I was way too deep in this already. I had been in love with him for years now, but I had no clue about how new this was to Min. I wasn't going to ruin it.

So instead I caressed his cheek softly and sighed. "Minjae, as much as I want to be with you like this the whole day...or a week...we have to work."

Hearing the word "work" apparently made him drop back to reality. He fluttered his eyes completely open and bit his lip before pushing me off of him softly. "Right..."

I got up, offered my hand for him and pulled him up from the couch. "Let's get going. I've booked a studio for the day."

He frowned and narrowed his eyes. "We're not working downstairs?"

I raised one of my eyebrows, amused. And, of course, wanted to tease him a little. It was only fair by this point, after the torture of the damned chokers. "Did you really think I could focus on work there, way too close to both of our bedrooms? With no one else home?"

He blushed adorably again and shifted his eyes to the floor, making my grin only widen. But as this wasn't the time to tease him, I held my tongue and didn't continue with something even more disturbingly suggestive. And I knew just the right kind of distraction for both of us.

"Well, as Tae probably took the SUV...we can take my car.

Madder Love

Amused, I watched Minjae's face first light up like a candle and then a frown making its way slowly between his eyebrows.

"But...isn't it better to take a cab straight to the back entrance or something? There'll be a crowd for sure," he said, hesitating.

By crowd, he meant reporters. Sasaengs. Fans. Generally curious people. They had been practically camping around the company ever since our comeback. Of course I knew why he was reluctant to go with my car, which didn't exactly blend to the crowd. But it wasn't anything we hadn't dealt with before, and I knew he would want to go.

"Come on, just live a little." I grabbed his hand to drag him towards the door but he hesitated.

"I gave Seong-gi a day off..." He casted his eyes down.

Seong-gi was his personal bodyguard—a grumpy, extremely unapproachable giant. I never liked him, but Minjae seemed to get along with him fine, for some reason.

I rolled my eyes. "He's annoying as hell anyway, and I'll protect you."

"Aish, fine! But let me get my things first," he said, and I let go of his hand. Reluctantly...but I did.

Minjae must've been at least a little excited, since it took him no time at all to grab his wallet, a cap, and a pair of huge sunglasses—as if they'd even help one bit to hide his identity. To be fair, the sunglasses also helped to hide things like bags under one's eyes, which was why I didn't joke about it. Minjae clearly hadn't slept very well last night.

We headed to the underground garage. I smiled softly when he started to rush us through the corridors, looking like he got more and more excited about the ride the closer we got to the garage. Yet, I still worried a bit now that I actually had something to lose. Reluctantly, I fished my phone from my pocket and dialed a number I hadn't used for more than ten times in my life, despite it being on my speed dial.

After a few beeps, Joe, my personal security guard and one of my closest friends, answered.

"Well, this is rare. What's up, Do?"

"Taking the Porche today," I replied nonchalantly, although I was feeling nowhere near nonchalant internally. Joe didn't need to know that though.

"Figured...I'll tail you," Joe assured me and hung up, just like I'd known he'd do. After the call, I felt better about this whole thing of taking Minjae out for a little ride.

Technically speaking, my personal guard's name wasn't Joe, it was Joo-hwan. But I had called him Joe for as long as I could remember. He was like the most annoying big brother you could have, but I somehow still got along with him.

As it was his work to take care of me and my company's security, he would have followed us anyway. Discreetly at that; I never even noticed that he was practically always somewhere close. All of us were accustomed to having at least one of the security personnel close by, so we rarely remembered they were there. Joe knew our usual schedule by heart, and he had his phone in sync with my personal calendar to keep track of the changes. He'd probably already checked that we were going separate ways with the others today.

But this time was different. As I was going with Minjae, I wanted to confirm it. Besides, it wasn't *that* rare for me to call him, but I nearly never called him to his work number. With Minjae, I somehow wanted to be more official about it. Especially considering what had happened last time we snuck out. It hadn't been a very nice ending to our "date," having to run away from a paparazzo.

I side-glanced Minjae. He seemed even more excited now that he knew Joe was going to follow us. He practically bounced to the car and hopped right inside as soon as I unlocked the doors. It all made my smile even wider, and my heart clenched painfully all over again. I swore that man was going to be the death of me.

Now, Minjae wasn't your typical car person. He actually didn't like to drive that much. Like, at all. I wasn't even sure if he had a driver's license—at least, before the army, he didn't. In fact, he never seemed to be even interested in getting one. That minor detail certainly didn't stop him from riding the passenger seat and loving the flashy, over the top, fast and beautiful cars. Which was exactly why I had bought my carmine red Porsche 911 shortly after the army. Must impress the guy somehow, right?

But the Porsche was nothing like Tae's boring, safe, black Honda SUV. Instead, the flashy sports car screamed things like "rich," "famous," and "irresponsible"...practically all the things needed to draw crazy fans and paparazzi. I still couldn't help but take a little detour to the highway, for the sole purpose of entertaining Minjae who was practically purring along with the car's engine, a wide grin permanently plastered on his lips.

It was still all too soon when I pulled over right in front of the main entrance of our label's headquarters. Sure enough, the area was already crowded. Someone spotted the car, and we were surrounded instantly. It wasn't like I had kept it a secret that I owned this particular car and frankly, the car was kind of impossible to hide anyways.

Sighing, I hopped out of the car. Thankfully, Joe was already there. I tossed him the keys to my car and glanced at him. He nodded, and I knew that he'd drive the car to the parking hall for me.

We were blinded because of the flashes of cameras, but it was nothing we weren't used to. We were inside in no time, without much of a hustle. Granted, Joe had helped heaps together with the security staff of the HQ.

Minjae, on the other hand, wasn't very pleased. "Hyung, why exactly didn't we go through the back entrance?"

I shrugged and tried to sound somewhat indifferent. "Gotta give them something to write about." To my relief, that answer seemed to be good enough for him—he only started walking ahead.

The truth was something else entirely. But I just wasn't going to casually admit him that I wanted everyone to see us together as much as possible. I had my suspicions that the DoMino pairing had originally formed because of the possessiveness that I had never learned to control. And now, I wasn't even going to try anymore. What would be the point?

Unfortunately, Minjae had other ideas. "Should we tone down the fanservice a bit?" he asked when we had made our way to the studio—and were once again—alone. "I mean, isn't it kinda too real now?"

"Well, it is real now, isn't it?" I asked while pulling him into a hug. Minjae just seriously needed to chill a bit. It's not like we were going to get exposed.

"Honestly, I'm not even sure..." Even though he had a faint smile lingering on his lips, he sounded worried.

"Oh, need proof?" I leaned in for a kiss but was unfortunately stopped by Min who put his index finger on my lips right when I was reaching the good part...his lips.

"Hyung, we need to work. That's why we're here," he said, downright scolding me.

"Right..." Why did he have to be such a workaholic again?

Minjae eyed me judgingly for a moment, but I could see through his pretenses. He wanted to be alone with me as much as I wanted to be with him. The only thing stopping him was work, and he proved that right in no time.

"Aish! Fine! I'll make a deal with you," he started. Somewhat amused, I raised one of my eyebrows a bit. I admit I was curious about this deal he was proposing. "Well, not a deal exactly...but if we finish this thing today, we can have tomorrow off. *Completely*. If we don't tell the others, that is."

Needless to say, nothing could have made me focus on work better than that.

It took us a while to get the studio up and running. And after that, it took a while for Minjae to open up his voice. Eventually, he settled behind the mic on the other side of the glass, eyes closed. I let my eyes wander a bit on the beautiful man before pushing the button of the speaker system and leaning closer to my mic on top of the mixing table.

"From the beginning—once entirely before breaking it apart, so don't pay attention to the smaller mistakes, okay?"

He nodded, and I hit play.

The lyrics were beautiful now that they were completed. But it was, again, the chorus that got me immersed completely. Minjae's deep and rich voice pulled my heartstrings as strongly as it did the first time I heard the chorus some time ago, back at the home studio.

I'm going mad
My heart beats
It's bittersweet
Is this real?

We're bad
Your touch is sweet
All too sweet
It's not real

I could hear that he had polished the lyrics quite a bit, but it still fit the melody perfectly.

My head kept repeating the chorus over and over again, much like last time. Back then, I had gotten so immersed with the song that I had nearly kissed Minjae right there at our studio, during a minor argument, nevertheless. I had been struggling for so long with my feelings towards him that I was no longer able to completely control myself. Especially the one morning when I had walked in on Minjae sitting on Tae's lap in our living room. To be honest, even thinking that now made my blood boil. Yes even after Minjae had cleared up the misunderstanding between us.

In retrospect, it all seemed silly and unnecessary. We could have saved so many arguments and heartbreaks if I had manned up and confessed earlier. In the end, it had taken years, self-pity, denial, avoidance, jealousy, Minjae getting seriously pissed at me before any of that had happened. Oh, and one pretty heated argument, when Minjae had finally snapped and admitted he had feelings for me.

Although, it all had made me realize some things. It finally was clear to me now, that although I could act strong and confident...

It was actually Minjae who was the stronger one of us in the end.

Right Bed

Minjae and I, we made a good team whenever we both bothered to focus on work. That's why we worked together while recording so much in the first place; we got things done. Like this day, we got the Minjae's solo track wrapped up nicely—although it had taken us the whole day and the whole evening, excluding a couple of breaks and a lunch. We were probably the last ones to exit the company's premises around midnight, switching on alarms on our way out.

On the way home, Minjae fell asleep in the passenger seat. When I was safely parked in our garage, right next to Tae's SUV, I was probably supposed to wake him up...but how could I? He looked so peaceful and sweet in his sleep that I couldn't bring myself to disturb him.

Instead, I killed the engine and lost myself in my own thoughts while looking at Minjae's beautiful face. He had curled up adorably in the leather seat, with the oversized shirt's sleeves covering his hands completely while they were crossed over his chest. A few strands of his nearly white hair had managed to escape the cap he was wearing, now covering his eyes. With his pouty, plump lips hanging slightly open, he breathed slowly and steadily in his apparently very deep slumber.

The need to kiss him nearly drowned me.

A light tap on my window forced me back to reality. Of course, it was Joe, probably wanting to know if he would be needed for the rest of the day. Or night. I had some things to discuss with him, so

I shushed him and proceeded to exit the car ever so silently, trying my best to not wake Minjae up.

Not knowing where to start, I started pacing around not too far from my 911. Joe just waited patiently for me to start talking, toying with his own car keys, and cocking one of his eyebrows up. I reminded myself that what I was about to tell Joe was something that he absolutely needed to know, in order to keep us all safe.

But how did you tell one of your own security staff, and one of your best friends, that you were in love with a man? A fellow bandmate, nevertheless? And that man might have feelings for you too, and that means you two are probably, hopefully going to be together. Which, in turn, will bring some serious safety issues along with it, hence making the security staff's life much, *much* more complicated.

"Now, let's talk strictly about business first," I started and eyed the now serious looking Joe carefully before continuing. "You still remember the thick as fuck paper bundle me and my company made you sign years ago? And then again after the army?"

"You mean the non-disclosure agreement?"

"Yeah, that. And now you hopefully remember that I can sue your ass and your future generation's asses to the moon and back if what I'm about to tell you ever reaches the wrong kind of ears..." I trailed off when I noticed Joe's eyes brightening several degrees.

"What? Did you finally grow some balls and confess to Minjae that you have it bad for him?" he asked.

I choked on my own damn saliva and had to figuratively pick my jaw up from the floor before I could muster up some actual words. "How did you..? What..? When? *How?*"

"Oh please, everyone else could see that you two have been in love except you two idiots. If you haven't noticed, the whole world practically ships it," Joe said with a relaxed half-smile lingering on his normally stiff lips.

"You're not disgusted or something?" I confirmed, still not quite believing what he'd just said.

Joe laughed. "No, I'm not disgusted. In fact, I swing that way too."

I blinked. "What?"

"Yeah... It's more common than you think."

And just like that, a ton of weight dropped from my shoulders, and I could breathe way more freely than any other moment in the past month. "Oh, okay. And for the record, Min's mine."

"Yeah, obviously," Joe said and rolled his eyes. "My taste is different from yours anyway."

"And it was him who confessed first," I admitted, earning a mocking smirk from Joe.

I got lost in my thoughts. I wanted to make tomorrow somehow special with Minjae but had no idea what to do with him. Maybe a date? How was that supposed to work? Not like we could stroll around the city anymore.

Plus, I had never been on an actual date before. I had no clue how those things worked. Sure, there had been a couple of one-night stands before, but they had happened drunk. Mostly it was me getting too frustrated around Minjae and getting it on with some random folks at company parties and such, all a few years back. They didn't exactly make me an expert. I didn't regret them, but I didn't exactly like to think about them either.

"Well, now that you know about us, and apparently also know some other things...what are you supposed to do on a date with a dude?" I asked, suppressing the hesitation that was attempting to make its way to my voice.

Joe barely blinked before answering. "You know, it's not that different. Whatever you'd do with a lady, I guess? Besides it is Minjae we're talking about..."

I gave it a thought, but I got exactly nowhere. It wasn't like we could just go to movies or a nice fancy restaurant dinner. And that wasn't only because we were both men. It was more of a famous person issue. How were you supposed to enjoy a date surrounded by paparazzi and fans for sure? I'd have to haul Minjae to somewhere very remote, where no-one would know us. And I doubted there even were such a place left nowadays...

"Well, we can't exactly go wine and dine in peace, now, can we?"

"No, but aren't you thinking too much?" Joe countered. "Maybe you should just think what Minjae would like? I bet he isn't one for fancy dinners anyway. And what about you?"

A smirk I couldn't stop, tugged one of the corners of my lips upwards. If only I hadn't promised Min we'd take it slow...

"Me? I'd just drag him to a hotel room and..." I drifted off when I heard the door of the 911 open and saw a very tired looking Minjae heave himself up from the front seat.

Joe winked. "You know, maybe you should do just that?"

"Hmm, maybe." I watched Minjae walk our way.

He looked adorable, rubbing his eye with the sleeve of his oversized shirt. The sight made my heart melt once again...until I noticed he was pissed. Whoops.

"Why didn't you two wake me up?" he asked with a disapproving tone.

I just shrugged at Minjae. He shook his head and we all headed to the elevator. Joe got off with some good night wishes when we reached the first floor where the staff's quarters were. Minjae and I continued to the top floor. Minjae got all sleepy again and nearly passed out while still standing, so I had to practically carry him to his room. The apartment was silent and dark—the others were probably asleep already.

Carefully, I laid Minjae down to his bed. I watched for a while as he tried to keep his eyes open but failed miserably. Chuckling slightly under my breath, I stroked his cheek before planting a soft kiss on his cheek. I whispered to the already sleeping Min a good night and headed to my own room next door...nearly emptying my stock of self-discipline in the process.

Sighing, I tossed the keys and my phone to the side table, put my clothes to the laundry bin, and hopped in the shower of my en suite bathroom. I took my time in there, relaxed my muscles, and handled some other business as well. Needless to say, I'd had some build-up lately down there, mainly because of the constant teasing I had to endure from Minjae. And pathetic as it might have been, I had to handle things somehow...right?

I probably could have jumped him today, or like a month ago. But as desperate I was, I still wanted the first time with Minjae to be a bit more special than a quick fuck in our dorm. Maybe getting a hotel room wasn't such a bad idea after all. Plus we shouldn't have anything special the guys couldn't handle themselves Saturday morning. Maybe we could visit my mom; she must be lonely nowadays, since my dad had passed away and my little brother Jae-ho had moved away from home, too.

The newly formed plan wasn't much, but it was something. At least, it would be something Minjae would enjoy, albeit not being a real date. He always loved visiting Mom's place. And Mom would love to see Minjae, too; it'd been a while.

I wrapped a towel around my waist and exited the bathroom, ready to put the plan into action. Grabbing my phone from the table on my way, I sat to the edge of the bed and started texting Joe. To his personal number, of course. No need to make *this* conversation official. Besides, he was the one that always did my hotel room reservations—I couldn't possibly book them myself. That would be just plain stupid.

You know what? Get us the hotel room after all... in Daegu, I typed, then stared at it for a while before hitting send. And then right after, I sent another text: *A fancy one. And a boring car to get there.*

It didn't take long for him to answer. *Consider it done. Good luck ;)*

I hit Min with a text, too, just to tell him to come and wake me if he woke up alone in the middle of the night again. To be honest, I kind of wanted him to wake up and crawl to my bed, but that was just a fantasy of mine. Had been since the night of our comeback concert when he'd stayed. It was awesome to get to hold him in my arms while falling asleep. A feeling I'd never forget.

After staring at the phone mindlessly for a while, I hopped up from the bed and hunted down some pajama pants from my walk-in closet. After putting those on, not even bothering to get a top, I headed back to bed. Just as I sat down again to the edge of my bed, I heard a light knock on my door. A wide smile spread to my lips, as I could already guess who it would be.

Surely enough, it was Minjae who walked through the door.

And he was wearing the damn same, oversized black satin pajamas as last time. I was most probably going to say something to him but fell plain speechless before the sight in front of me. It was just downright criminal how hot he could look while wearing simple pajamas, hair all messy, and traces of sleep still weighing his eyelids. I swear, the sight was so hot I could barely control my situation downstairs getting way out of hand. Again.

Forcing myself to think about anything else than the man in front of me, eventually, I got my shit together.

"I hope I didn't wake you up?"

"No..." he started, but didn't sound very convincing, and he must've even noticed it himself. "Yes...but it's ok."

I tugged his sleeve and asked him to stay, if for nothing more than to revel in the nostalgia.

A shy smile spread on his lips and I tugged again, ultimately pulling him down to my lap. He had showered too, and I could smell a faint trace of some shower gel when I buried my face against the nook of his incredibly soft neck—thank the gods that there wasn't a choker this time. Otherwise, I couldn't have been held responsible for the consequences.

It took all the restraint I had in my body to only wrap my hands around his tiny waist and nothing more. Minjae wrapped his hands around me too, and we stayed that way for a while. I must admit, it was incredibly nice.

We had wasted so much time before. Now that we tried to find time for us, there never seemed to be any. And for a moment, I couldn't handle the fact that we only had tomorrow and the next night to be together. Who knew when we'd be able to be together after that again, with our insanely tight schedule.

Apparently, Minjae's thoughts were pretty much in line with mine.

"I don't want to sleep, Do... Feels like a waste of time," he whispered and squeezed me tighter.

"I know. We still should." I let my grip loosen around him.

Minjae crawled under the sheets and I followed suit, after turning the lights off. Just like last time, he turned away from me immediately. I wrapped my hand around his waist and pulled him close. He fit there perfectly. The heat radiating from his smaller body pressed against my bare chest was an amazing feeling I could get used to... and surely hoped I would, someday. Although, I wasn't entirely sure this feeling would be a thing anyone could ever "get used to". But right now, it was so overwhelmingly calm that I nearly fell asleep right away, just like last time. He shivered adorably when I nuzzled my nose against his neck.

I was about to say my good nights for the second time that night, when Minjae took a deep breath and whispered hesitantly, "Do-hyun, what are we now? Exactly?"

My body stiffened. He even used my full name, usually meaning that he was serious. Normally he called me Do or hyung.. Were we really having this conversation now, in the middle of the night, in my room at the dorm? To be honest, I had envisioned something a bit more romantic. Maybe the hotel room, roses, wine... I mean, that would have been what Minjae would have deserved after the countless times of me being a possessive, jealous jerk who couldn't keep his calm and made him feel bad more than once. All because at first, I couldn't face the fact that I loved him, more than just a friend or family. After that, I just couldn't admit it to him in fear of his reaction. Oh, and the whole misunderstanding with Tae and all.

I eventually gave up on thinking altogether. Might as well get it over with then, although Minjae would have deserved so much more. But maybe I could make it up tomorrow...

"I don't know Min, what do you want us to be?" I finally replied, and I mentally slapped myself—way to dodge the subject. I felt Minjae freezing in my embrace. "Well, I love you...and I'd like to officially be your boyfriend."

He relaxed considerably.

"I'd like that, too," he whispered, his voice soft and husky.

"Good. 'Cause you can't get rid of me now, even if you tried," I murmured against the nape of his neck, making him shiver again.

It had always mesmerized me how sensitive he was around his neck—probably the reason I was so obsessed with it in the first place. It made me want more, and it made me want to make him beg for more. My mind clouded, just like it always did when I was this close to him. The situation in my pants just got worse. Thank god my pajama pants were so loose. Otherwise, it would've become extremely uncomfortable.

Not being able to help myself, my hands made their way under the loose, silky smooth pajama shirt of Min. I knew he was in good shape due to constant dancing and working out. After all, I kept myself in shape too. Goes with the profession. But it didn't make me go any less crazy about caressing the smooth surface of his skin. It burned feverishly under the touch of my fingertips while I traced the edges of the firm but lean muscles on his abdomen.

Minjae trembled a little, and I smiled against his neck when the sensations made him involuntarily arch his back and press his behind against my now very prominent hard-on. I was half expecting him to retreat and maybe even dart away from the whole room when feeling it. But the little minx surprised me once again: instead of retreating, the little tease started to grind his behind against my crotch. I froze in shock—how was I supposed to maintain any control?

At this rate, it would be me instead of Minjae who'd beg for more.

"Did you lock the door?" I asked. It was just a strained sound against the nape of his neck, but it got the point across.

A nod was all it took for me to lose control over my body completely. I practically ripped the buttons of his shirt open and started to place soft kisses first to his neck, and after pulling the shirt down, down to his shoulder. My hand started to wander again on its own on his firm abs, not quite believing I finally got to do this in reality, and not just in my dreams. I wanted to feel all of him at once, and I reached for his chest. I felt it start to rise and fall rapidly as his breath quickened.

It had always been me who lost the control, so this time I wanted him to be the one losing it. With my left hand under him, I held him against me while my other hand started to make its way south. Minjae tried to turn, probably getting shy. But as I was determined to make him feel good about this, I didn't let him. Eventually, he settled down and gave up, letting out a quiet whimper.

Now, I wasn't exactly known for being the most patient guy in the world. And I wasn't exactly a virgin either. But I felt like, for Minjae, I could wait an eternity. Right now, all that mattered to me was him: what he felt, what he wanted, what he desired. I was almost scared of my thoughts—usually, I went after what I wanted and had no regrets.

"Minjae, please tell me to stop if I go too far, alright?" I whispered when I reached the waistband of his pants.

He just breathed a quick "don't stop," and squirmed in my embrace.

If possible, I became even more turned on by that statement and my groin was now downright aching. For now, I still insisted on ignoring my own urges and focused on the beautiful man in front of me. By simply being there, he made my chest feel tight of emotions I didn't even know existed. He deserved so much more than me, but it made me extremely happy that he'd chosen me, despite all my flaws.

Slowly and carefully, I caressed his erection through the layer of the smooth fabric of his pajama pants. I continued that way for a while, making sure he wouldn't regret not making me stop while he still had the chance. The deprivation nearly made me lose control all over again, but I managed to keep my cool and eventually made my way under and past the waistband.

Minjae was surprisingly well hung, despite the small frame of his body. Gently, I caressed his length and listened to him moan and pant against the blanket he was now holding on for dear life. His body shivered and shook in my embrace as I stroked him. In ecstasy, I listened as he whimpered my name over and over again when I worked him towards his limits. He arched his back, damn near making me come too by pressing his perfectly round and firm butt against me and my member once again.

"Do! Wait, I d-don't want...not...yet..." Minjae stuttered, nearly sobbing, now finally properly flushed and desperate for more.

"Shh, just let go," I whispered softly against his ear.

Minjae tipped his head back then, so close to his release that his body was right about to burst in my arms. He was trembling. His legs stiffened up against mine under the blanket and his toes curled. My chest exploded with feelings; it was just that incredible to realize he let me see him this fragile, all of him exposed, just for me.

"Saranghae," I breathed in his ear.

It was his undoing, and he immediately reached his peak.

The lights of Seoul made their way to the room through the window just enough for me to see and admire Minjae's gorgeous face as he rolled to his back when I released him from my grip and backed off a few centimeters. His warm brown eyes were still nearly pitch black with lust and I bit my lip in awe in front of the sight as he slowly came down from the high.

I hunted down some tissues from the drawer of my nightstand and proceeded to wipe the evidence of Minjae's release from his abdomen. Grinning widely, I realized I might've fallen even more in love with him, if possible.

"What about you?" he asked and lightly touched my still very prominent hard-on through my pants.

I took his hand in mine gently and moved it away. "Min, it's okay, I can wait."

He hesitated for a moment before concern spread to his face. "You don't want me? Don't you want to, like...go all the way?" he asked, biting his lip, adorably embarrassed by the topic at hand.

I couldn't believe it. After all that, he still doubted I didn't want him? What the hell?

"Trust me, I do. I just want the first time to be a tad more special than this," I admitted and smiled softly. "Besides, I'm no expert...but common sense and some knowledge about basic human anatomy tells me we'll need to get you way more prepared for it."

He stiffened up and blushed even more deeply. "It'll hurt?"

"Probably. At least at first. And we don't have to do it ever if you don't want to," I said, although not very excited about the possibility.

"I want to."

The man never failed to amaze me. I kissed him gently on his soft lips, before replying. "Alright then. But not now."

He pouted slightly but nodded anyway.

"Which reminds me, how would you feel on a trip to Daegu tomorrow?"

"It's a three-hour drive," he said.

"I know. But we both could use an escape, and Mom's waiting for us to visit..." I trailed off.

"Fine, we'll go. But you won't tell her about us, right?"

"Not if you don't want to," I said, amused by his concerns. Truth be told, I thought that Mom already suspected something. She always had.

"Well, it's your mom. But your father..."

I raised my eyebrow slightly. "Dad's not gonna wake up from the dead just to judge us."

Besides, I had already told my family that I was gay years ago. While Dad had been kind of sad about it at first, he had accepted it soon enough. We just never talked about it with him, and there wasn't much to talk about since there was no-one. Mom stated she'd already known it, so she was over it in a nanosecond. Granted, Minjae didn't know about this, so he might have seen it differently.

"I don't know..." he said, adorably biting his lip again.

"Look, let's just see how it goes?"

"Fine," Minjae said and snuggled beside me.

I pulled the duvet over both of us.

Slow Motion

"We're here," I announced, parking the car.

I cut off the engine and turned to glance at Minjae because he didn't answer. He was still sleeping, peacefully oblivious to the fact that I'd spoken. The man had curled up to an adorable ball on the passenger seat, shoes off, hugging his knees, sunglasses on and mouth hanging slightly open. It looked highly uncomfortable, but then again, Minjae could sleep just about anywhere. Especially when he was being sleep deprived.

Last night and staying up late had taken its toll on me too, but I bet Minjae had been awake much later than me. I reached over and lightly shook his shoulder in an attempt to wake him. Still nothing. He stirred a bit in his sleep and mumbled something incoherent. I gave up.

While I was stretching out on my seat behind the wheel, my mind randomly reverted back to last night and I couldn't have stopped the smile happening even if I tried. Minjae sure had changed me, in more ways than I cared to admit, even to myself. With him, I could be patient and calm, more mature—at least nowadays. I didn't care to linger too much on my past mistakes.

From the rear view mirror, I could see Joe approaching my car, and I rolled the window down. We could have driven here with him, but I hated the way he drove—like an old man—when I was a passenger. Yeah, I knew he'd have to drive carefully due to him being my security guard, but it would have taken three days instead of three hours to get here with him driving us. The annoying part? I knew he could step on the gas if he wanted to.

Like now. When he reached my window, Joe only announced he'd be gone to do a security check on our hotel rooms for the night. I nodded, and he gassed away with the BMW leaving us alone in the large parking garage of my mother's apartment building.

The garage was a fancy one. We were practically surrounded by brand new, luxury cars, making our rental Honda look old and shabby in comparison. Well, it really wasn't that old and shabby, but it was plain and normal like most of the other cars on the street, meaning that our whole trip here had been free of any hazards with reporters and fans.

I'd bought the apartment in this fancy building for Mom after Dad died. It was an unexpected heart attack, which turned out to be lethal. Mom had been down for a long time but was now starting to get better. Still, the guilt kept creeping on me—I really should visit her more often. The old house—my childhood home—in the countryside was just way too far from everything. In addition, it was becoming too much for just Mom to handle by herself.

This new building was nearly as secure as our dorm back in Seoul. I wouldn't need to worry about reporters and such making their way here, and I could have some peace and quiet when visiting.

Speaking of Mom, she was waiting for us upstairs, and Minjae was still sleeping. I tried to shake his shoulder again, but I got the same reaction as before: nothing. Maybe kissing him would be as effective as a wake-up call as it was silencing him. I leaned closer...only to be abruptly cut off by a huge, older man knocking on the passenger seat's window with a pissed-off look on his face.

After my initial heart attack, I recognized Seong-gi and took deep breaths to calm myself. I got up from the driver's seat, exited the vehicle, and slammed the door shut.

"The fuck are you doing here?" I asked, probably letting a tad too much of my annoyance showing through to my voice.

Seong-gi gave me a sly smile and raised his eyebrow. "Watch your tongue, brat. I'm here to protect Minjae, of course."

I scoffed. "You won't have to protect him from me."

"Are you seriously telling me that, right after I caught you groping him just now?"

"I didn't grope him, we're toge—" I stopped mid-sentence to actually think. Wait, he didn't know about us? At *all*? Weren't we supposed to tell our guards everything that would put our safety at risk? Then again, Minjae might have been too shy to admit anything to just about anyone. "Get lost."

Seong-gi strode around the car and towered over me, a hostile aura surrounding him. "Oh, you might think you got him all wrapped up, brat, but you're a bad influence. You're just going to get him hurt in the end like you always do. This whole gay thing isn't safe around here. So no, you're not going to get rid of me."

Apparently, he knew but didn't accept it. Well, there was some truth in there somewhere, especially around the dangers of being gay. But he might as well have shoved his concerns straight up his ass because I wasn't going to let anything happen to Minjae from now on. He was mine. I protected what was mine.

"Look, I don't care what you think about us. But let me remind you that we're not some teenagers anymore and can make our own decisions. And our sexual orientation isn't your business in the first place."

"I don't care if Minjae's gay. I'm only pointing out that it's dangerous. It's you I don't trust. Or like, for that matter."

"We have one thing in common then," I scoffed. Right when the passenger door opened and Minjae crawled up, rubbing his eyes with the sleeves of his shirt.

"Both of you just shut up. I'm too tired for this," he stated while getting around the car.

Apparently, he had woken up during our argument and was now majorly pissed; he didn't really talk like that unless triggered. I winced and even Seong-gi took a step back, carefully eyeing

Minjae like he was about to explode I guess Min didn't normally talk like this around Seong-gi, either.

We both fell silent, and Minjae eyed the both of us then glanced around the empty garage before continuing. "Do, don't talk like that to your elders. It's rude," he said and turned to face Seong-gi. "And you...with all due respect, it's really none of your business. We're together, whether you like it or not."

We all fell quiet after that. Seong-gi still fumed, but to my ultimate satisfaction, he did back down when I assume he realize he was on Minjae's payroll so couldn't exactly piss him all the way off.

As Minjae continued to eye both of us with ice cold glances, the corner of my mouth turned into a slight smile; the somewhat insecure Minjae defending our newly found relationship spread a warm feeling to my guts. I even dared to glance towards Seong-gi victoriously.

"Well, finally," a woman, sounding an awful lot like my mother, said behind us.

Everything turned to slow motion as we all turned towards the woman.

Revelations

Sun-hee Park looked stylish and confident standing in front of the lifts. At that moment, she watched all of us with an amused smile and a raised eyebrow. She wore a navy blue blazer and matching trousers, paired with reasonable heels. Her brown hair was styled into relaxed waves. She had light make-up on, and her brown eyes were twinkling. To be honest (and even if she was my mom), I must say she looked way younger than she actually was. I guess city life suited her better than the life she had on the outskirts of Daegu, trapped in a shabby country home. I didn't miss that crappy house, and based on her freshened up appearance, she didn't either.

"What? Why do you all look like you've seen a ghost?" she asked, amusement dripping through to her voice.

I glanced at Minjae. He was frozen to his spot, all paled up except for the light blush that'd crept up on his cheeks. Apparently, he wasn't all that confident about us now that Mom was involved. Calmly, I watched my mom's words slowly register to the brain of his.

"Mrs. Park, I can expl—" he started nervously, but I cut him off by taking his hand in mine.

Minjae glanced at me with a panicky look on his face. But what was the point in hiding it now? Mom would find out soon enough anyway. She was intuitive like that—always had been. She hadn't ever voiced her suspicions out loud, but I knew she knew. I knew from the way she referred to Minjae as her son-in-law and teased me about him. It had bothered me before when I thought my love for Min was one-sided. Now, it was just a relief to know she'd be okay with us being together.

"Eomma...we're together."

Minjae shot me a glance that resembled a deer in the headlights, but Mom let out a small, relaxed chuckle. "I'll repeat: finally," she said, smiling widely. "Let's get inside. I only came down here to check what took you so long." She headed towards the lifts.

I gave Min a reassuring smile and tucked his hand, making him finally loosen up a bit and let out a relieved breath. Together, we started heading towards the elevators with Minjae, leaving Seong-gi staring at us three like the hell had just frozen over.

Unfortunately, Mom also noticed that Seong-gi was going to stay behind.

"Mr. Kim, would you like to join us?" she asked, turning around when we reached the elevators.

Sigh. Of course, she just *had* to ask.

"Mrs. Park, I sincerely thank you for the invitation, but I'll have to refuse. I wouldn't want to interrupt family time. I'll wait here," he said, faking a miserable expression and glancing around the garage.

What a sly bastard, I thought. It was obvious to me that he wanted to make my life miserable.

"Yes, stay here," I said, with a voice that hopefully translated as 'you're not welcome.'

"Do-hyun, behave!" Mom barked at me with a disapproving expression. Like I was four all over again. "Mr. Kim, I'm sorry about my son. I assure you; he has inherited the behavioral issues from his late father. Please join us. I insist."

"Well, if you insist..."

Seong-gi offered me a victorious smile in turn and entered the lift with us. Although he despised me from the bottom of his heart, for some reason he'd always liked my mother. My stomach turned about the idea that he might actually try and *flirt* with her, now that dad was out of the picture. Don't get me wrong, I would like Mom to get over Dad as soon as possible, since she still was relatively young to be by herself...but not with him. The last thing I wanted, was that he'd be in my life even more than before. I had to hope that he'd have some decency left in him and would refrain from trying anything with a widow.

My hopes and dreams were crushed in a nanosecond, as my mom "accidentally" brushed Seong-gi's arm on the "cramped" elevator. Seong-gi smiled at her and I felt a nearly all-consuming urge to vomit. But the whole thing made Minjae smile again after being so tense before, so I swallowed my needs to be pissed off. Instead, I squeezed his hand, which was still locked with mine, and offered him a hopefully reassuring half-smile.

The elevator's doors opened straight to mom's apartment, as she had the penthouse. At first, she had argued that she wouldn't need that much space. But back when we were inspecting it, I saw she loved it. Besides, I considered it an investment rather than something I plainly bought for her.

The light poured into the apartment from the enormous windows and lit up the open floor plan. After taking my shoes off, I dragged Minjae to the living room and plopped down on the blindingly white couch. He seemed hesitant to join me at first, but when he saw Mom and Seong-gi going to the kitchen, he relaxed and sat beside me.

"Do-hyun, I'm sorry. I didn't mean to blurt it out like that to Mrs. Park." He fiddled with the silver bracelet on his wrist.

After pulling him closer, I offered him another hopefully reassuring smile.

"Min, it doesn't matter. It's over and done with, and she didn't mind."

"Yeah... I guess," he said, but avoided my eyes.

I took a deep breath. "I came out to my parents years ago. I believe she has suspected that I have feelings for you from way back then. This kinda isn't that big news to Mom."

That made him snap his gaze from the floor up to my eyes. I smiled at him warmly and traced the small of his back with my fingertips. As the silence dragged on, I grew a bit nervous, but still tried to keep my calm for him.

After a long, strained moment, he finally spoke. "H-how long?"

As I wasn't sure what he referred to: me coming out, or how long I'd had feelings for him. I replied to both. "Well, I hope this doesn't freak you out, but I've been in love with you since debut...and I came out to them like a couple of years after that."

Another silence moment. I could practically see the gears turning in Minjae's head when he did the math. I waited patiently and tried not to think how freakishly long I had been hopelessly and secretly in love with him.

Just when I was going to completely freak out by the stagnation, Minjae finally opened his mouth.

"It's the same for me," he said, but it was only a barely-there whisper.

I still heard it, clear as a day. My heart first stopped and then picked up the pace. First, I couldn't believe it. Then came the remorse—the first time I realized how much he must've been hurting because of my actions. All the avoiding, all the cold words, all of the times when I lashed out to him, trying to cope with my feelings which had made me question everything I had thought to be right at the time. I also regretted all the time I had wasted—no, *we* had wasted—both not being able to voice our true selves.

Last, I felt relieved. I felt relieved about the fact that, clearly, Minjae wasn't freaked out by me. In fact, he was the same—even more than I had initially thought. And I felt relieved because I finally didn't care about others' opinions after the army. The army had made me see Minjae in a new light, after missing him like crazy for two very long and lonely years.

Suddenly, going slow wasn't an option anymore. I wanted to drag him to the guest room that instant... but unfortunately, I was painfully reminded that we were, in fact, in my mother's house when her voice reached us from the kitchen, asking us to join her and Seong-gi for lunch. I pulled the blushing Minjae to give me a quick hug. After I kissed him softly on his lips and pulled him up from the couch, we both headed to the dining room.

The day went by agonizingly slow. We had some home-made lunch, talked with mom. I tried to piss Seong-gi off. Mom scolded me...the usual. Minjae was kind of awkward around Mom for a while, but Mom refused to even notice. Instead, she acted as if nothing had happened at all. I was forever grateful for that, since it made Minjae loosen up and relax after a while.

Nearly forgetting that we were supposed to work at the studio back in Seoul, I fully enjoyed the day off. I did, however, remember to send the audio file of Minjae's solo to Jiwoo in the afternoon.

Eventually, dinnertime came around, which got me busy thinking about my escape plan. Mom seemed to assume we'd stay for the night, and Minjae assumed we'd head back to Seoul. He was still oblivious to the fact that we had a hotel room to go to. Seong-gi kept glancing at me with a knowing look, almost like he was waiting eagerly to see how I would squirm my way out of this one.

My rescue turned out to be Joe. During dinner, Seong-gi happened to receive a call from him about something *of dire importance*. It was only moments after he zipped out of the suite to address the issue back home that Joe texted, he would be ready for us downstairs shortly. Looked like I owed him one for the second time that day.

As dinner wrapped up, I excused myself and went to the bathroom to buy myself a moment to think. After taking a leak and washing my hands, I splashed my face with cold water to calm down and focus. I wanted to keep the hotel thing a surprise for Minjae and, of course, Mom didn't need to know. A simple, small lie wouldn't hurt anyone, right?

Just as I was reaching for the door handle, Mom's words stopped me on my tracks, though.

"So, when are you planning to go public with Do-hyun?" she asked Minjae.

I wanted to hear the answer for that too, so I cowardly hid behind the door and yes, I eavesdropped. It took a while for Minjae to answer.

"Mrs. Park, you're really not against us being together?" Minjae asked, his voice just barely reaching my ears.

"Min, I have asked you several times to call me with my given name," my mom scolded.

I could nearly hear Minjae smiling. "Sun-hee, then."

"That's better. And for the record, I have nothing against you. In fact, I've seen you as my son-in-law for a while now."

"Sun-hee, we can't get married..."

"Here. *Here* you can't get married. Yet. But don't you see that you have the power and influence to actually make a difference? And that is why I think you should go public."

Whoa, wait, what? Way to dump this on Minjae so suddenly. At the same time, I cursed myself for being practically an open book to Mom. She always seemed to know what was going on in my head.

There was a long silence before Minjae answered.

"I don't know... At least not now. It's still new," he finally answered, a pause between every word.

"Nonsense. I've seen you circling around each other for years." Why did everyone see us together before we saw us together? "Besides, I know Do would want to."

"He would?" Minjae asked silently.

I could feel the conversation turning awkward; it was time to intervene and save Min.

"I'd want what?" I asked while walking through the door.

"Nothing." Minjae blushed just like I had anticipated.

I mentally congratulated myself for a successful conversation killer move. I apologized to Mom that we had to go since we had work tomorrow. It was a half-truth at least. We'd simply decided to skip it already.

With that one, hastily delivered, lie, I was able to successfully drag Minjae out of the house with nothing more than a couple of suspicious glances from Mom. And most definitely, before Minjae could wrap his head around what was happening.

At this point, I was just eager to get us out of here and to the privacy of a hopefully fancy hotel room.

After Dark

On our way to the hotel, I glanced at Minjae who was pouting on the passenger seat. He was confused—rightfully so—since he figured out that we weren't going back to Seoul.

"Just tell me where we are going!" he whined for the fifth time.

"I told you, it's a surprise. Trust me, you'll like it."

"Oh, I'm done with surprises for the rest of my life," he said and continued acting miserable.

Despite that, I was in a great mood while following Joe's taillights through the city. When we reached the hotel, Minjae finally caught up to what my surprise was, and his eyes lit up. Yes, he had seen his fair share of luxury hotels, but hopefully he was as enthusiastic about spending some alone time with only the two of us as I was.

Joe led us straight to the private part of the hotel's carpark. As soon as we stopped, Minjae bounced up from the passenger seat and greeted the woman waiting for us to arrive. She looked around our age, or maybe a year or two older. She was wearing a formal, black knee-length dress paired with black heels. Her warm brown hair was tied up to a sleek chignon. Based on the appearance, she was most the hotel's employee assigned to guide us to our room. Her eyes brightened when she clearly recognized us but remained a well-trained professional and gave us no further reaction..

I nodded to the woman out of habit before heading towards Joe's car, parked oddly far from ours. I'd hidden the overnight bag, which I'd secretly put together, in his car. Joe had other ideas though. He got up from the driver's seat and made a point to walk to the back before opening the trunk. I narrowed my eyes, but followed him anyways, although I was sure I had tossed the bag to the backseat.

"I added a couple of items you might need today..." he said with a lowered voice while handing me the bag from the trunk.

I side glanced at Joe. He winked back. He sounded like a drug dealer and curiosity got the better of me...so of course, I made the mistake of opening the bag, only to spot a pack of condoms and a bottle of lube right there on top.

"Well, thanks," I said with a mocking, unamused tone, closed the bag, and strode back to Minjae who was now happily chatting with the host lady near the elevators without giving Joe a single glance.

Joe let out a small chuckle behind my back before slamming the trunk shut and locking the doors. After that, he headed to the stairs, told us his good nights, and confirmed that he was just a phone call away if something happened.

Though I hadn't meant to imply that Minjae and I would be having sex that night, I admitted that—as annoyed I wanted to be— I was actually grateful for the extras Joe had tossed to the bag. It was good to be prepared, and it wasn't like I could casually stroll to a store to buy these kinds of things. At least, not without making the evening news. The fact that Joe had gotten them for us was a huge relief.

I zoned out with my thoughts until we reached the suite door.. The host lady handed us the keycards and we made our way in. She gave us a small tour and showed us how the basic things worked around the room.

Joe had done well with selecting the hotel and the room. I'd first had my suspicions, since it was a large chain hotel, identical to the one we had from the same company back in Seoul. But the suite managed to exceed my expectations. We entered a spacious living room area, styled with dark interior design and with a huge black leather couch dominating the space and a wide-screen TV on the wall. There was a door leading to a private balcony on the back of the living room. To the right, a separate bedroom housed a huge, comfy-looking king-size bed. The lights on the bedroom were adjustable, and it had an en-suite, extravagant bathroom. The bathroom had an enormous hot tub and a modern looking shower that probably had every kind of setting you could dream of.

After tossing the bag on top of the bed, I followed Minjae and the host lady back to the living room. She poured us two glasses of champagne and left the bottle to the cooler on top of the sofa table. She assured me that she'd be at our disposal any time. I handed her a generous tip. Tipping wasn't actually common here, but she had done a good job showing us around, so it felt like the right thing to do.

"Thanks, Hyunmi," I said, finally catching a glimpse of her name tag. She gave us a small smile and discreetly exited the room, leaving us alone.

When I turned, Minjae was still in awe. He kept circling the place silently, occasionally sipping the champagne and testing the adjustable lights. Warm fuzz settled in the pit of my stomach when I watched him walk around, touching the furniture, and eventually making his way in front of me again.

"I hope you like it. It's for you." I took his hand in mine and led him through the door to the balcony.

When we got outside, Minjae took a nervous sip of his champagne again before replying. "What for?"

The chilly evening was tolerable with my jacket on, but that didn't stop me from sitting on the balcony couch and pulling Minjae down close to me for warmth. He leaned on me after placing his glass to the table in front of us and I pulled him even closer.

"Our first official date of course," I started and took a deep breath. "I'm sorry, but I couldn't think of anything else since we can't just casually go out..."

He smiled and rested his head against my shoulder. "It's perfect."

We stayed that way for a long while. At first, we silently enjoyed the closeness of each other, then we talked about music—the usual. To me, it was still time well spent. Nowadays it was getting so hard to even have a nice conversation with him, let alone spend some quality time with just the two of us. The past month of pure torture had made me hyper aware of that.

When I lightly brushed Minjae's hair away from his face so I could properly see his amazing eyes, he decided we'd have one of those more serious talks. He got out of my embrace, turned to face me fully, and started to play with his bracelet. I could see he had something on his mind, so I waited patiently yet again; it was the only way to get anything out of him while he was nervous.

"Do-hyun, do you want us to go public?" he finally asked. As he didn't know I had eavesdropped them, I had to think about my answer for a moment.

"Yeah, sure...someday," I said and watched his reaction carefully. To my relief, he didn't seem entirely opposed by the idea, judging by the almost smile on his face.

"It seems risky," he said after pondering my words for a little.

"But it could also make our life a lot easier." I shrugged. "Besides, it isn't like we won't have support. I mean, I'm sure the guys wouldn't mind, and my family is already okay with it."

"Oh, yeah, that reminds me... Tae kinda knows about us, I think," Minjae said and started to chew his lower lip, suddenly avoiding my eyes. He was probably thinking I'd get upset. Before that might've actually happened, but I had changed.

"Yeah?" I raised one of my eyebrows in amusement. I couldn't deny I was surprised.

"Yeah...umm, he kind of guessed that I had feelings for you, the night before the comeback concert. Then he figured out some other things, too..." he admitted.

That bastard. So, Tae knew we were kind of dating, but still had insisted on ruining my plans of being alone with Minjae for a whole month...? Unbelievable.

"I'm sorry." Minjae.

His hushed voice melted my annoyance away. "I'm not mad at you." I pulled him into a hopefully reassuring hug.

"Good." He wrapped his hands around me.

Minjae shivered then. The sky had already turned dark. Time just flew by with him. I didn't even notice it had turned seriously cold and I suggested we head back inside. Minjae nodded and I led him in. I was just about to crash to the couch after tossing my jacket to the armchair and continue our conversation where we left off, but Minjae had other ideas...

With a sudden confidence boost, he took my hand and dragged me straight towards the bedroom.

Something Sculpted

Minjae seemed determined, I'll give him that. Still, it wasn't that much of a task for me to stop him when I halted at the threshold. A slight smile crept on my face when he turned around with a confused expression, cocking one eyebrow up as if to ask, *What's the hold-up?*

I knew it was irrational, but the truth was: I was terrified. I knew he really wasn't going to break or anything, but compared to my tad taller and broader frame, he was so lean and thin he looked like a perfectly crafted porcelain doll that could break from the slightest touch.

And I was going to do way more than just touch.

I didn't quite know how to voice my concerns, but I started with, "Not...so fast."

"So fast?!" His clear frustration made me chuckle uncontrollably. He blushed and he turned his gaze to the floor. "I mean, isn't it what we came here to do...?" His sudden lack of confident almost made me regret laughing at him, but not quite.

"Define 'it'," I teased. I loved to see him flustered. More so, I loved to see him flustered because of me. Plus, it was a good distraction from my real concerns.

The blush deepened on his face and he tugged his hand, trying to pull it out of mine. I only held on tighter and turned us around to take a step into the bedroom, pulling him in with me. He still didn't answer me and kept averting my gaze, so I lifted his chin up with my index finger and forced him to look at me.

"Minjae, we didn't come here to have sex. We came here for a date," I said, as his closeness intoxicated me yet again, and I leaned closer.

I was about to reach his neck with my lips when he turned his head away. At first, I thought it was to make room for me, but then he stopped me by planting his hand on my chest.

"You don't want me," he said. It wasn't a question; it was a statement. He said it like it was just a fact, with no other options available. I let out a frustrated groan, and pushed him gently against the wall, pinning him there. I rested my forehead on his shoulder.

"There's nothing in the world I want more than you," I took a deep breath. "I... I'm just afraid. Of hurting you."

His arms made their way around my waist then and started to trace my spine in a soothing manner. "You can't hurt me. Not with this."

I wanted to argue, but before I got one word out, Minjae shushed me. He cupped my face and leaned in for a kiss. I closed my eyes when our lips connected.

My concerned thoughts seemed to disappear into thin air almost instantly. All I could wrap my head around was how demanding his soft lips became. Minjae's extreme duality made my head spin like it always did when he deepened the kiss, tracing my lips with his tongue, and letting out a small moan.

The sound made me back off a bit, with the very last drop of restraint I had in me.

"Minjae, are you sure?"

He looked me dead in the eyes when he answered, "I'm sure."

Minjae looked absolutely gorgeous while I lost myself in his deep brown eyes, searching for answers one last time. He looked confident and calm now, and certainly sure. Gradually, I let the urges take over my body when I connected our lips again. The kiss felt different now. It felt so special with this new frame of mind, where I completely gave up and let my body do what it really wanted. It might as well have been the first time.

My heart started to beat faster and faster when Minjae parted with me and led me towards the bed, hastily turning the lights down low on his way. He pushed me to sit on the edge of the bed and boldly climbed on my lap. He kissed me again. Wondering how long his confidence would last this time, I let my hand start to wander on his back while our lips moved together, sending sparks to my soul. Minjae traced the hem of my shirt before lifting it up. He pulled it over my head, tossed it somewhere, and started to unbutton his right after. His eyes glazed up right when he pushed me on my back, unbuttoned the rest of his buttons and tossed his shirt to the floor. I grinned at his impatience as I lay down on the soft bed. But my eyes betrayed me as they eagerly roamed on his well-defined torso.

I didn't get to admire his now naked upper body for long, though, since Minjae topped me over and started to explore my body with his lips. He started from my lips and I answered his sloppy kiss with equal eagerness. Shortly thereafter he moved to my neck. I got lost to the sensations and closed my eyes. His hands traced on the skin of my abdomen, leaving behind a strange, burning trail.

Eventually, he reached my jeans and we got rid of those together, leaving only my boxers on. He squirmed away from his extremely tight ones on his own and laid on the bed while I fished out the bottle of lube and a condom from the bag and placed them on top of the nightstand.

Taking my time exploring his body with my eyes, I became speechless. To me, he was perfect from head to toe. Minjae's platinum hair had spread on the plush pillow, messy as always. His eyes had darkened with lust while they shamelessly roamed my body, almost managing to make me feel self-conscious before he turned his burning gaze away. His incredibly smooth skin glowed in the low lighting, making him look even more like something sculpted rather than a human.

He tried to hide the one scar he had on his right shoulder with the duvet which he had gotten years ago. I remembered how he got it, clear as day, because I had panicked so much. It had been an accident on a rehearsal stage. The stage lift broke, and he fell. That scar was the only thing that told me he was a human in the first place.

I got so lost to the sight in front of me, I didn't even notice that he was getting shy all over again. He started to get under the sheets, all blushed up. When I did notice, I smiled and laid down beside him, making it impossible for him to squirm under the blankets. Although I liked to tease him and make him feel flustered, right now I wanted him to feel like he was the most beautiful man on earth—which he honestly was to me.

"Don't hide. You're perfect," I said, surprised by how deep my own voice sounded.

"Shut up," he huffed and turned his back to me, blushing even more.

Luckily, I had already figured out the perfect way to distract him from his own insecurities. I inched closer, wrapped my hands around his waist and pulled him against my chest before going for his neck with my lips. Even hovering my lips close to his soft and delicate skin between his jaw and collarbone made him shiver…how adorable.

While placing soft kisses on his neck, I traced my fingertips on his side. Starting from his thigh, I made my way up and over the curve on his hip, to the slight dip on his waist, before heading back down. It wasn't the first time I'd touched his skin, but I was still surprised how soft and velvety it felt under my fingertips.

When I reached his hip again with my fingers, I slightly sucked the soft spot on his neck. Though it wasn't enough to leave a mark, it was enough to make Minjae finally relax and get his confidence back. He turned around, pushed me down on my back, and made his way on top of me. He leaned in and we kissed deeply—I let my instincts take over when our lips danced together with growing urgency and I let my tongue brush against his lower lip. In the heat of the moment, I wrapped my hands around his waist and turned us over, still devouring his lips with mine. We were both gasping for air when we finally parted.

"I want you," I whispered, making a point by pressing my erected member against his.

"I want you too," he simply answered with blushed cheeks, swollen lips, and clouded eyes.

That statement was all I needed as a final confirmation. I grabbed the lube from the nightstand and started to make my way down on his body with my lips. His nipple was rock hard when I traced over it with my tongue. He arched his back and bit the joint on his index finger when I trailed my tongue over his apparently sensitive abdomen, all the way down his barely-there happy trail.

When I finally reached his underwear, I curled my fingers under the elastic and yanked them down. I also got rid of mine and then turned my attention back to Minjae's now fully erected dick. A nearly all-consuming need to taste him overpowered me. Every concern, every insecurity, had already left my mind when I leaned in and slowly twirled my tongue over it, just once, tasting the slight sourness of the tiny bead of precum.

Minjae stiffened, probably surprised, but when I took him all the way in my mouth he let out a strained whimper and grabbed the bedsheets. I figured he didn't really mind what was happening, and I went further down to the point where his dick touched my throat and sucked. I continued that way for a while, sliding up and down. I glanced up and saw Minjae's heated face—the sight was so hot my own cock started to throb with pure need.

Not being able to restrain myself any longer, I stopped sucking him and started preparing him for me. After covering my fingers with plenty of lube, I hesitantly circled his entrance and carefully entered one finger in while stroking his shaft with my other hand. Minjae froze and flinched when my index finger slowly made it past the tight ring. For a moment I was sure this wasn't going to work since he was so fucking tight I barely even got the one finger in.

Minjae relaxed gradually and preparing him got way easier. After a while of touching around, being careful to not make any sudden moves, I entered another finger. My eyes were fixated on his face the whole time I prepared him, watching him squirm while I worked my fingers in his hole. He was already in a whole another world and kept moaning and whimpering, gripping the sheets, and squeezing his eyes tight.

Eventually, the sight made my patience run out. Quickly, I rolled a condom on, lathered on some more lube, and aligned my cock in line with his hole. With one firm movement, I pushed all the way in. He was just so damn tight; I swear my sight momentarily blacked out. Minjae let out a small, pained whimper, clearly holding back, and I opened my eyes. One tear of pain ran down his face. My heart broke. I panicked and started to pull out, but Minjae had other ideas...

"No! Just let me adjust..." he said with a firm voice and trailed off, holding me still.

My heart cried for his pain, but somehow I managed to stay still. Whispering some hopefully soothing words to his ear, I waited patiently, although it was nearly impossible with his tightness around me. Gradually, he relaxed and nodded to me in a sign that I could move. Still, I took it extremely slow at first, to make sure it was bearable. Slowly but surely, Minjae's expression turned from pained back to lust and I dared to pick up the pace a bit.

Every movement got me closer to the edge. Every whimper of Minjae made me lose myself a bit more. Every touch we shared made me feel like I was one with him.

Minjae whispered that he was getting close. I propped myself up a bit and reached for his shaft. He started mumbling and moaning my name when I stroked his length in rhythm with my thrusting. Out dragged, hot breaths mixed together, when we rocked towards our mutual goal.

I kept my gaze on his gorgeous, flustered face all the while when we both inched closer to our climax. He was just so beautiful;

my mind couldn't put it to words. Eventually, he stiffened, bit his lip and frowned—and came all over his stomach. I let out a satisfied groan when I followed him over the edge shortly after, riding off the after-waves of his orgasm.

The expression on his face afterwards was mesmerizing, something I'll always remember. He looked like a complete mess, a beautiful one at that. With his hair all messy, eyes still clouded, lips swollen, he looked thoroughly fucked...and completely mine.

Still feeling high and exhausted to the core, I couldn't keep myself propped up any longer and crashed on top of him. Praying he didn't get crushed under the weight, I mumbled some apologies and tried to roll over...he didn't let me.

Instead, he wrapped his hands around my waist and looked so deep in my eyes it felt like he was looking straight through to my soul. He pulled me even tighter against his chest before letting out a faint, exhausted whisper, "Saranghae."

American Pancakes

A wide smile crept on my face when I woke up to the sunlight beaming brightly to my eyes. Minjae was still in my arms, sleeping peacefully with his naked back against my chest. The light bounced off from his hair and skin; he looked mesmerizing…and gorgeous.

He'd fallen asleep before me, after we showered together, and slept the whole night continuously, for once–at least to my knowledge. My heart swelled on my chest when memories of the night momentarily took up all the space in my head.

I groaned from my sudden arousal and couldn't help but tighten my grip around Minjae's waist and reach for my favorite spot on his neck with my lips. Inhaling that intoxicating scent of his made my head feel light, and I closed my eyes as I continued devouring the neck of the sleeping man in my arms.

Though he didn't get to sleep much longer since my actions woke him up. Still admiring the glow that his skin seemed to radiate, I watched him first stir in his sleep and finally flutter his beautiful brown eyes open. When he turned around to face me, I got surprised—he wasn't his usual grumpy self this morning. Instead, he smiled, and his eyes glistened nearly as bright as the sun.

Now that was a sight I could get used to.

"Good morning," he mumbled with his incredibly sexy, husky morning voice.

"Good morning," I replied before leaning in for one of those mind-blowing kisses I knew he had in store.

Unfortunately, Minjae had other ideas.

"Morning breath," he mumbled through his hand which blocked my way.

"Watch me care," I said back, prying his hand away from his face and finally reaching his lips.

He eventually wrapped his hands around my waist. Soon enough, we were one hot, panting mess, rolling around on the bed while both of us tried to get their hands everywhere at once.

When we finally calmed down, Minjae had somehow ended up halfway on top of me with his leg tangled between mine and his face buried in my neck. Lazily, I stroked his lower back with my hand while the other was comfortably tucked behind my head. Minjae fit there perfectly. I could have stayed this way for the rest of my life.

Unfortunately, reality started to creep in our happy bubble in the form of a ringtone, ringing annoyingly loud somewhere in the room. It was the tone I specifically set for Tae.. I had no idea what the time was, but I suspected it was nearly ten since he was calling. We were probably supposed to be in Seoul, preparing for the promo event scheduled for this morning.

I didn't make one move to get up from the bed and answer him. Then again, neither did Minjae.

"I don't want to go back..." Minjae whispered.

What could I have said to that? I didn't want to go back either. It didn't just mean going back home; it meant going back to hiding. Not to mention back to being busy. My phone rang and rang somewhere while we both continued to stubbornly ignore it. The first call ended eventually but was immediately replaced with a different ringtone. Even though it was my regular tone, I could've thrown a highly educated guess that it was either Jiwoo or Joonseok. Minjae's phone rang somewhere too.

Finally, the last caller was Joe, who also had his own ringtone.

"Minjae, I have to take it. It's Joe," I stated to the pouting Minjae and practically had to tear my way out of his grip. After spotting my jeans on the floor not far from the bed, I searched the pockets and found the phone and swept the screen to answer.

"What?" I barked.

I heard a chuckle on the other end before Joe said, "I hate to burst your bubble, but they're all harassing me with endless phone calls. I think we should head back."

"I know. I'll handle them. Just let us have some breakfast and get rid of the rental. We're riding with you."

"Sure thing," he said and hung up.

For a few long seconds, I stared at the phone in my hand and sat on the edge of the bed. Minjae made his way behind me and wrapped his hands around my waist.

The two callers before Joe had been Tae and Jiwoo, as expected. I picked the least evil of the two and called back. It took exactly two beeps before Tae answered.

"Where the fuck are you? And where's Minjae?" he demanded to know and continued to throw me insults and profanities about all the work we had to do and something about how Joonie was worried sick, Jiwoo was pissed, and Chris was suspicious. I let him get the steam out and waited patiently for his rant to be over while Minjae nuzzled his nose against my back.

Nothing could ruin my mood with Minjae here..

"We're in Daegu," I stated calmly after Tae's rant finally ended.

"The fuck are you doing in Daegu?!" he shouted back.

"Visited Mom. Look, you don't get to be pissed. You knew about me and Min and you still chose to make my life a hell...so just deal with it."

"Oh..." he huffed, trailing off before the realization fully hit him. "OH! Umm...yeah, well, get back soon. I'll cover for you here."

"Thought so." I smirked and ended the call. Served him right.

I tossed the phone on the pillow and leaned back. Minjae rested his chin on my shoulder and squeezed me tight. I felt conflicted—yesterday had been the happiest day of my life, then today crushed me right under the weight of reality. Honestly, I could sense that

Minjae had the same conflicted feelings, which made me worry about him too.

"We have to go back?" he asked with a somewhat whiny tone. He too seemed to be disappointed.

"Yeah. But I'm honestly not sure if I can take another month without you," I said, sadness taking over my voice while I traced Minjae's arm with my fingers.

"Then don't," he simply stated.

"What do you mean?"

"Well, since Tae already knows, I think we could start the public thing by telling the other's when we get back home."

I rested my head against his shoulder. That sounded like a dream come true at this point. "Really, we don't have to tell them if you don't want to."

"Believe me, I want to. At least that way it'd be easier to find time to be together...and slightly less of the hiding involved."

"Well, I'm ready if you are," I said, fully grinning.

"Actually, I'm not worried about me. I don't have any family besides GRiD, remember? It's you I'm worried about."

I turned around and pulled him into a tight hug.

"Stop worrying so damn much," I said and reluctantly let him go to get up and order some breakfast.

"Someone has to," he said and rolled his eyes.

I grinned and threw him some clothes from the bag and made my way in some loose jeans I'd packed. Faintly remembering the hotel telephone was in the kitchen, I strolled there and speed-dialed reception. A pleasant female voice answered, and I ordered some American pancakes for Minjae and me. I knew he'd like them; he had always ordered them for breakfast whenever available in the hotels we'd stayed in the past. When I got back to the bedroom, Minjae was finally getting up from the bed. He was mumbling something about the clothes not matching.

"I ordered pancakes," I stated at the threshold, ignoring his whining about my awful fashion sense.

I heard Minjae take a deep breath and curse slightly under his breath. I turned back and saw him wince as he was standing up. I was by his side in a nanosecond.

"What's wrong?" I asked and hovered my hand near his elbow, ready to catch him if he fell. Which he looked like he was about to in any second.

The corner of his mouth turned up in a slight smile while he blushed and averted my worried gaze. "I'm just a bit s-sore..."

The Night of Confessions

"Aish, stop apologizing. I'm fine," Minjae said while violently stabbing his pancake with the knife.

It was just like I had predicted—however careful I had tried to be, he still got hurt in the end. And it was all my fault. I felt awful. I opened my mouth to protest and apologize for the hundredth time when Minjae's ice cold gaze made me close it again in defeat.

Sulking, I chomped down my part of the breakfast. After leaving a huge tip and making sure we didn't leave our personal belongings behind, we headed to the garage with Joe, who joined us at the elevators. I had planned on cuddling with Minjae the whole way home, but he darted right to the back seat of the BMW and slammed the door shut right in front of my nose.

Joe chuckled. "What did you do this time?"

"Apologized," I mumbled, tossed the bag to the trunk and heading to sit in the front seat instead.

Soon enough, we were on our way back to Seoul. The reality started seriously weighing my shoulders down with every passing minute we got closer to home. It was a weird feeling—normally I would have been thrilled to get home. This time I was disappointed that we even had to leave the hotel and sad that we weren't going to have that much time to be together anytime soon.

And I still felt awful about hurting him.

I assumed we were still on about telling the guys that we were together. I might've looked like one that doesn't worry to Minjae, but the reality was that I was slightly terrified to get home. I was still sure I wanted to tell them, but at the same time, I wondered what their reactions would be. Well, at least Tae had taken it lightly. Maybe Chris and Joonie would be the same. But I couldn't guarantee it. And then there was Jiwoo too, who was nearly as close to us as the guys. Would we tell her? How would she react? Probably at least give us a lecture about scandals and how they've ruined perfectly good careers in the past.

The thing about scandals was that it broke the carefully crafted illusion all celebrities have created to both protect and promote themselves. Sometimes scandals ended careers. Sometimes they were efficiently used as publicity stunts. But they were never planned, which made them hazardous.

Being famous wasn't even remotely like most people believed it was. It wasn't like we were opening our whole personal life to the public. People don't generally realize they are fed an image, a strategic presentation of a person—not the actual person. Our fans might've thought they knew us, but the reality was that they knew what we and our publicity team wanted them to know.

Our fans knew only the so-called stage personality of Minjae—to them, he was confident, shameless, and for many of them: a sex object. As unrealistic as it might've sounded when you knew the real Minjae, he was the "mister abs" on stage, making sure to flash some skin from time to time. Not to even mention all the raunchy choreographs he made. But the fans knew nothing about his insecurities, or that he had an extremely cute side to him too. Well, the cute side he showed sometimes, but never the insecure side.

They thought I was only an arrogant, somewhat good-looking brat, who somehow miraculously made it big despite coming from a family living in poverty. I was all that, but most of them didn't realize how much time I had to spend on the gym to get and maintain this body, not to mention the endless dieting. They knew nothing, and probably didn't even want to know about the countless hours of work I had to put into it before I even got signed. And I was only a 17-year-old kid back then. I had to work as a trainee for over a year before we even debuted, and *then* it had been an uphill battle for years before we got somewhere. Then we did our stint in the army, and we were suddenly thrown back to square one.

GRiD as a whole was basically a carefully carved story, one that had next to nothing to do with reality. The reality was boring, reality didn't sell albums or the seats of arenas and stadiums. A fairy-tale named GRiD did. And if this ended badly, that story would be broken. And Jiwoo knew that. It was her job to keep that from happening.

The drive back home went by all too fast and way too slow at the same time. We were all quiet the whole way. Minjae fell asleep on the backseat midway. I concentrated on staring out the window, deep in my own thoughts, watching the scenery change. For once, I was grateful that Joe drove like a grandpa, and it took us nearly four hours to get back to Seoul.

Eventually, whether I liked it or not, I saw our apartment building standing tall in front of us. Just like a thousand times before, Joe drove to the garage on the underground floor. I was momentarily blinded by the sudden darkness of the garage after looking out to a bright sunny day for hours. My heart sank when I got my sight back and immediately spotted Jiwoo's car parked right next to Tae's SUV.

Minjae woke up when Joe parked the car next to my Porsche. After stretching and telling us he had things to do, he waved us his goodbyes and headed to the elevators. I sighed, got up as well, opened the trunk, and took our bag. Minjae had gotten up too and waited for me by the elevators with a frown in between his eyebrows.

"You still mad at me?" I asked when I reached him. We stepped inside the metal box which would take us upstairs.

"Of course not," he started and took my free hand in his. "I'm just a bit nervous."

I knew exactly what he meant. It was a nice confirmation that we were still up to telling the guys about us though. As the lift came to a stop, I placed a light kiss on his plump lips before letting go of his hand, all right before the doors opened. We both took a deep breath before stepping in.

On our way to the living room—where I predicted the others were waiting for us—I quickly tossed the bag in front of my bedroom door. Getting ready for scolding and a lecture or two, we both walked the short way to the living room like we were preparing for the doomsday.

I was right about them waiting for us in the living room, but everything else I had predicted was completely wrong. We both halted at the threshold, the sight taking me by a surprise, and I guess Minjae too. They were all acting pretty much normal, even cheerful. Joonie was cooking in the kitchen part of the open space, while Chris and Tae were casually chatting with Jiwoo around the living room table.

Jiwoo even greeted us like she was genuinely pleased to see us. I glanced at Minjae, who looked back at me with a bewildered expression that I was sure I had on my face as well. It was Minjae who shrugged it off first and sat on the couch.

"What's with the unmatching outfit?" Jiwoo asked Minjae.

"Do-hyun packed," he stated nonchalantly and pointed towards me with his thumb. "So...where's the lecture about us ditching work and such?"

I crashed to the nearest armchair and turned my eyes toward Jiwoo, equally as curious as Minjae.

Jiwoo chuckled first and gave us a smile before answering. "I didn't come here to give lectures for grown-ass men. Besides, I think I've laid the schedule a bit tight for all of you guys, so your disappearing on me is kinda my own fault. Frankly, I'm sorry."

My jaw dropped and I just stared at her like she was an alien from a different planet. That wasn't the Jiwoo I knew; that was a stranger. To my relief, Joonie still acted like himself.

"But please give us a heads up next time. I was worried sick," he yelled from the kitchen.

Minjae was the first one of us two to recover. "So, noona, what are you doing here then?"

"Oh, just visiting. What, can't I just visit you without ulterior motives now?"

"Yes, but you always have something," I clapped back.

She smirked. "Ahh...I've been caught. I came here to talk about Minjae's solo piece. I listened to it yesterday and so did some other's back at HQ and—"

"And?" Minjae asked and straightened himself up on the couch.

"And it's great! In fact, it's so good we're currently being pressured by the label about turning it into a group piece instead and publishing it as the next single. The same goes with Joonie's solo—he and Tae already agreed to this."

"Whoa, wait. What?!" My neck cracked to how suddenly I turned my eyes back to Jiwoo. "There's no time for that!"

"I know. Which is why I've negotiated that we'd publish this album as is right now. Then we'll repackage around five months from now, adding these two songs and anything else you might come up prior to that. That is, if you agree. It's entirely up to you two."

Normally, I would have been against all repackaging bullshit. But five months from now would mark right about after the halfway point to our world tour, making it a great move businesswise. Also, it would give us much more time to polish them up, rearrange and re-record, film the music videos and such... And we wouldn't be in such a hurry to do an entirely new album. The fans would get their hands on new material sooner than they'd even expect. It sounded like a win-win situation to me. What sealed the deal for me, though, was that I'd be able to spend more time with Minjae when our schedule loosened up a bit.

Unfortunately, It would also mean Minjae would lose his solo. I was sure that there would be other opportunities to make a new one for him, but I wanted him to have all the spotlight. He was talented and deserved it. Besides, that might've been an important song for him. I heard it in his singing and the lyrics.

"Well, I'm down. But it's practically Minjae's, so it's up to him" I glanced at him.

At first he looked a bit conflicted, but eventually the crease between his eyes smoothed out. "On one condition: the chorus stays as is."

"Noona, you'll stay for dinner, right?" Joonie yelled from the kitchen, startling us all.

Jiwoo looked like she was about to roll her eyes but only yelled back, "Of course." She turned back to us. "It's settled then."

We both nodded.

Tae, Minjae, and Jiwoo started to chat about something that had gone down today. Something about the collaborative special stages at MAMAs. Apparently, some popular groups' leader had specifically requested for Minjae to do one of the collaborative performances with him. I had a hard time keeping up with that given everything that happened, but I was glad Minjae was getting some recognition.

After that, Chris, Tae, and Jiwoo just continued their discussion from before we arrived. Minjae and I shared a questioning glance—we both didn't have any idea of what had just happened. Though, I had a hunch on why Jiwoo had been exceptionally nice to us today...

"I'm in serious need of a shower and a change of clothes," Minjae stated as he gave me a meaningful glance and headed towards his room.

As soon as Minjae was completely gone, I got up. "Admit it, you didn't give us the usual lecture because you wanted to soften us up for the album thing."

"Guilty." She raised his arms up in a sign of surrender and started laughing full-heartedly.

Eager to get back to Minjae, I didn't linger to chat. Instead, taking over his room started to sound appealing in my head. It was always fun to watch him pretend to be annoyed.

Joonie stopped me at the threshold to the hall, however. Thankfully it was just to hand me a couple of bowls of leftover lunch.

"Thanks."

"You're welcome," Joonie said, eyes twinkling. "I'm right to assume you can take the other bowl to Minjae?"

"Of course."

As I strolled down the hallway to Minjae's door was left ajar. I made my way in and closed the door as silently as possible while balancing the noodle cups in my hands.

Inside, Minjae was already in a full panic mode. I stood there at the entrance, patiently watching him pace around the room like a cornered wild animal. When he finally noticed me, he stiffened still as a stone. To my relief, his shoulders dropped in relief when he noticed I brought lunch.

He snatched one of the cups from my hand without saying anything at all, sat down on one of his armchairs, and started munching the lunch down eagerly. I followed his lead and took a few bites. As I wasn't really hungry, I gave up when Minjae was done with his bowl and left my cup on his desk before hopping on his bed. After getting comfortable, I tapped the space next to me.

Letting out a long sigh, he plopped down to sit on the bed beside me.

"Jiwoo's staying," he hissed silently. Apparently, we were whispering now.

"Yes, I noticed," I whispered back with a small, silent chuckle.

"Are we gonna tell her, too?"

"This whole thing was your idea, so it's up to you. But it's kinda perfect timing."

"What do you mean?" he asked, still whispering, but now also frowning.

"For one, she seems mellow today—that's rare. Also, she deserves to know," I stated, just as quietly.

He pinched the bridge of his nose for a short minute before responding, "Fine. But after dinner. I'm hungry."

"Still?" I teased, earning a light punch to my shoulder.

I wrapped my hands around his waist and pulled him on top of me. He struggled for a while but as always, I won. He gave up and got himself comfortable, resting his head on my chest with his legs tangled in mine. He mumbled something about crushing me under his weight, to which I chuckled. He felt as light as a feather to me.

At one point, I stroked his fluffy hair gently. A minute and some more flew by. I don't really know how much time passed like that; time became a meaningless drone to me. Unfortunately though, Minjae was keeping track.

"Hyung, it's nearly dinnertime..." Minjae started.

Reluctantly, I let him go. Surprising me, he sneaked in a short kiss before darting to his bathroom. I couldn't erase the smile on my face when I watched him go. With dragging feet, I reluctantly made my way to my own room. Our overnight bag lingered in the hall. I picked it up, and for once, didn't unpack immediately. I just tossed it next to my bed. After taking a quick shower, I threw on some random comfy jeans and a t-shirt and plopped down on my neatly made bed.

Staring at the plain white ceiling, I let my mind wander. I was neither terrified, nor worried any longer. I realized that at the end of the day, Minjae was the most important thing to me now. I had enough money to last me a lifetime. I was sure Minjae's bank account wouldn't be any less loaded. Although he didn't earn as much as me from royalties, he had many side projects like choreographing for other groups and such. GRiD itself was good business, especially touring. If it came down to it, we could just quit. We could even move to another country... a more open-minded one. Start over.

The problem was that I didn't want to. And I knew Minjae didn't either. Even I had to admit, the advantages of being a celebrity and my love for making music outweighed the downsides to this profession by a ton. I knew Minjae loved this life, and he loved it here. We all loved our fans wholeheartedly, even though we couldn't really show the reality to them.

Minjae wouldn't be able to leave Tae, Chris, and Joonie behind, even if they were to break his heart by rejecting our relationship, which I highly doubted they would. Jiwoo was a big question mark, but she didn't seem old-fashioned. If she'd be against us, it wouldn't be because we were gay. It would be because us coming out to the public or getting outed would be a scandal.

A knock on my door and Chris's voice telling me that it was dinnertime dragged me back to present. It was pointless to wallow on my thoughts anyway. I'd find out the outcome soon enough.

The dinner went by like it always did—noisy and boisterous. Joonie had once again managed to make chicken, rice and vegetables served in different ways taste like heaven on a plate. As seniors, Jiwoo and Tae kept pouring us all beer and soju throughout the dinner. Chris took a few videos to the Crew and posted them on Twitter. Even Minjae relaxed next to me, probably due to the alcohol hitting his system. He was wearing one of those choker necklaces, and I caught myself once again staring at his neck from time to time.

The dinner turned into plain old drinking real fast, and there never seemed to be the right time to bring up the topic at hand. Minjae seemed to notice that too and became increasingly fidgety every passing minute. Under the table, I squeezed his thigh and winked, trying to get him to relax again. He only gave me a small smile, and we continued to fool around with everyone, waiting for the right opportunity to appear.

Which never did.

My phone buzzed in my jeans pocket. I fished it out, frowning, nearly no-one except Minjae ever texted me and he was right beside me. My frown deepened when I noticed it was, in fact, Minjae who had sent the text. I hadn't even noticed he had had his phone at hand. He was chatting with Chris about something regarding the new album, clearly ignoring me and the text he had just sent. Discreetly, I opened the text under the table, because apparently it was something to be hidden.

They're getting drunk, I'll just say it before that, the text said.

Just when I lifted my eyes from the phone, Minjae downed a shot of soju.

"Quiet!" he yelled, earning everyone's complete attention at once.

The whole room fell silent. Everyone—including me—was in shock that Minjae had raised his voice. He rarely did. I gulped—*this is it, then*. Minjae took my hand in his under the table and cleared his throat.

"So...me and Do…we're together. Like, *together*-together. Just for your info," he said with a surprisingly firm voice. He even gave me a warm, wide smile before downing another shot.

It was dead silent.

I took back one shot too before daring to raise my gaze from the table to seek for the reactions. Tae smirked smugly, which wasn't a surprise. Joonie's smile had a bit more warmth to it.

"Ugh, we know. No need to make a statement, geez," Chris said, eyes rolling.

Finally, my eyes found Jiwoo's, who was watching both Minjae and me with an unreadable expression. She toyed with her beer and narrowed her eyes but didn't say anything for a long while. When the silence continued, even Chris turned to look at her.

"So yeah, that happened," I said to Jiwoo, just to break the strained silence.

It seemed to snap her awake from her frenzy. "I'm just confused ..." She trailed off after shaking her head, making her long curls bounce. When no one said anything, she continued. "I mean, haven't you been together, like... years?"

Everyone let out a long, relieved breath, including me. I took a sip from my beer and inhaled again, suddenly very aware of my own breathing. "No, it's been like a little over a month," I said with a glance at Minjae.

He smiled back, clearly relieved by Jiwoo's response.

"A month?!" Jiwoo downed a shot, too. Apparently, that was now a thing.

Tae choked on his beer. Joonie let out a chuckle. Both of them threw back their own shots. Chris just eyed us all amused, before having a hysterical laughing fit. After he calmed down, he, too, took a shot.

"Well, damn," Jiwoo said, fanning her face with a magazine in an overly dramatic manner. "Now *that* was a surprise."

Gradually, everyone went back to drinking and chatting. The only slight change compared to before was that Minjae and I continued holding hands. We had fooled around before, yes, but this time it all felt way easier when you didn't have to act like you didn't really care. And we wouldn't have to hide when at home anymore, which was a huge relief.

All in all, it almost felt like it had been too easy for us to come out of the closet as a gay couple. Even when it was just for the closest persons around us, for now. Considering our profession and the publicity of it all, it was nearly impossible that we wouldn't get at least one problem down the road. But for now, everything seemed okay for the first time in ages.

Choker of the Day

Later that night, Jiwoo pulled me to the side when she found a moment I wasn't glued to Minjae.

"Now, seriously speaking...are you two planning to go public with this?" she asked.

I couldn't read her weird expression at all, so I answered truthfully. "Yeah, maybe someday."

"Well, when that happens, please tell me first. There's no need to make it a scandal," she said nudged my elbow with hers in a playful manner.

"Of course," I replied. It was a no-brainer for me.

She twisted a finger through her curls, not making eye contact. "Honestly, I was a bit surprised. I mean, I've seen you circling around each other for years, but I never really thought something would come out of it."

"Yeah? So, you didn't really think that we had been together for years?" I asked.

"Of course not; that was for Minjae's sake. He looked like he was about to faint. I trust you enough that I know you'll tell me these things. I'm not only your manager you know, but you're also all my closest friends. At least I'd like to think that way. And I am genuinely happy for you two. I don't know why you looked like you had seen a ghost." She chuckled.

"I just didn't know how you'll take it since we are, you know...gay. And sorta famous ones."

"Oh please. I'm older than you all but I'm not that old," she said, paired with another chuckle and headed back to the living room to the others.

Still a bit out of it, or maybe just under the influence of alcohol, I watched her go. I'd agonized over telling her for nothing. She was not like our first manager before her, who had been a cold, emotionless scumbag bossing us around. *Ugh.* I preferred to not even remember his name.

Jiwoo practically skipped across the room and started dancing together with Joonie and Minjae who had turned the living room into a dance floor. The furniture was all pushed aside to make room for their drunk fooling around. Chris shook his head to the sight and went past me to his room. Chuckling, I shook my head and headed to the bathroom to take a leak.

After I was done with my business, Minjae was waiting for me right outside. He leaned against the wall, swaying a little. As soon as he saw me, he bit his bottom lip, gazed me under his thick lashes and played with the fucking choker-of-the-day.

Something snapped in my alcohol-hazed brain. It took only one swift movement, and I had Minjae pinned between me and the wall.

"Now, tell me...what's with these lately?" I whispered while curling my index finger under the velvet ribbon on his neck.

"The chokers?" Minjae confirmed. "Joonie and I got a bunch of them for free from this one brand a few weeks ago. Why?"

I pulled him in by the necklace. He gasped, leaned closer, put his hand over my chest and grasped a handful of my t-shirt in his fist.

"They're driving me mad," I whispered breathily to his ear before pressing my lips to the sensitive spot between the ribbon and his earlobe.

"Good," he breathed, tipping his head back, and wrapping his hands around my neck.

Fuck.

My mind went totally blank and blood rushed straight to my groin. A groan I tried to muffle against the skin on his neck, came from somewhere very deep inside me. I swear this man was making me go insane. We needed to get out of there, now. Minjae must've read my thoughts and hopped in my arms, wrapping his legs around my waist. I barely caught him on time, and with growing urgency, we somehow miraculously made it to the door of my room. I put him down, opened the door and hastily dragged him inside.

As soon as we both got in, I locked the door behind me. Minjae pushed me against it immediately and started yanking my clothes out of his way. I heard a faint ripping sound when he pulled my t-shirt over my head, but I couldn't care less. I wasn't that patient for his t-shirt either, so I guess we were even after that.

Minjae clashed his lips against mine as soon as we got rid of the shirts. I responded to him with the same eagerness, my worries about hurting him apparently washed down with the alcohol. But Minjae was even more impatient than me, weirdly enough. As soon as we parted for a breather, he immediately went for my neck with his lips. I practically saw stars when I leaned my head back against the door.

He didn't stop there though. After he was done with my neck, he went further down. Making me a hot, panting mess on his way, I might add. I regained my sanity momentarily when he started unbuckling my belt. I tried to stop him—no way he needed to do this—but he just swatted my hands aside. I glanced down and was met with the hottest sight I had ever seen in my entire life.

Minjae was on his knees in front of me and was now palming my ever growing erection through the front of my jeans. Slowly, he opened the button and pulled the zipper down while staring me straight in the eyes with his hazed up ones. The rush we both felt earlier was all but forgotten by now. He took his time pulling my pants down. As soon as I was freed from the prison of my jeans and underwear, I couldn't do much else than watch Minjae bite his lip when he wrapped his warm hand around my shaft. I almost let out a loud sound of pleasure, but fortunately remembered we were still at the dorm and quickly bit my left knuckle.

This man will be the death of me, was the only thought crossing my mind. Repeatedly, like a broken record.

Minjae certainly took his time to get himself familiarized with my manly parts. It felt like his hands were everywhere at once, and I was right on the edge of losing it multiple times. But it wasn't until he wrapped his warm and wet mouth over it that I was sure I'd go over the edge instantly. Miraculously, I was able not to.

It was torture. Sweet, hot, and extremely pleasant torture…but still torture. My free hand which wasn't chewing down my knuckle made its way on its own through Minjae's hair when he bobbed his head up and down on my length.

Closing my eyes was a mistake. It only heightened the sensations. I flashed them open as soon as I got them closed and pulled his hair gently to get him off my dick. Letting out a relieved sigh when he released me from his mouth, I helped him up from the floor. As soon as he was up, we got rid of his pants together.

Impatiently, I dragged him further in my room and practically tossed him on top of my bed. He didn't mind; he just laid on his stomach and arched his back for me. I was tempted to stand there and admire him. But of course, I didn't have the patience for that. At all.

Thank god I didn't bother to unpack the bag earlier. The lube was still right on top. After climbing to the bed next to him, I ran my hand down his spine, making him shiver and arch his back even further. I would've teased him even more if my own dick wasn't already throbbing almost painfully.

After lubing up my fingers and his entrance, I somehow managed to take my time prepping him up. Minjae was at least as much of a hot mess as I had been earlier while I prepared him. He was whimpering and whining against the sheets and pillow, scared to make too much noise. Any other day, anywhere else, I would've wanted him to just let go and make as much noise as he wanted, but this was the dorm.

I completely lost it and barely remembered to grab a condom after Minjae grabbed my shoulder, yanked me closer, and whispered in my ear, "I need you. Now."

Barely even remembering it, I don't think I've ever slid a rubber on faster.

Minjae squirmed under me when I raised his hips and entered his still tight asshole. This time, I knew to let him adjust to my size and kept still for a moment. Pinning him down against the mattress, I started placing sloppy kisses all over his neck and shoulders, still very much distracted by the velvet ribbon circling his neck.

He started panting and moving his hips a bit, so I figured he was at least somewhat adjusted. I started slow, but as I had been so close to cumming several times already, I picked up the pace as soon as I was sure he wasn't hurting too much.

I was sure I'd come first this time, but again, I was utterly and completely wrong. Apparently, the friction from the mattress and me hitting his prostate made him get over the edge in no time. His muscles clenched around my dick and I pushed in as deep as possible. With a groan, I released deep inside him and crashed on top of him.

For a while, we both caught our breath. Eventually, I carefully pulled out and rolled onto my back. Minjae rolled on his back too and we just stared each into each other's eyes, thoroughly exhausted but completely happy. When his eyes started to droop, I figured it was time to get us both cleaned up.

With utmost care, I tucked my hand under his back and the other under his knees and lifted him up. He clung to my neck when I carried him to the bathroom and laid him to his feet under the shower. His legs were still a bit shaky, so I let him cling to me while I washed both of us with warm and soothing water.

After putting him back under the blankets, I crawled into bed next to him and wrapped my hand around his waist from behind.

"Minjae...are you hurt?" I asked softly, worried I'd messed up again.

He turned around in my embrace and smiled. "No. It was amazing."

But there still was another concern lingering on my mind which I couldn't brush aside. "I—, um, I almost forgot to use a condom. I'm *so* sorry."

He still smiled. "I noticed. Look, I was a virg....umm, I've never done this with anyone else. So if you're clean, I think we're good either way."

My chest exploded with all kinds of feelings. Minjae was a virgin? Yes, I knew he was inexperienced, and so was I, but this...I nearly forgot to even answer him.

"Yeah, I'm clean." I was sure. I had been tested.

"Then don't worry about it," he said and placed a soft kiss on my lips.

Black Liquid Gold

Alcohol is often fun...until the next day arrives. I woke up to a massive headache pounding in my skull. My mouth tasted like shit and my throat was as dry as a desert. Swallowing literally felt like I'd eaten sandpaper the previous night. Groaning, I got up to a sitting position, instantly blinded by the sun shining straight to my eyes. The rays felt like they were scorching my eyeballs, resulting in me whining like a baby.

A faint mumble sound emerging from under the blankets made me take a sharp turn, which I immediately regretted. The sudden movement made my head downright exploding. Wincing, I held my head between my palms, trying to keep it from falling completely apart. While taking some deep breaths, still trying to get the headache away, I heard that same mumbling voice again. Only this time, I was able to decipher some actual words.

"Oh, please keep quiet. Also, shut the fucking blinds."

It was Minjae's grumpy morning voice. Carefully opening my eyes just a tiny bit, I spotted a man-sized lump beside me on my bed. Minjae had buried himself completely under the blankets, only a few strands of his platinum hair stuck out from the top. I chuckled at that sight.

If I was hungover that much, I could've only imagined Minjae had it worse. Frankly, I felt sorry for him.

"Want some water?" I asked, surprised by how hoarse my voice sounded.

After hearing a faint, barely there, "Yes, please," I slowly got up from the bed with shaky legs. I made my way around the bed towards my first goal: the window. I tried to block the sun rays with my hand. but I wasn't very successful, and the light was killing me. It was a struggle. After finally getting the blinds closed, I let out a long sigh of relief. I think I heard one from under the blankets too.

My mini fridge was across the room. Even though it was easier to move was after it got darker, it was still a struggle. I might've tripped on some clothes on the floor on my way, possibly making a bit of noise while I was at it. When I finally reached the fridge and yanked it open, I let out a frustrated growl because there was nothing. I had forgotten to fill it up.

"Are you incapable of doing anything silently? Geez..." Minjae hissed from the bed, still buried completely under the blankets.

Ignoring him, I fished out some sweatpants from my closet, threw on a bathrobe and stomped out of the room, cursing under my breath for not remembering to fill my fridge. Unfortunately, the outside world on the other side of the door was still as bright as fuck, so turned right back. After grabbing a pair of sunglasses laying on top of a drawer, I headed back out on my mission.

My feet weighed a ton, but I somehow managed to slowly walk my way to the kitchen. Halfway there, my nose picked up the faint, alluring scent of just-brewed coffee. It smelled like paradise.

Tae had already brewed coffee and was setting up a huge hangover breakfast for us all. I plopped down on one of the bar stools on the counter and just trying to survive while Tae looked energetic as ever. He wasn't much of a drinker, unlike the rest of us, so he rarely got hungover. Smart bastard.

"Hungover?" Tae asked, smirking and handing over a glass of water.

"Yeah," I croaked and eagerly took a sip. "Got some of that black liquid gold?"

He nodded. "I'll pour you a cup."

"Make that two, Minjae is in a pretty bad shape as well..."

"He's got you all wrapped around his finger already?" he teased while roaming through the cupboards, trying to find something. "Let me get you some breakfast, to-go then." Maybe Minjae had him around his finger too.

"He's always had me—" I started but got cut off by an equally as—if not worse—hangover Joonie.

"Stop making a mess at my kitchen," he muttered to Tae while plopping down to the bar stool next to me, looking honestly a bit greenish.

Maybe Tae had been a little more affected by the previous night's alcohol consumption more than I originally thought because he jumped when he heard Joonie's voice behind him. He recovered quickly though.

"It's not your kitchen. It's *our* kitchen..." Tae said and trailed off, his eyes scanning the cabinets above him. "But where do you keep the trays?"

Joonie chuckled and pointed to the cupboard on the left corner before getting back to wallowing in misery beside me. Tae served him some coffee and returned to arranging the breakfast for me and Minjae. When he was done, it looked mouth-watering. There were eggs sunny side up, bread, fruits, juice, and two steamy cups of coffee.

Carefully, I picked up the tray, muttered some thanks to Tae, and rushed back towards my room. I was so ready to get back to the darkness and under the blankets, hopefully getting to cuddle with Minjae for the rest of the day.

I had left my door cracked open, so it wasn't hard to weave through with the tray in my hands. Minjae was still curled under the blankets, his back towards me, but at least his head now stuck out.

"Took you long enough. Got water?" He turned around, hair all disheveled and eyes drooping. He looked absolutely adorable.

"Better," I replied, smiling.

I laid the tray on the bedside table and quickly tossed the bathrobe and the sweatpants off before crawling back to bed. After propping myself up against the headboard, Minjae followed my lead.

"That smells amazing." The corners of his mouth tugged upwards.

I handed him a cup. "You'll have to thank Tae for this."

He took a sip and closed his eyes with satisfaction lingering on his lips.

For a while, we concentrated on eating some bits and pieces of the breakfast and chatted. Minjae looked like he was slowly livening up, and I certainly felt better after the cup of coffee and some food. After we managed to down most of the breakfast, we both just kind of slumped further down on the bed and stared at the ceiling. I got a little down over the fact that our extended weekend was now over, and we'd be all busy from tomorrow onwards.

The MAMAs were approaching fast, as well as the world tour...not to mention our new album release. And the worst part was that Minjae and I would have completely opposite schedules. Unless we were recording, touring, or training, Minjae and I had different responsibilities. I was mostly trapped at the office, polishing tracks with Tae or some other producers, or perhaps promoting us somewhere as they liked to call me a visual. Meanwhile, Minjae would be busy with the stage performances.

This wasn't the time to worry. We still had a few hours of alone time together. Instead, I rolled around and pulled Minjae against my chest. For once he didn't fight me. He just sighed and made himself comfortable.

"Do-hyun...a lot has happened in such a short time..." He started.

"Too fast?" My stomach flipped with nervous guilt. I had promised him we'd take it slow.

"No, no... I'm just trying to wrap my head around it." He paused, and I stared at him, lost in his beautiful brown eyes until he found his next words. "And I wonder if I can ever face Mrs. Park again." He released a chuckle under his breath.

"Look, Mom's fine. Damn, even Tae, Joonie, Chris, and Jiwoo are fine. Everyone's fine."

"Yeah, and that's exactly what I can't wrap my head around."

"Then don't, and let's just cuddle." I pulled him closer.

With a nod, Minjae curled up in my embrace, fitting there in such a perfect way no one else could. I tightened my hold, before placing a soft kiss on the back of his neck. He shivered then weaved his fingers through mine before sliding our joined hands from his waist, across his chest, all the way up until his lips reached my fingers. I almost melted on the spot.

Neither of us spoke, and we didn't feel the need to. The best thing about dating your best friend, was definitely this—not feeling the need to fill up every single moment with useless blabbering. Despite dating for such a short while, we were already so comfortable together.

Minjae even fell back asleep, not quite snoring but huffing and puffing with his mouth hanging agape. I didn't dare wake him. I reached out for the remote on the nightstand as silently and carefully as I possibly could, turned on Netflix, and hit play on the first movie it suggested with the sound turned down to a level it was barely audible.

My intention was to watch the random flick until I, too, fell asleep, but watching Minjae sleep was far more entertaining than the movie. With uttermost care, I untangled my fingers from Minjae's tight hold without waking him up and moved the tangled strands of pure white hair aside.

Despite the hangover, it was beginning to look like one of those rare absolutely perfect days. I wished I could've stayed there beside him forever. Despite having the tendency to screw things over, I hoped that this—what I had with Minjae—would continue to face no more obstacles. I wished I could've guaranteed things would stay this way until the end of time.

Unfortunately I was not capable of giving such promises.

Celebrity Crush

"Remind me again, why do I have to attend these boring as fuck interviews while Minjae and Joonie get to have fun at the mock-up stage?"

Of course, I was annoyed. The days had started to blur together again. I barely even saw Minjae over the past days. The rare occasions when we were together during daytime, we were always working and there were always others around. Basically, it meant no fun. The only difference was that we slept in the same bed almost every night now. Minjae's bed. And yes, I mean that we *only* slept. We were always so exhausted that we practically passed out whenever home.

Minjae was the exhausted one, really. I was mostly left with blue balls. Though that didn't bother me all that much. At least I got to hold him in my arms most nights.

We'd been training like crazy for the MAMAs and the world tour, and Minjae had the more demanding part. He was in the planning committee and had a collaboration performance with people from other groups. Joonie was in on that, too. That was all in addition to promoting, which me, Tae, and Chris were mostly handling without them.

"They're not having fun. They're working. And for the hundredth time, you're our visual. Thus, you have to be visible," Tae replied from the front seat.

Joe was behind the wheel, driving us to a parking hall. Tae made sense, being the one and only logically thinking of us all, but it didn't mean I wouldn't have rather been with Minjae.

"Yes, I'm handsome. But so are Chris, Joonie, and Minjae. Besides, if being good-looking is a requirement, I don't get why you're here," I mocked. Not that Tae wasn't good-looking too in his own way—just not by Korean beauty standards. He was way more popular overseas. That didn't mean I wouldn't rub it in his face whenever I had the chance.

Chris chuckled beside me but got cut short as soon as Tae glanced at him with icey, narrowed eyes just as Joe parked the car.

"Look, I get it. You wanna cuddle with Minjae. Newsflash, we have to work," Tae said as the car halted to a parking spot.

"Yeah, yeah...but lemme say I'm glad we're heading to tour," I hopped out of the car, closed the door behind me, and smoothed out my outfit.

Tae slammed his door, and we both headed towards the entrance. Chris followed suit.

"Sorry to burst your bubble, but we'll be having a lot of interviews and such on tour too. Especially in the US," Tae said.

"Yeah, but they're way more fun abroad," Chris added.

Tae and I nodded simultaneously. Abroad, they were actually eager to interview us. To them, we were "exotic". To them, we were still new. To them, everything was genuinely interesting, especially our music. Here, they all tried to get us to spill something scandalous as we were otherwise old news.

Someone from the staff of the radio station met us right after we entered the lobby and led us to the studio where we were having the interview. The radio host was on a full swing with his afternoon show. We snuck in and Tae ushered me to take the seat closest to the cam. We got comfy as we waited for the host to start the interview. A commercial break happened and the host took the chance to introduce himself.

He was a new one. I remembered some of the nicest and most professional ones from back in the days, but most of them were now doing other things. We were stuck with the newbies. Their names and faces all blurred in my mind, and I forgot this one's name as soon as he said it.

They had sent us the questions beforehand, and Jiwoo had reviewed them. I hadn't bothered to even read them. The questions were the same in every freaking interview. They'd asked about our break; we'd answer something vague. Then they'd asked about our upcoming album, which was at least a little more interesting topic. Me, Tae, and Chris answered those questions a more eagerly, especially Chris, who had a hand in the production and song writing for the first time. The host that day was shocked about that, like the last ten hosts before him. I didn't get it; how could they not know by now? I mean, didn't they research like, at all? Then they'd asked if we still insisted on doing everything ourselves as it really wasn't the industry standard around here. Our answer was always, "of course". It was the same answer we always gave these kinds of questions, right from day one.

The conversation was steered to our world tour. It was all the basic questions at first, like how we felt about the concerts selling out. Had we missed touring? Etc. Autopilot kicked in, and my mind flew entirely somewhere else...

Until the guy asked the dumbest question I had ever heard.

"So, who's your celebrity crush?"

I stared at the dude dumbfounded. He couldn't be serious right? I mean, we were celebrities ourselves. And we were talking about our world tour now. I couldn't understand how this related to that in any way. So, with a straight face and clearly not thinking at all, I answered, "Chang Minjae."

There were a whole two seconds of awkward silence before the host played it off as a joke along with Chris and Tae. Those seconds were one of the longest in my life. After doing some damage control, joking along with the guys, I drifted back to my earlier state of being braindead.

When the host started asking questions about our private life, it was time to actually wake up. And since I blurted out that my celebrity crush was Min, of course, the host asked about him. Where was he? Why wasn't he here? What was going on between me and him? That wasn't the first time I'd been asked these questions, either.

My go-to answers back in the day had been either "no comment" or some flirting action with Minjae. You know, fanservice. Leave them guessing and never provide any actual answers. They'd always assumed we were only close friends, acting accordingly to the social standards around there. To play it safe, I didn't venture off the script anymore. Instead, I gave him the answers Jiwoo had written for me. The dull ones.

To my ultimate relief, we got the interview wrapped up soon after. I braced myself for the scolding I thought I'd get from Tae. It never happened though. Instead, he congratulated me for successful fanservice when we were heading back to the dorms. What a weird man. On top of that, he gave Chris and me the evening off.

Chris glanced at me with a bewildered look on his face. "Do you know what happened to Tae-hyung?"

"I have no idea, but let's not jinx it," I replied back at him, equally confused. Usually if everything on interviews didn't go exactly as Tae had planned, he would've been annoyed.

"Guys, I'm right here. And nothing happened. I'm just tired of babysitting you two," Tae scoffed from the front seat.

"In that case, Joe can give me a ride straight to HQ," I stated and dug my phone out from my pocket to text Minjae. He wouldn't mind if I came to his rehearsal, right?

"Umm," Tae began but said nothing more.

I lifted my eyes from the screen to see Tae and Chris exchanging glances with a meaning I couldn't read. "What?"

"I don't think that's a good idea," Tae finally said.

"Why?"

"Just better let them do their work in peace, okay?" Chris clearly tried to sound nonchalant about it, but the tone of his voice betrayed him.

What bullshit. Since when did we let each other work in peace? Something was definitely off.

I shrugged to convince them I'd dismissed the topic. But more than ever, I had to figure out what was going on. It was only a hunch—a strange feeling. A tingle going up my spine—that they wanted to hide something from me...something that involved Minjae.

As soon as we reached the dorm, I pretended to have some business with Joe and stayed behind. But when they disappeared to the elevator and the doors closed, I hopped back to the backseat of Joe's BMW.

"HQ, now," I barked to Joe, who hadn't even bothered to get up from the driver's seat. He knew me way too well for that. In fact, I was surprised that Tae and Chris hadn't said anything more about the matter. Thank gods Tae was off his game, otherwise he would've caught my bluff no doubt.

Or...perhaps the strange feeling was just my imagination running wild?

"Figured you'd want to go," Joe said before steering the car right back out from our garage and straight towards the company headquarters.

LBR Entertainment had started small, that's when we were signed. At first, it was a small recording studio, and we were dumped in a tiny apartment during the training period and recording of our first album.

We had all slept in the same damn bedroom in bunk beds and barely had enough money for food. Even that was mostly thanks to Joonie, who worked some part-time jobs as a waiter back then. We basically trained in the streets because we didn't have money to rent any large enough spaces for the choreographies Minjae mustered up like a machine, even back then.

Many things changed since then though—and I liked to think that the success of GRiD had something to do with it. Nowadays, our label had a couple of other groups as well and many solo artists on their list, but we had been the first. I think Tae even bought a part of the company recently and became a shareholder.

I knew that building like the back of my hand. It was my second home; that was how much time I spent there. It was a modern, somewhat tall building located at the heart of the commercial area in Seoul. Filled with offices—including my very own office—meeting rooms with all different sizes and purposes, countless training facilities, high-end recording studios...and of course, the thing I was heading to: the two-floor mockup stage. My footsteps echoed on the silent hallways as I made my way towards the stairs leading to the giant hall-like space.

If my turf was my office or the recording studios, this was Minjae's turf on the company premises. Because of that, I had been here countless hours before. If not practicing with the whole group, then I was here watching and helping Minjae whenever I could. That day, the stage was arranged to resemble this year's MAMA stages. Although it was missing most of the props, it was a sight to behold.

I stayed in the shadows, not wanting to disturb the hard working Minjae. He shouted instructions for the backup dancers with some dude I had a hard time recognizing. They were too far. I spotted Joonie sitting in the corner, watching. I quickly made my way beside him.

He noticed me before I sat next to him on the floor.

"Oh, hi. What are you doing here?" he asked, surprise evident on his face.

"Finished work early," I replied. "Tae didn't think it was a good idea to come here. Wanna tell me why?"

Joonie let out a small, delicate chuckle before answering. "Just watch and please try to keep your cool."

I furrowed my brows. What the hell did he mean by that? What the hell was going on here?

Jealousy

I reluctantly turned my gaze back towards the mock-up stage. All of the dancers, including Minjae, went to their starting points around the stage. Someone turned the music on. It was a familiar beat—something that Tae and I had worked on a couple of months back but eventually discarded as it didn't fit for the theme of our new album. It must've made the cut for MAMAs.

All at once I recognized the dude that was shouting orders a moment ago with Minjae. *Daesung.* A dark-haired dancer from Stargazers, another idol group that'd started around the same time we did. I believed he had shortened his name to Dae on the stage. He was hot. Even I could see it, though he didn't even compare to Minjae's complete gorgeousness. I had met him a few times, mostly at award galas and always briefly.

The tabloids liked to think we were sworn enemies or something, but in reality, that wasn't the case. For one, we had both made it big, so we didn't have to compete. For two, most of the idol world got along just fine.

I had no opinions on the guy. Yet.

My eyes fixated on Minjae right when his part on the choreo started. He'd always been able to capture my full attention with his dancing. You could see the hard work he put in, but there was pure talent there too. Perfectly in sync with the beat, he moved his body like no one else could, owning the stage. I couldn't take my eyes off him; his dancing was that mesmerizing. It took a hold of me like a drug.

But as soon as the choreography evolved, boy did I have some opinions on Dae. The worst part of it all was that the whole choreography screamed Minjae—he had designed similar routines for the two of us in the past. It was sensual, slow, and touchy. It brought the best out of contemporary dancing beautifully...except that this time, it wasn't me on the stage. It was this dark-haired punk with his filthy hands all over my Min.

Jealousy.

The feeling was no stranger to me. After years of watching Minjae perform, I had made myself more than familiar with it. Jealousy and I were best buds by this point. Still, the rage that burned inside me, consuming me, took me by surprise. My hands started to sweat and shake uncontrollably. I closed them in tight fists, trying my absolute best to control the urge of ripping this Dae guy's limbs off one by one. I was failing.

The rational side of my brain tried to tell me that this was only work for Minjae, and I had no reason to be this jealous. It was just dancing. It was nothing I hadn't seen before. The not-so-rational side of my brain argued that this was far more explicit than anything I had witnessed before. The way I saw it, Minjae was acting like a slut and this Dae-person seemed to enjoy it far too much. My body stopped obeying my mind completely, resulting in me barely noticing my feet making me stand up from the floor and dragging me closer to the stage. Joonie tried to stop me, but I shrugged his hand off my shoulder and shot him a dark glance. He raised his hands in a sign of giving up, and I turned my attention back to the stage.

That was a mistake.

When Dae circled behind Minjae and hovered his lips pretty damn close to my spot on Minjae's neck, I snapped. Minjae leaned his back on Dae, who, in turn, curled his hand around his waist, grabbed a fistful of Minjae's white decoy tank top... and proceeded to rip it right off. Right then and there, directly in front of me. I froze to the spot, my veins filling with ice.

Of course, that was also the exact moment when Minjae lost his focus and started to laugh.

"Aish! Dae-hyung, you know you don't have to rip every damn shirt apart, right? It's enough if you do it on the actual stage." Minjae chuckled and lightly punched his shoulder in a friendly manner. He didn't even seem bothered one bit that he was half naked in front of everyone.

Someone stopped the music.

Dae smirked. "I know."

That was it. Fuck this guy. And Minjae while we were at it. Most of all, fuck this performance.

The sound of my sweater's zipper opening made Minjae snap his towards me. I tossed the sweater towards his naked torso with narrow eyes that contrasted his, widened with shock.

"Wear that. We're leaving. Now."

After that, I turned my glare towards the now amused-looking Dae. "Rehearsal's over for today." My voice dripping with venom.

"But we just started," Dae replied, still with that annoying little smirk on his face, which I so very badly wanted to punch right off of his face.

"I don't care," I growled while grabbing Minjae's wrist through my way-too-big sweater. If I hadn't been completely losing my mind, I would've thought that he looked adorable in it.

"You can work with Joonie-hyung. We'll continue here tomorrow morning at eight," Minjae hollered to Dae and the others right before I dragged him through the exit and then straight to the changing rooms.

Not saying a thing, Minjae started to change to his regular clothes and eventually gave me my sweater back. I put it back over my t-shirt and crossed my arms over my chest, tapping my foot while waiting for him to change the rest. As soon as he was back to being his normal, clothed self, I grabbed his hand and texted Joe that we were leaving. Now.

Though, I didn't get very far. A small whine from behind me made me halt completely, like my feet were suddenly glued to the floor. When I turned around to look, I saw a Minjae's face distressed and instantly let go of his wrist with guilt dropping to the bottom of my stomach. I had, again, gone too far.

I took a few deep breaths to calm myself and closed my eyes. "Look, I'm sorry. Just...you need to stay away from that guy."

When I opened my eyes again, I saw Minjae looking at me with one eyebrow raised. "Why?"

"I don't trust him." I shrugged. It was a nagging feeling in my stomach, but that guy was up to something, and I knew it.

"I can't. And I won't. This is work, Do. You just have to deal with it," Minjae said, unamusement obvious in his blank expression.

I sighed and pinched the bridge of my nose. "Fine. But otherwise, stay away from him."

Minjae walked right in front of me, wrapped his hands around my waist and hugged me. His warm body melted some of the anger and jealousy away. My arms automatically wrapped themselves around his waist. He cupped my face and glared me straight in the eyes before his gaze softened a bit and his lips turned to a crooked smile.

"Are you jealous?" he asked in a mocking tone and leaned even closer.

His face was merely five centimeters away from mine. He was again so close that I barely kept my sanity intact. Damn near I didn't start to stutter when his eyes searched mine.

"No... Well, not anymore," I admitted after Minjae let out a small chuckle.

Minjae kissed me on the lips right then and there, not caring one bit we were on the company premises. Not that it mattered since the hallway was empty. My heart picked up the pace, and the ice that filled my veins just a moment ago all but melted away. All I could think of was his lips—his body pressed against mine.

As angry and jealous as my mushy brain wanted to be, my body didn't let me. I tried to resist; I really did. I was still angry as hell. But as my lips started to move with his, I become less and less successful. Smiling against my lips, he let his tongue trace my lower lip, just a teeny tiny bit.

From day one, Minjae had known the best ways to calm me down, now he just had some more effective ways to do it. It was unfair.

So yes, the kiss was a good distraction.

That was, until my eyes closed. The hair on my neck stood up. A shiver ran down my spine. Something felt off, like someone was watching us. I snapped my head back as I pushed Min away and looked around the hallway, but I saw no one.

I was about to go around the corner to look if there was someone, but reality came back to me through Min's voice.

"What's wrong?" Min asked with a hushed voice. I sensed that he could feel it too.

Slowly, I turned my eyes back to Minjae, who now had a wrinkle of worry between his eyebrows. I shook my head to clear it a bit and took his hand in mine.

"Nothing. Just let's go home," I said, and we continued our way to the carpark in a strange silence.

But I couldn't shake off the feeling that someone had watched us back there.

Promise

"Do, I have to go practice," Minjae said with a strained voice.

We were having a rare evening off. After dinner, I had Minjae pinned against his room's door, and my game plan was to distract him enough that he'd forget rehearsing the choreo that still made my blood boil. If he was going to be hot and heavy with another dude on stage, I'd be damn sure to make him mine in private.

"Mhmm," I muttered against his neck which I attacked with my lips.

To my complete disappointment, Minjae didn't give in. Even though he let out a small moan when I sucked the delicate skin on his neck, he was still persistent to go downstairs to practice. In fact, I could sense his growing annoyance in his reluctance.

Just then, he pushed me away and I tumbled a couple of steps back.

"What?"

"I don't have time for this. It's less than a week to the MAMAs and I'm nowhere near ready. And you crashed our practice the other day, for fuck's sake," he said and opened the door.

"Yeah, just in time to see you acting like a slut around that douchebag," I muttered silently to his back.

I admit, I was overreacting, and acting like a douche myself. Not to mention that calling him a slut might've been taking it a bit too far. But it hurt just too damn much. I couldn't believe Minjae would still rather be practicing than be with me on our rare day off.

Minjae, on the other hand, wasn't having it. Slowly, he turned on his heels and glared at me with an icy stare. "What did you just say?"

"You heard me." I didn't want to say it, but it came out anyway. I regretted it, despite the lingering anger.

"I don't know who pissed on your cereal this morning, but it surely wasn't me or Dae. So, can you, like, back off?" He shoved me further away from him to make a point. "And let me do my fucking work!"

With that, he was out the door in mere seconds. The loud bang from the door, which nearly fell off its joints when he slammed it shut, rattled in my ears. I stared ahead, not being able to move a muscle for a solid minute. Finally, my brain started to function enough to wrap my head around what happened.

Fuck.

To no one's surprise, I'd pissed Minjae off, majorly. Again. I groaned and ran my hand through my hair, getting extremely frustrated. After slowly backing off from the door, I sat to the edge of Min's the soft and warm bed. It felt so wrong to be there when Minjae was not happy with me. I took a few deep breaths and somehow managed to make my way to my own room and plopped on top of my own bed.

My own bed wasn't nearly as comfortable as Minjae's. Also, my room was way too boring, too neat. Minjae's room was messy, yes, but at the same time, it was cozy. In comparison, mine felt too cold and empty. Organized. Bland. It didn't even look like someone actually lived there.

And the reason for that was, well...kind of embarrassing. Over the years, I had made a highly annoying habit of cleaning and organizing every damn time I screwed up. And that had happened a lot in the past. Seeing the tidiness of my room downright pissed me off nowadays, so I avoided it as much as I possibly could.

I'd fucked up again, and my accessories needed some arranging, I sat down to the floor in front of the big ass drawer that held them. It was downright pathetic that it was the only thing that needed some tidying up anymore. Even that was mostly because Minjae usually plowed through them whenever I needed help with my fashion sense—which was often. At least the memories of playing dress-up with Min made the corners of my mouth turn up.

The bottom drawer held my collection of bandanas and other scarfs, beanies, etc. I folded them neatly and even bothered to sort them by color. The second drawer held belts and other larger accessories, and the top was for my jewelry. The top one was divided into smaller parts; one usually held necklaces, other bracelets...but now they were all tangled up to one big, messy ball.

With the argument on my mind, I got to work.

It was a mindless job, which gave me time to think about what happened with Minjae. Yeah, I might've gone too far with the jealousy once again... But honestly, did he absolutely have to act such a fucking slut every fucking time on stage? Especially with someone other than me. From another group, even.

Besides, that Dae dude gave me the chills. First of all, he looked like a scumbag. The one time Minjae and Tae had had something on stage during "Contrast" at our comeback concert had already been way too much, and Tae didn't weird me out nearly as much. . Too lost in my own thoughts, I handled one necklace a bit rough and ended up snapping it in two. With a long sigh, I tossed it to the trash bin.

It took me ages, but eventually I got all the jewellery sorted out. A satisfied huff left my lungs when my eyes glanced over the rings which I had on top of the drawer in a glass showcase. They were already neatly arranged to their designated places on the velvet platform. As I always picked out my own rings, they were kept in order. Minjae thought I was obsessed with rings and often made fun of me because of that, but that wasn't exactly the case. It was that there was this one particular ring that I hadn't wanted Minjae to inspect too closely.

Which wasn't in its place…Nor in my hand. Actually, I didn't see it anywhere. I lifted the glass top and went through every damn ring. But the one I was looking for wasn't there.

My heart rate sped through the roof when I ploughed through the whole drawer, ruining that which I just finished organizing. Nothing. No ring. The only other sensible option was my walk-in closet, which I turned upside down. Not there either. I started to feel like fucking Gollum from the Lord of the Rings as I rummage thought every last corner of my room. But the damn ring kept itself stubbornly hidden from me.

Frustrated and out of breath, I crashed to my armchair and buried my face in my hands. I couldn't have lost that ring; I had managed to keep it safe and secure for years. It couldn't go missing now.

"Just think, Park Do-hyun," I muttered to myself.

When was the last time I wore it?

Usually, I wore it all the time. Yet, I still couldn't remember the last time now that I needed to. I hadn't had it the whole last week. I hadn't had it when we were in Daegu with Minjae. I hadn't had it the best night of my life, when Minjae and I admitted our feelings for each other.

The last time I was sure I had worn it was the day of our comeback concert at Gocheok Sky Dome. I remembered playing with it backstage after getting upset at Tae for interrupting the original choreography of "Contrast". But I also remembered putting it back to its place after that, so that couldn't possibly be when I'd lost it.

No! I haven't lost it yet. Keep thinking. *What happened next?*

I'd put the ring back in the showcase. I'd showered. I'd changed to my pajamas, and then Minjae had appeared to my room with my phone, and I'd asked him to stay. He'd stayed, at least until I'd drifted off to dreamland. I remembered waking up in a good mood the next morning and had slid the ring back on... And then I had walked in on Minjae sitting on Tae's lap at our living room, having that damn vlive.

It hit me.

After that, we had a fight. He'd left crying. I'd darted after him but hadn't caught him in time and ended up apologizing through his locked door for ages until Joonie had interrupted me. I'd gotten back here...and went straight to the bathroom. I'd taken the ring off and placed it on top of the sink, next to the soap before rinsing my face with cold water.

Hastily, I darted to the bathroom only to find the sink empty. The damn ring wasn't there either. My knees gave in and leaning to the wall, I glided down to sit on the cold floor. Then, my eyes caught a glimpse of something glimmering on the floor near the sink.

Ahh, found it!

The ring was just a thick, simple, cheap, titanium band. It wasn't anything special, at a glance. And it was well worn and old. It clearly didn't have any monetary value. Worth had nothing to do with my obsession. It was the message that was engraved inside that mattered to me. I had to squeeze my eyes to even see it, as time and constant wearing had taken its toll on the text.

I remembered the moment I had gotten the ring like it was yesterday. It was one of the first fan meetings we had had back in the day. I remember being bored, annoyed and tired. It had been a long day and the meet and greet had already taken over two hours.

Then this cute girl around our age had made her way through the table, smiling blindingly bright and chatting with all the others cheerfully. She had been a rarity; she hadn't had any plushies, letters or any other gifts for us. She didn't try to touch us excessively, she didn't scream, she didn't play favorites. She was just genuinely happy she got to meet us.

Eventually, after chatting with all the other guys for a bit, she had made her way to me. I'd been the last one on the row. She hadn't chatted with me as she had the others. Instead, she just handed me this one, simple ring and held her pinkie finger up.

"Keep this safe for me, promise?" were the only words she had said to me.

At the time, I had been confused. Nevertheless, I had linked my own little finger with hers, offered her a polite smile and promised to keep it safe. She had flashed me the brightest smile before scurrying off. I remember glancing at the engraving and not understanding it at all since there were just mine and Minjae's names and one word written in hangul—약속; yaksok. Promise.

Later, I learned that she had probably been one of the first DoMino shippers. A then-teenage girl the Japanese would've called fujoshi—a rotten girl. The term itself was ugly, but it simply meant female fans who enjoy any media works or fanworks with a romantic relationship between men.

As we had capitalized on them heavily, we obviously didn't mind them. That would've been hypocritical of us. Plus, they were actually kind of fun to be around. At the very least, most of them weren't as aggressive as some other fans with trying to touch or kiss or anything like that.

Smiling, I slid the ring to its place in my pinky finger and heaved myself up from the floor.

The ring reminded me that at the end of the day, Minjae mattered me more than anything else. It was time to do some more apologizing. After all, I had a promise to keep. So, I got up, determined to make things right. I figured he'd be in the dance studio downstairs. He was always there whenever he was upset.

All my anger and jealousy had toned down quite the lot, so I strolled through the hallway with a lighter step, all the way to the stairs and eventually to the dance room's door. It was locked, but I entered the code without thinking it twice. After a beep, the lock clicked open.

The room was dark, not one light was turned on. I frowned at first in confusion, but then spotted Minjae sitting on the floor in the dark. He leaned his back against the mirror and hugged his knees, hanging his head. The immersive feeling of guilt washed over me, getting stronger every hesitant step I took towards him. Eventually, I made my way beside him and plopped down on the hardwood floor, too.

Minjae didn't move a centimeter. In fact, he didn't acknowledge me at all. He didn't even lift his gaze from the floor. His eyes were glassed over. He just plainly stared at the floor, seeing nothing. I tried to touch his arm, but he flinched and pulled his arm away. I dropped my hand, turning my eyes to stare at the floor too.

Damn. I had screwed up even worse than I thought.

"Look, I'm sor—" I started, but Minjae cut me off.

"Do-hyun, this isn't going to work like this." He never stopped staring at the floor.

I snapped my eyes back to his face, panicking. "Don't say that!"

His eyes met mine. I was surprised by the look on his face—heavy creases between his eyebrows, body shaking.

"Well, what am I supposed to say?" he asked, annoyance in his voice. "You can't keep saying things like that and then assume just saying sorry will make everything magically okay again."

"I know, I'm sor—" I tried again, but stopped when I realized I was only doing exactly what he accused me of.

Minjae got up. "I'm only doing my work, for fuck's sake. It's not like I'm shagging with everything that breathes. This isn't going to work out between us if you snap at me every time I'm performing with someone else. We're idols. Plus, you do it, too!"

My eyes were wide and my mouth hung open. I wanted to apologize again but that wasn't what he wanted. I couldn't mutter a single word. Minjae stared at me for a while. I just sat, speechless, on the floor. Then he turned around and stomped to the door. With his hand on the door handle, he looked at me over his shoulder and let out a sigh.

"Let's just get MAMAs over and done with. Then, we can talk," he stated with an even, cold, and disappointed tone. He hesitated for a bit, probably still waiting for me to say something, giving me a chance to say anything.

The silence dragged on. My words were still stuck to my throat along with a lump forming at an alarming speed. My heart clenched painfully inside my ribcage and my stomach nearly turned around.

"Right?" he added with a slightly softer tone after the silence turned to a strained one.

I couldn't do much else than nod.

Minjae walked out the door and closed it gently behind him.

Trust Me

Not sure how long I stayed there in the dark, playing with the promise ring, losing track of time. I had fucked up. That was clear enough. Not that it was anything new to me. Or Minjae. But why did it hurt so damn much this time? My head was a mess, and it was hard to breathe. Leaning my back to the cold surface of the mirror, I tried to sort out my thoughts.

I'd had at least a million fights with Minjae throughout the years. The outcome had always been one of two options, and our disagreements never lasted long. We either sorted them out right away or apologized and everything was good between us.

This time, Minjae hadn't even let me apologize. He hadn't apologized, either. Not that there wasn't anything for him to apologize for. It was true that he was only doing his job, and by now I should be used to that. But the thing was, I wasn't used to that and didn't *want* to get used to that, ever. He should have known that by now.

It hurt like hell to realize Minjae might be right about us not working out like this. After all, he was a celebrity as was I, and we had to keep up with the image that had been established over the years—the personalities the fans that were paying our bills loved. I knew it was the polar opposite of what Minjae was in real-life, but it was there, and it bugged the hell out of me. I really, really loved him, but there wasn't denying that I absolutely hated how he acted around other people. I detested the way he acted when performing.

If our somewhat newfound relationship would last, it would mean we would have to change. At least, I would have to change. I wanted Minjae all for myself, but that wouldn't happen as long as we were famous. Which wasn't something you could turn on and off. If you reached celebrity status at a high level, you'd be a celebrity for life. You couldn't decide one day that that's it, you don't want to be famous anymore and then magically you'd be a commoner.

But I also didn't want to lose Minjae. He was hands down the most important person in my life. I loved him, and that meant I'd have to love all the parts of him—public and private. After tasting the sweetness of being in a real relationship with him, I didn't want to let it go. I could change for him, and I would change if that's what it took for this thing to work out. This time, though, I'd change for real, not pretend to have changed as I'd apparently done this past couple of months.

Fuck. Being in a relationship was *hard*.

With that, I stood up and made my way straight to Minjae's door. Yes, I knew he wanted to have some space until the MAMAs, and I respected that. But there was something I had to do before all that.

There was no hesitation in my steps now, and I was determined to make this work. I knocked on his door, hoping he wasn't asleep. I would've just waltzed straight in, but after today, that would have been rude. First step to change: don't be a dick.

The door opened halfway, and I was met with an exhausted-looking Minjae who was peeking through the opening. His eyes were kind of puffy, and his hair was even messier than usual. He'd cried, and man did it sting that it had been my fault. Once again.

He didn't say anything at all, just glanced at me with tired eyes.

"Can we talk?" I asked with a hushed voice.

He just nodded and walked back in. I followed suit and we sat side by side on his bed.

"I'm tired. Let's get this over with," he said, his voice cracking a bit at the end.

I sighed. "I'm going to try to change. Though I'm not gonna lie, it might take some time."

He rubbed his eyes. "I'm tired of being walked over. And it's too late to cancel the MAMA performance with Dae now."

"I know. I'm going to work on it."

"Look, I get it. This is hard, and I want a breather. Let's just take some time off until the MAMAs are over, okay?"

Six days. I could do that. Maybe. "...If that's what you really want?"

There was a long pause when we just stared each other in the eyes before Minjae spoke again. "It is."

"Alright then."

A silence. Then I leaned closer. If I was going to be willingly apart from him for six days straight after getting used to at least sleeping with him, I was certainly going to make him realize what he'd be missing during that time. When our lips met, my heart sunk a bit since he didn't kiss me back at first. But then he did, and we shared one long, desperate, and passionate kiss. It was filled with unsaid promises, regrets, apologies, and longing. When we finally parted, I wished him a good night and made my way in my own room next to his.

Later that night when I laid on my bed, I decided I could do this. I'd stay out of Minjae's way, and I'd behave. It was only six days, and I would survive it. And I'd prove to him I could be a decent human being for once. Closing my eyes, I drifted off to sleep.

Time is a weird thing. It changes depending on who are you with—what are you doing and whether or not the memories you've made were just that: memorable. The five days before the sixth day being MAMAs went by agonizingly slowly because most of the time I was bored without Minjae. But when looking back, the days went by in a flash because I remembered next to nothing about them.

The first day had gone by in a blurry haze. When I woke up, Minjae had already gone wherever he had to be that day. I preferred not to think about that too much or what he'd been doing, most probably with Dae. My morning coffee had tasted bitter. I'd made my way to work and spent the day at my office at the company's HQ. Our new album was released a few days prior, and I'd held a long vlive, telling our fans all about the process of making it while playing it through track by track. It'd been a good distraction, and a tradition I had developed over the years. That was our sixth full-length album already, in addition to countless mini albums.

Dinner had been unusually quiet since I didn't fool around with Minjae like usual. The others noticed it. It'd been awkward as hell. But Joonie had once again made some pretty good food so at least I had that going for me.

The second day I'd spent at our gym with Tae and Joe. Trying to act normal, I'd lost myself in lifting weights. At the end of the day, I'd already began to feel sore, but as I'd missed a few workouts lately, it'd seemed like a good thing. But everything had started to feel a bit dull without Minjae, and I'd already noticed how much I'd taken for granted. The small moments had started to mean everything to me now that there weren't any.

No waking up from the same bed. No "good morning, Do"s. No trying to make each other skip work even though we knew we couldn't do that. No going to work with the same ride. No sneaky kisses. No hugs. No fooling around at lunch. Or dinner. No "good night, Do"s.

Hell, honestly? Everything had started to feel very mundane.

The next day, every muscle in my body had been on fire. It'd been a struggle to even get up from the bed. The day had been packed, so did I get up, nevertheless. Following a strict schedule had been a relief though. It'd been nonstop. Get up. Stretch the sore muscles. Eat breakfast. Go to rehearse our "Contrast" MAMA performance one last time. Try to avoid Minjae. Shower. Change. Have an interview. Have a meeting. Work on some tracks with Tae.

Have a vlive with the whole group. Avoid Minjae. Have dinner. Light workout Shower again. Sleep.

The fourth day had pretty much been the same as the day before. Though instead of having our own rehearsals, we'd had the dress rehearsal for MAMAs at the actual stage built in the Dongdaemun Design Plaza (or DDP for short). Luckily, "Contrast" was way before Minjae's performance with Dae. That meant I hadn't had to stay and watch.

I wasn't stupid. Even though I was determined to change, I knew that wouldn't happen overnight. And I certainly wasn't going to torture myself through that.

Also, Mom had called that day. She's been worried about Minjae and me since she hadn't seen new pics of us in the tabloids. What a fucking weird reason to be worried. Then again, Mom was a weird person. I'd tried to assure her that everything was fine, and she wouldn't need to worry. She hadn't believed me. She'd said she was coming to Seoul to see our MAMA performances, threatening to kick my ass if I had insulted Minjae in any way...little did she know.

Finally, the fifth and the last day before the day of MAMAs arrived. I was proud I had made it that far. I was having a day off, so I worked out at the gym with Joe once again, but this time I was a bit more cheerful. Then it was time to stress out about my outfit for the MAMAs, this time without Minjae. Frankly speaking, it was freaking me out. I contemplated consulting Joonie, but I was met with a surprise as soon as I got back to my room from the gym: one of my suits was laid on my bed.

It was a black, pinstriped one—Gucci—paired with a new, plain and black dress shirt. But instead of a bowtie, there was this platinum, chainlike piece of jewelry I guessed was supposed to go in the bowtie's place. The cufflinks laid next to the suit were also platinum ones. There were some earrings to every single one of my piercings, arranged so I'd know which went where. A pair of my finest dress shoes rested on the floor.

But what caught my eyes was the piece of paper on top of the suit. I swore my heart doubled in size when I read the text on it written in familiar handwriting…

Wear this and trust me. -Minjae

Mnet Asian Music Awards

Mnet Asian Music Awards: a massive award ceremony rewarding established artists annually. For several years the ceremony had been a series of shows in different cities across Asia, but this year it was one huge show in Seoul—where the ceremony had first started when it'd been a smaller event for only Korean artists. And we were a part of it, again, after being away for three years.

We all arrived at different times. Minjae and Joonie were the first ones to leave the dorm early in the morning because they were in the show's planning committee. Tae and Chris helped with the last sound check, so they had been there earlier than me, too. I was the last one of us to arrive at the venue, just before the red carpet event, since I had next to nothing to do with the show. I was merely a guest, and one of the performers of one song. We gathered in the area with other celebrities where the staff was supposed to pick us up when it was our turn to go.

Just before entering the red carpet, I checked my outfit for the last time, hoping I got it right despite Minjae not helping me. I glanced over at Minjae and caught him smiling at me for the first time in six days. That probably meant he was either approving my outfit—which he had picked out himself—or that he was ready to put our argument, our longest fight in history, behind us. Hopefully both.

I smiled back.

I didn't get a chance to exchange a word with Minjae before we were picked up by the crew to enter the jungle of cameras, reporters, flash interviews, and fake smiles called the red carpet. The noise was deafening right from the start, when each one of the reporters shouted at us to look at them. Flashes from the endless sea of cameras blinded me when I plastered on a cheerful expression and tried to make sure I looked straight into the lens of most of the front row of cams.

When it calmed down a bit, we agreed to a couple of interviews from the most respectable news agencies—now that we were big enough to have that choice. Back in the days, it hadn't been like that. We'd had to take what we got to get ourselves covered.

They asked about our outfits, and to my relief, Minjae and Joonie helpfully provided those answers. They also asked if we expected any awards this year, which was more like a complimentary question since the obvious answer was a no—we'd only *just* made a comeback and our album had been released way after they had announced the nominees. We only had one nomination and it was for the Mwave Global Fan's Choice, an award that was decided by international voting. It was a miracle we were even invited as performers and not guests.

We posed for the cameras for a while when we reached the area with the MAMA backdrop. It was our cue to leave when all the reporters turned their attention to the next artists' arrival at the carpet. I made the mistake of glancing back as we exited, only to catch a glimpse of Dae's face. He glanced right back at me and grinned—but for some reason, it wasn't that same smug grin he'd had the other day at the mock-up stage. It weirded me out. I wasn't sure why, but he didn't have that aura around him that made me hate his guts like last time. Maybe it was because right now, he didn't have his hands all over Min…or perhaps I'd really begun to change. I truly hoped it was the latter because I'd still have to endure the "hands all over Min" part tonight. Out of common courtesy, I flashed him a small smile back.

This is going to be a long evening.

After that, it was nothing but a seemingly endless waiting. Tae, Chris, and I were provided beverages and snacks while we waited and waited backstage. Minjae and Joonie had disappeared somewhere to do their duties. We couldn't go to our designated seats at the venue until after our performance, leaving us bored out of our minds. At least "Contrast" was going to be one of the very first ones to be performed so we wouldn't have to wait for long.

As anxious as I was to see Minjae, I knew I would probably not see him until we were on stage. The choreography didn't involve us appearing on stage at the same time, so we wouldn't even have time for our pre-stage routine. My heart ached a bit at the pure thought of missing that.

I started to feel the usual nervousness creep up on me when the clock ticked ominously towards our performance. Unfortunately, my confidence never extended to our music; when we'd first started I even had stage-fright. Thankfully, that'd eased up over the years. But it always lurked in the back of my mind and got slightly more prominent whenever I couldn't see Minjae right before I hit the stage.

Thankfully, when I entered the stage, the adrenaline hit me. The spotlights blinded me enough to not see the audience. The bigger than life choreography that this song had, came straight from my spine, and I let my body take over my nerves and do its work to get me through the performance.

Minjae looked me straight in the eyes when it was time for our fanservice part of the choreo. He wore a smile that promised a lot of things after we got through this whole evening. At least, that was what I wanted to believe, since I refused to think it was just fanservice. We ended the song with huge applause and returned backstage.

Instantly, we were attacked, surrounded by stylist, hairdresser, and make-up artist noonas. They freshened us up in record time. In less than ten minutes, we were already being guided to our places by the part of the audience that was designated to nominees, performers, and invited guests.

Tae ushered me to sit next to Minjae. I didn't mind, even though I knew it was for fanservice. I could feel all the cameras from the crowd already zooming in on us. Finally, things felt like they were going to normalize from that moment on. My eyes lingered on Minjae's gorgeous face nearly the whole time, while he was enjoying the show. His expressions varied from one end to another. Just like always, there was no middle ground for him.

The music and the audience were so loud there wasn't a point in trying to make a conversation. Which may've been for the best since we still hadn't fully resolved our argument yet. I'd still have to endure his performance with Dae, but I was determined that I wouldn't let that get in between us.

Someone from the staff came for Minjae a little over halfway through the show. He was just getting up to go backstage with Joonie for the collaboration stages when I grabbed his sleeve and yanked him closer.

"I trust you," I said to him loud enough for my voice to reach over the noise and let go of his sleeve.

He shot me a short smile and scurried off. I turned my gaze back to the stage. Trying my hardest, I pretended to enjoy the show while I prepared myself mentally. I knew he was an amazing performer, but that was just it. He was too good. Too convincing. And I wouldn't be there with him—instead it would be Dae.

I could feel every camera turned toward me on my neck. I couldn't ignore the performance. I'd even have to pretend to like it. Good thing I had turned out to be quite a good actor over the years.

It was Joonie who started the piece. At first, it was just him, alone on the huge stage. He sang a short part of one of his solos from years ago, but as this act was more about dancing, he cut it short, and the music changed. Joonie was an amazing dancer too— despite being our lead vocalist. He didn't need a huge fuss around him to make it a good show.

When the beat started to pick up, there were a bunch of female idols around him, pretty famous ones too. Joonie fit in it like no other male idol could, as he was more than a little feminine. Always had been. And he was wearing the exact same kind of high heels as the girls, to top it off. It was almost funny to think about how back in the days he hadn't been as confident about his feminine features...despite the fact that his stage personality "Sweet" was designed to emphasize that part of him.

I leaned to the left, to praise Joonie's performance to Tae, who was supposed to be sitting next to me. He wasn't there. Not once had he ever skipped out on a Joonie performance in the past. I couldn't think of any, not even one. Whatever. Maybe he needed to use the restroom that badly.

When the beat dropped after the long build-up, the main stage spotlights turned off and the extension part closer to the audience, closer to us, lit up. Unfortunately, that also meant I'd probably see every damn detail, clearly.

Minjae appeared right in the middle. He wasn't wearing the decoy tank top like he had in rehearsal, but instead a long-sleeved button up—an oversized satin one. It was white and so thin that it was practically a see-through, especially from how close I was to the stage. I got mesmerized by his moves, which his shirt only highlighted.

Dae still hovered his lips way too close to my spot on Minjae's neck, but he didn't rip Minjae's shirt apart. He just opened the top button and that was it. The performance continued with no more disturbing scenes. Minjae stayed fully clothed throughout the whole thing.

I watched in awe, not quite believing how drastically those two simple things changed how I received the performance.

It was still seductive enough for the audience which was screaming collectively for the performance. There was no doubt that a new ship had formed tonight in the idol fandoms. But that didn't even bother me. Little did the fans know that this performance had been turned down several notches from the original.

And at that point I knew Minjae had done that solely for me, and my heart swell with pride and love. Apparently, I wasn't the only one that had made a decision to change.

In Private

The rest of the show went by fast.

Minjae eventually made his way back to his seat next to me. As soon as he got himself comfortable, not looking so much as winded, he glanced at me with one of his eyebrows cocked. I couldn't even put words to how grateful I was for his change in the choreography, so I smiled back at him brightly and took his hand in mine. It would easily pass as fanservice since it was something we did fairly often, even before we were nowhere near an item in real life. Thankfully he seemed to understand the wordless gesture as he didn't let go of my hand.

Only vaguely I registered it was time for the fans' choice award when I heard the host announce our name within the list of nominees. In my wildest dreams I didn't have any hope we would actually win it, so I was mostly focusing on stealing glances at Minjae's gorgeous face when the host started with the usual, "And the award goes to…"

When he continued straight away with "GRiD," it still didn't hit me.

It was only after the whole audience took a deep breath before starting to chant our names top volume, when my brain managed process the information…

We had won.

I looked around with my jaw hanging slightly open and noticed that only Tae had stood up. He was ushering up Joonie beside him.

Chris was just staring ahead with an empty gaze while Minjae looked at me as if to ask, "Really?"

Figuring out it was happening in reality, weirdly enough, I grabbed Minjae by his elbow and practically lifted him up to stand. We all started following Tae to the stage, the way there feeling incredibly long as it felt like I was walking through the mud. Yet, it started to feel more and more real the closer we got, and the fans didn't stop screaming once. I really adored GRiD Crew. Now more than ever, for not forgetting us during the long break.

When we did reach the stage and the spotlight caught us, the audience became even louder if possible. They calmed down only when the host handed Tae the microphone and we all gathered around him for the speech. All I could think of, was that I was grateful Tae didn't even try to hand me the mic. I shivered; no way I could've come up with anything to say on the spot.

"So, uh…" Tae started, before giving a second for the audience to calm down. "I think I can speak for all of us when I say we weren't expecting to get this award…or any award for that matter. But as always, our GRiD Crew, you all surprised us in the best possible way. It has truly been a blast to get back with this incredible support you're giving us. So, thank you. Truly. We love you!"

We all bowed to every possible direction, and I tried my hardest to not trip to my own feet on the way back to my seat.

Soon enough, the whole ordeal was behind us, and we headed to the afterparty. Minjae and I weren't even the only ones that let out a long sigh of relief when we were finally sipping some champagne at the back of our company's limo, headed to one of the biggest hotels in the city. It was the same chain of hotels I'd stayed at with Minjae a month back at Daegu...what a nice flashback.

The bar, nightclub, and restaurant were reserved solely for people that had performed or were nominated at MAMAs. No reporters, no media whatsoever, no fans were allowed in the whole building. That meant it was one of the only events throughout the year where celebrities could let loose…and needless to say, they had a reputation to turn a bit wild from time to time.

The limousine came into a stop right in front of the main entrance of the hotel. There was a short red carpet, and the sides were swarmed with reporters. After getting through that, we would be free. Well, for the most part. And that was probably the only thing that got me to get up from the car and not try to disappear. After one last wave for the cams, we were inside in a flash.

We didn't have rooms reserved, as our dorm was right here in Seoul. Our label didn't think we needed those. Unfortunately, that also meant that I wouldn't get to drag Minjae right to one of the rooms and keep him there until sunrise, doing things I had wanted to do for a whole six days. Instead, I'd have to endure the party as long as Jiwoo thought it wouldn't be too rude to leave. As we all were worn out and hungry, we headed straight to the restaurant. I knew we had a reserved table, but they had even prepared us a cabinet to have some privacy.

One long and noisy dinner later, I found myself at one of the tables of the night club with a beer in my hand. There were several celebrities and other people from the industry all around me, but I wasn't really interested in socializing. I had better things to do…and especially watch.

The whole time my eyes were on Minjae, who headed to the dance floor first thing when we arrived. Together with a huge crowd full of other dancers all across the industry, they filled the whole thing to the brim. Minjae was clearly having fun, grinning, and downing shot after shot with them. I didn't have the heart to drag him home yet, even though Jiwoo had already given us a pass. She'd already left herself, as well as had Tae, Joonie, and Chris.

A light tap on my shoulder forced me to rip my gaze from Minjae and turn around. I regretted not ignoring it when I ended up staring right into Dae's face. Somehow, he didn't irk me as much as I had anticipated though, so I gave him a small nod to let him know I had noticed him before turning my eyes back to the dance floor and Min.

"A word, in private?" he asked, loud enough that I could hear it over the music.

What could he possibly have to say to me? I followed him out of the nightclub to one of the hotel's corridors. Out of the night club and the common areas, the silence was deafening, heightened by the carpeted floor muffling out even our own footsteps. It creeped me out, to say the least, but I ignored the weird feeling in the back of my head as I was way too curious to hear what Dae wanted to say.

Dae stopped at in little lounge area, and we each sat in one of the armchairs. I raised one eyebrow at him, waiting for him to say what he had in mind. There clearly wasn't one soul in this part of the hotel since everyone staying for the night were still probably at the party in the nightclub.

"Look, Do-hyun," he started. I didn't hate him as much as I used to, but exactly who was he to use my first name even thought we had never introduced ourselves?

Dae didn't notice my annoyance, though. "You and I didn't have the greatest start. I had no idea you and Minjae were together, so I—I thought it'd be okay," he continued, rubbing the back of his head nervously.

My heart skipped a beat. Why—how? How did he know?

"And now you do know?" I asked. I neither wanted to confirm or deny until I knew what he knew.

"Yeah, Minjae told me. You know he changed the whole choreography for you, right?" He sounded sincere with his words, and yet I was sure Minjae would never tell anyone about us without asking me first. Something didn't quite add up. Then again it seemed like the two of them had hit it off with the friendship thing quite well.

"Yeah, looked like he did." And I was so grateful for it.

"To put it frankly, I'm sorry," he said after an awkward silence.

"It's alright. Just keep your paws off my man from now on," I said jokingly, stood up and offered him my hand.

As he took my hand, I pulled him up from the chair and we patted each other's backs. "Will do," he answered.

Maybe it was that they had toned down the choreo, or that Dae now knew about us and sincerely didn't look like he was going to try anything with Minjae—and we most certainly wouldn't be the best of friends anytime soon—but I could cut the guy some slack.

After an awkward silence when we both couldn't think of anything to say, I decided it was my chance to get the hell away from this creepily silent corridor.

"I think I'll head back now, goodby—" But I was cut off by Dae.

"Wait," he said, holding out a white key card. "Here, a peace-making gift. It's to my room for the night, but I have my eyes on Mina. She promised I could crash at her's." He winked. Yeah, that sounded like something someone would do at these kinds of parties.

"Uhm, thanks, but I think I'll head home for the night," I said and started to leave.

"Minjae has the other card to that room. Told him he'd find you there. So, you might want to reconsider." He shoved the key card into my hand. I glared at him, question after question popping in my head. He ignored me, turned around, and strode away, leaving me standing there with the card in my hand, dumbfounded.

"Wait, what's the room number?" I finally hollered after him, just before he was disappeared around the corner.

"708," he hollered back.

The room number sounded oddly familiar, but I didn't give it much thought and walked to the elevators. It never even crossed my mind to doubt anything or anyone. Not even Dae. My mind was so full of Minjae I could hardly breathe, let alone think clearly. I wanted to be alone with him so bad it physically hurt. And our home, the dorm, was way too far away.

Still a bit out of it, I pushed the button to call the lift. Hoping Minjae would show up, I started to grow a bit nervous, a tingle going up my spine. I had my doubts he'd appear since technically;

we still hadn't fully resolved whatever was left to solve with our argument six days ago. We hadn't had the chance to really talk tonight. Finally, the lift on my right opened its doors. Stepping inside, I pushed the button of the seventh floor and turned to look at the closing doors, hands in my pockets.

Just when the doors were about to close, I heard Minjae's voice. "Do, wait!"

Forever

I stopped the doors from closing. Minjae ran straight into the lift right on time for the doors closing again. Then he was there, all too close for me to have any self-discipline, trapped in a metal box. Other than Minjae's dragged breathing, it was dead silent. The lift started to rise.

"You didn't have to change the choreo..." I finally muttered.

"I know," he replied, still a bit breathless but now standing upright and looking me dead in the eyes. "But I did. Let's put this whole thing past us, please?"

I pulled him into a hug, totally giving up on holding myself back. "Let's. These past six days have been the longest in my life."

He hugged me back, wrapping his arms around my waist and nuzzling his face to the crook of my neck. "I know. They were the same for me."

And with that, Minjae attacked me with his lips. I answered his kiss just as hungrily. Inhaling the mix of sweat from all the dancing and the cologne he was wearing for the evening made my head spin...in the best way possible. The deprivation of even his touch for the past days made my pants feel tight already. The rest of the ride to the upper floors we were clinging to each other, already making up for the lost time. Too thirsty to wait. Too hungry to have patience. My heart raced and the only thing I wanted and needed right now was the privacy of a hotel room and Minjae in bed, naked.

When the doors of the lift opened, we parted hastily and out of breath. Luckily it wasn't a long way to the door of our room for the night. As soon as we got the door open, I noticed it was almost identical to the one we stayed back at Daegu. Though it was merely a passing thought since I forgot even my name when Minjae jumped to my embrace, wrapping his legs around me. The room and everything else around us disappeared as I carried him straight to the bedroom. We didn't even bother to turn on the lights.

We fell on the bed, and for a while, we were a tangled mess. Ripping each other's clothes off and tossing them to random directions around us, we finally made it somewhat naked. Minjae's boxer briefs were the last one to go. As soon as he was fully exposed, I took his dick in my mouth and sucked, making it from semi-hard to rock hard in the span of just a few seconds. Minjae whined and squirmed under me, not leaving me room to even doubt if he wanted this or not.

"I need you, now," Minjae moaned, sounding pretty disappointed I released his cock from my mouth.

A small bead of precum leaked from the slit. Slowly, I licked it off, while lifting my eyes from his dick, across his defined abs, all the way to his flustered face.

"We don't have any lube," I said and wiped the corner of my mouth with my thumb, still miraculously being able to form one coherent thought.

"To hell with lube, just fuck me already," he hissed, bit his lip and slid further down, directly under me. I would have been surprised if we hadn't already established the other night that Minjae turned into a needy mess while drunk.

This time, I embraced it and every single even remotely sane thought flew out of my mind. I no longer wondered if he meant it or not, for fuck's sake he was right there for me to take and even begged me for it.

After all the things that had happened, I wanted to tease him a little, though.

"Someone's getting needy here," I teased and held two fingers in front of his mouth. "Open up then."

Minjae took the fingers in his wet and warm mouth. He started licking and sucking them, closing his eyes, the sight blazing a fire somewhere deep within me.

When he was done, I teased his pucker for a moment before entering the two fingers Minjae had lubed up with his saliva to his tight hole, as gently as possible. He winced slightly and moaned against my lips. It didn't take long for me to find his magic spot, his prostate... By then he was already whimpering my name.

Not being able to hold myself much longer, I spit to my hand in hopes of lubing up my dick. After getting that somewhat spread, it was as good as it was going to get. Replacing my fingers in his ass with my cock, sliding past the tight ring, I thrusted as deep as I possibly could.

It was harder without lube. Somehow though, that made it even hotter, the tightness and the friction driving my already corrupted mind completely mad. Minjae looked like he was at least uncomfortable, maybe in a bit of pain...but he did nothing to protest, only stayed still. Letting him adjust way longer than ever before, I kept myself occupied by taking every bit of Minjae's neck back to my possession. It was my revenge to him teasing me on stage.

Certainly, I took my time, kissing, biting, licking, teasing him to the edge of insanity, holding his hands firmly in place above his head so he couldn't protest. In no time, Minjae was practically begging me to move—to do anything really. He whined for me to stop teasing him.

As I was losing my mind too, I couldn't keep teasing him any longer. We started to rock together in a slow rhythm, Minjae getting louder every passing second. I might've teased him a bit too much, since he came in no time with a loud moan, making a mess of his abdomen with his own cum. His muscle spasms around my dick made me go really close to the edge as well, but with enough willpower, I was able to hold it.

"Sorry, babe, we're not even remotely done yet," I said out loud, and couldn't help but smirk. He started whimpering and squirming uncomfortably under me again when the last waves of his orgasm vanished.

Ignoring his whining and still holding his arms over his head, I continued rocking towards my own goal. He mumbled some incoherent things, still way out of reality. My lips started to roam on his neck again, sucking and nibbling my favorite spot. All I wanted was to suck so hard I'd mark him mine, but even over the lustful haze of my mushy mind, I knew that would be a bad idea.

To my ultimate surprise, Minjae's cock started to swell again. Bewildered, I picked up the pace, pounding into him harder...he seemed to like it. He even started begging for more again. I used his own cum as lube and started to stroke his dick in rhythm with my movements. Feeling his legs stiffen up, which were still wrapped around mine, I danced right at the edge for a long time before I felt him getting closer as well. It took all the concentration I had to stay at the edge and not cum, but somehow I made it to the point when Minjae clenched almost painfully around me and let go. We came almost exactly at the same time.

Riding off the high, I crashed on top of him. I didn't want to move. My eyes started to droop, and the only thing keeping me from falling asleep with my dick still inside him was his hand which started to stroke my hair gently. When I finally got around to pulling out, he winced but then smiled. He looked just as tired as I felt. I helped him up and to the bathroom with care; after all, that was rougher than what we had done before. He clung to me the whole time when I washed the complete mess out of both our bodies, trying to be extremely gentle with his, as I bet he was sore as fuck after that.

But damn that was hot. And messy. Hot and messy.

After the shower, we both dug ourselves under the blankets and cuddled the world away. No words were needed. It was just the two of us now in the whole wide world, and I couldn't have been any happier. Aish, I loved that man. In fact, I had a hard time deciding which I liked in bed more, the insecure Minjae, or the slightly drunk and confident one. Maybe he'd be a perfect combination of both someday... I mean, we did have forever together, right?

I was going to be damn sure to not anger Minjae as much as I had this time ever again.

Farewell Gift

It's almost funny how the fall feels so much longer when you're dropping from the top of the world, all the way down to rock bottom. Hard. Sometimes having completely shitty luck made me wonder if I could ever have one brief moment of happiness without a painful reminder of the harsh reality. Every fucking time I felt happy, the next day came, grabbed my balls, and crushed them.

Way too early in the morning, I once again woke up in a hotel room to a phone ringing and Minjae snuggled beside me, plus one hell of a hangover. I forced myself to crawl out of the warm bed. Minjae stirred a bit at first and then fluttered his eyes open.

"What's going on?" Minjae sat up on the bed and rubbing his eyes. "Please make that fucking noise stop."

"It's Joe's tone. Where the fuck is that damn phone?" I continued feeling around the floor for my suit jacket where I believed I'd left it.

It was still fairly dark, as the blinds were closed, and there was no way I was putting the lights on yet. Eventually, I did find the ringing phone and grunted something incoherent at it before realizing I hadn't even answered yet. I swiped the screen and repeated the same grunt while trying to put on the boxer briefs I had found on my way to the phone.

There was a long, dead, creepy silence. I was about to hang up on him, assuming a pocket-dial. But before my finger reached the red button, I heard him loud and clear. "You've been outed."

I blinked. Breathing became difficult. I was frozen. Paralyzed to the spot. Eventually and with enough willpower, I forced my mouth to speak. "What?"

"You've been outed. You and Minjae. You're all over the news," Joe said, his voice stiff.

No. Fucking. Way. "How?"

"I don't know. Yet. There's this photo of you two spreading like a wildfire. Turn on the TV."

Minjae was already there beside me, hastily putting on his clothes. Maybe he could sense something was wrong. At that moment, I didn't care. I forced my feet to move me to the living room part of the suite, spotted the remote on the side table, and turned the tv on.

As soon as the screen flashed, my heart stopped beating. Breath stuck to my throat. My mouth turned dry. The phone in my hand dropped, landing on the couch. On the tv screen was a picture of us, kissing. The photo was as clear as day, leaving no room for doubt. Both of our faces were on full display. It was taken from a hallway...LBR Entertainment's very familiar hallway. I couldn't do anything but stare at the screen. I couldn't even feel my heart beat. When the news anchor started speaking, my knees gave in, and I crashed to the couch.

There wasn't a single thought crossing my mind; it was simply...empty.

Faintly from the corner of my eye, I noticed Minjae entering the living room, fully clothed and gasping to the sight in front of him.

Great. Just great. I didn't even have the opportunity to break it to him easier. I still couldn't move at all, still couldn't form one coherent thought. I felt nothing. Joe yelled to the phone; I could hear his voice even though the phone was still on the couch. I couldn't pick it up.

Minjae recovered before me and grabbed the phone.

"Joe, it's Minjae. Can you pick us up?"

I heard Joe mumble something, but I couldn't hear the exact words.

"Okay. We'll be downstairs in 20 minutes. Inform Seong-gi," he replied to Joe, hung up, and tossed the phone aside.

At some point during their brief conversation, I gained the ability to play with my ring again. It brought me relief that at least I could do *something* through my shock.

Yes, I had wanted us to be public. But not this way. Not in a million years.

Minjae stared at me, probably worried sick, but I still couldn't move. Eventually, he sighed and forced his way on my lap. He had done the same thing at our comeback concert. That was the one move that made my heart start beating again, and I slowly regained my ability to move. Wrapping my hands around him and holding him tight against my chest, I buried my face to the nook of his neck. On the verge of starting to sob uncontrollably, I felt something wet dropping on my own shoulder.

Minjae was crying too. We were in this together. It wasn't only me being outed; he was buried as deep in shit as I was. I held him even tighter, holding my own tears back even though they burned right behind my eyes. All I wanted to do was to grab Min and disappear from the face of the earth.

I had sworn to myself that I'd protect him, and now we were outed. I didn't know how, but it happened. I'd betrayed him, failed him. I knew he didn't want this to happen yet, and certainly not in this way. The guilt washed over me, and I started mumbling "I'm sorry," repeating it probably a hundred times.

"Shh, it's okay, we'll get through this," he replied and continuing to mutter something similar every time I apologized. It almost made me feel worse.

Maybe a minute passed, or half an hour. Maybe two hours. I truly didn't know. But eventually my brain started to function again. I realized our best bet was to get us out of there as soon as possible and find Jiwoo. Besides, maybe I was overreacting.

Maybe, we could just pass this as fanservice or something. Or a joke. A bet.

Maybe.

"Let's get going."

Minjae nodded and we parted reluctantly, though I still kept my hand cupping his neck. With the other hand, I gently wiped his tears away from his cheek while looking deep in his eyes, hoping I'd find the strength to get through this from him.

If only I'd know then that it was only going to get worse.

In a flash, I had all my clothes back on. Well, at least somewhat on. I didn't bother to tug my dress shirt in my pants, but it sufficed. Minjae waited for me by the door and together, we exited the room, leaving the key cards on the table. It wasn't even our room, so we wouldn't need to check-out. Thankfully no one except Dae knew we were even here since the hungry hyenas called paparazzi would've been waiting for us outside if they'd known.

Coincidentally enough, as we passed a lounge by the elevators, Dae grinned and waved at us from one of the armchairs. As he was the least of my worries, I walked straight past him without even saying hello. Well, until Minjae stopped me on my tracks by grabbing my arm. I turned to look at him and started to open my mouth to usher him to hurry up, but he was staring straight at Dae with narrowed eyes, burning with rage.

"Why did you do it?" Minjae spat with pure hatred saturating his every word—tone I had never heard from him before. Not in any of the horrible fight's we had ever had.

Did…did he think Dae outed us? My unasked question was confirmed when I glanced at Dae, as it was basically written all over his face. He just continued relaxing with a smug smirk without a care in this world.

"Because I can. Oh yeah, and there's more where that one innocent photo came from. Here, a copy," he said and tossed a USB-stick towards us.

Minjae caught it while I froze to the spot again. Maybe that was a good thing though, I might've murdered Dae right then and there if I had been able to move. There was suddenly so much hatred towards that one person boiling inside of me, I was afraid I'd burst in flames right then and there. But also, there was the guilt of being careless burning with almost equal heat within me.

A million thoughts crossed my mind at once, making me dizzy. I should've trusted my gut, the instinct that told me he was up to no good right in the beginning. I shouldn't have acted so recklessly. I should have never, ever started trusting Dae, as I somehow had last night.

Then came the regret, a million emotions crushed my heart under their weight. I should've never dragged Minjae into this. I should've never even started this thing with him, just to keep him safe. Seong-gi was right all along, it wasn't good for him to be with me. And this very much proved him right.

But it was too late for regrets now. I'd have to be there for Minjae through this. Both he and I stayed silent, so Dae spoke again.

"Consider that a farewell gift, as I doubt we'll ever meet again. Now, everything I have on that USB is going to magically leak by the end of tomorrow unless, you make a statement that you are going to a long self-reflection period because of the picture, concluding in GRiD being history. Your choice. Make the right one."

"Why are you doing this?" Minjae asked with a strained voice.

"Ahh, I already told you: because I can. You two are just too dumb to even notice that this hotel and many others are owned by my family. After your short honeymoon at Daegu, it wasn't that hard to figure out you two were together, and then you walked right into my trap last night," he said nonchalantly. How could he sound so damn bored while playing with our fucking lives?

So Minjae hadn't told him about us. He had figured it out by himself.

"You should have stayed in the army," Dae continued. " Me and my group, we were doing so well. At least until you decided to casually appear back to the scene out of nowhere, messing up with our businesses. I'd like things to go back to the way they were. And now they will." With that, he walked out, flashing us a huge grin on his way.

The day had already turned from bad to worse, and we hadn't even had breakfast yet.

Minjae and I stood there for a long while, too shocked to move. Not quite believing what'd happened. We were being blackmailed on top of getting outed. Blackmailing wasn't even unheard of in this industry, but I'd never thought it would happen to us.

The way downstairs was a silent one after both of us recovered enough to get moving. Minjae handed me the USB like it was something slimy and gross. I dropped it to my suit jacket's pocket, hoping that it was all some kind of a bad dream, and I'd wake up any moment. Joe was already waiting for us downstairs with the hotel's staff member who led us through the hotel all the way to their back door where the BMW was parked.

Joe hopped on the driver's seat as Minjae and I sat to the back. Luckily, the reporters were focused on the front entrance, so there wasn't much of a hustle to get out of there. I would still be forever grateful for the fact that the back windows were so heavily tinted that even the best cameras couldn't capture a single feature of our faces.

The way home was also a silent one. Halfway through, Minjae grabbed my hand, and I turned my eyes curiously towards him. His eyes were again filled with tears that were threatening to fall.

I cupped his neck, pulled him closer and rested my forehead against his. "Minjae, shh...it's gonna be alright."

"No, it's not," he argued. "I should've listened to you. I shouldn't have trusted him." He closed his eyes and control his trembling bottom lip by biting it hard.

"Aish. I trusted him, too. So don't blame yourself. It's all on Dae."

"I'm so sorry," he whispered, his voice broken.

"I'm sorry, too. But we're gonna get through this, whatever it is."

Minjae just smiled at me with a sad look on his face then turned his gaze to the window. Of course, he knew I was trying to comfort him, but he didn't argue any longer. Maybe he was just too exhausted. I knew I was, despite barely waking up. I grabbed his hand which was laying on the leather seat in mine and squeezed, trying to get all my feelings through with that one touch. I hoped and prayed to all possible gods that whatever that USB-stick held, wouldn't be the end of us.

Speechless

Joe parked in his usual spot beside my Porsche. But the rest of the garage being filled to the brim was something that had never happened before. Too tired to think too much of it, we all headed to the lift and took a ride up.

We were instantly met with a disconcerting scene when we made it to our dorm. It felt like the whole staff of LBR Entertainment had been packed inside. The people we knew and the people we hardly had seen once or twice, were all talking on top of each other. The noise was unbelievably loud. News boomed in the background at top volume. Minjae clung to me.

No one even seemed to notice us when we made our way towards the living room. My mom was the first one to spot us when we reached the threshold, then she strode in front of us and pulled Minjae into a tight hug. Minjae crushed my hand, which he was still holding as his life depended on it. I spotted Tae, Joonie, and Chris sitting at the kitchen bar top with mugs of steaming hot coffee in front of them. I could've killed for a cup right then.

I turned my attention back to Minjae when Mom spoke.

"Are you okay?" she asked Minjae.

"I guess," Minjae replied when she finally let go.

Jiwoo spotted us across the room. She was talking on her cell but cut it short and hung up. As soon as she was close enough, I asked, "Why are these all people here?"

"HQ is surrounded by reporters and fans. We had to take over your dorm. Sorry about that," she started, and waved for Tae,

Joonie, and Chris to join us. "Look, it looks bad, but it isn't a big deal really. We'll handle it with the publicity team. We can play it off as fanservice. Try to not do anything stupid meanwhile." She started dialing another number on her phone and was turning away when I grabbed her elbow to stop her.

"Jiwoo, the kissing photo is the least of our problems right now," I said, the words sticking to my throat so firmly I had to force them out.

She raised her eyebrows. "Care to elaborate?"

I looked at Minjae who nodded. "In private. Is there any room left where we can talk in private?"

Jiwoo frowned. "Not upstairs. Your bedrooms have been turned into offices temporarily. But I think the dance studio might be free." She grabbed her laptop from the side table. Good, I didn't have to ask anyone to bring one.

We both nodded to that and started to turn around to head downstairs when Tae reached us. "Can we join?" he asked, gesturing towards himself, Joonie and Chris.

I nodded to them but asked Mom to stay behind. As I had no idea what the USB held, I would do everything in my power to not let Mom see it, at least yet. Zigzagging through the crowd, our silent party that included me, Minjae, Jiwoo, Tae, Joonie, Chris, and Joe walked downstairs. Minjae opened the dance studio, and we all released a relieved sigh since it was empty. And quiet.

We all took a floor pillow from the sides and sat in a circle in the center of the floor. I asked if anyone brought coffee, hoping it would help with the exhaustion. No-one had, but thankfully Chris headed back. It took him maybe three minutes to get two steaming hot cups of coffee which he handed to Minjae and me. I took a sip and I swear it tasted like a liquified orgasm. It was the first and probably the only good thing about this day. Up to that point, the day had only turned from bad to worse every time I thought it had stopped.

"We are being blackmailed with this," I said and held up the USB-stick. There was no evading the inevitable anymore.

Minjae winced when he saw it and Jiwoo snapped it out of my hand and plugged it to her laptop. "Now what are we looking for?" she asked, surprisingly calm.

"Dunno, could be anything. I haven't had a chance to look at it yet. But it was Dae who released the earlier photo, and he said there's more material. That's just a copy," I stated nonchalantly. There weren't enough feelings left for more than that at this point.

"Okay, weird. Why would he do that? What does he want? I mean he couldn't be after money, right?" Jiwoo muttered, poking at her laptop.

"He wants us to quit GRiD and disappear," I said.

There was a loud, collective gasp from all of those around us. They all turned their stares to Minjae and me with horror in varying shades lingering on their faces. I looked away; I couldn't bear to see it. Minjae clung to my shirt, and I curled my hand around him, pulled him closer and starting to stroke his side in a soothing manner. He closed his eyes and leaned his head against my shoulder while the others tried to recover from their shock.

Jiwoo cleared her throat. "Let's see what's in this thing before panicking."

We all nodded in unison, turning our attention back to her and her laptop. I braced myself because I could already guess what would be in it, though I still hoped it wouldn't be that...

"It's a video. Can I play it?" she asked me and Minjae.

Minjae shot her a fiery glance. "Dae's going to show it to the whole world. Just play the damn thing."

Jiwoo looked at everyone and they all formed a half circle around the laptop. It was placed directly in front of Minjae and me since we didn't make a single effort to move. Jiwoo hit play.

It was a short video, but did it get its point straight across? Definitely yes. And unfortunately, it was exactly what I had feared it would be.

It started with paparazzi photos from the mall—our little outing before we were even near being a couple. Then there was the already familiar kissing photo, making sure everyone would know who the main stars in this shitshow would be. Continued straight away with security footage from the elevator, where we had had our short but heated make-out session. Then there was footage from the corridor, right until we had made our way to the hotel room. There'd been a hidden camera in the room—the worst part of it all. If I remembered the layout correctly, it must've been hidden either in the bed's headboard or one of the night lamps. Luckily, there wasn't much to see since we hadn't bothered turning the lights on.

After the video ended, Joe slammed the laptop shut. Jiwoo buried her face in her hands. The others were just staring ahead, speechless. I planned the perfect murder of one specific individual while the silence strained on. Minjae sobbed silently, still clinging to my shirt. I pulled him to sit between my legs and squeeze him tight against my chest. There might've been a single tear escaping my own eyes, but I would've never admitted to that.

Privacy is something all celebrities have to compromise up to a point, but Dae had gone way too far. It wasn't even that we had been outed anymore...we were completely screwed over. It was basically a hell, designed specifically for the two of us. The worst nightmare that could happen to any artist, only ten times worse because I was fairly sure it was the first one involving a gay couple. At least in this part of the world.

It was Joonie who spoke first. "Well, it could be worse. He can't leak it since that's illegal on so many levels."

I didn't even bother to laugh, even though I was tempted to do exactly that.

"When has that stopped anyone, ever? I'm sure he has thought everything through," Chris said putting my exact thoughts into words.

There was another strained silence until Tae spoke. "I think Joonie has a point actually. What if we just...let him release it? It can't be that hard to link that hotel to him somehow. How else could he have access to the security footage?"

"He did say the hotel was owned by his family. In fact, he said he had found out about us when we were at Daegu in one of his family's hotels," I elaborated.

"See? Problem solved. I say we just let him release it and then press charges," Tae said with a smug shrug. Easy for him to say.

"Aren't you forgetting one tiny little detail though? It's us on the video! Ever heard of privacy?" I huffed. "I would give a billion Won if this would just go away."

"Well, hate to break it to you," Tae started, business as usual. It pissed me right off. "But who says he wouldn't leak this even though you would bargain with money or quit just like he wants?"

I hated to admit it, but he was right.

"Also, it would be the end of our careers. And I'm not even concerned about only Minjae and me at this point," A lump forming at an alarming speed in my throat as I spoke.

"...right," Tae admitted with a defeated look on his face.

After another silence, it was Jiwoo's turn to chime in. "Not necessarily... Look, we could play you two as the victims. Which, you are, right? You have an enormous fanbase. We'll just have to rely on their support. The fact that DoMino is the ultimate ship there is might give us a slight advantage."

"I could help with sailing that DoMino ship," Chris said, earning the undivided attention from us all. After he noticed us all staring, he added a quick, "What?"

"Care to explain?" Minjae asked.

"Umm, I—ahem..." Chris stuttered. "I just might happen to run the world's biggest fan account dedicated to DoMino." He blushed adorably and scratching his head, evading all our eyes.

"I knew it! The @crewinsidr one, right?" Minjae shouted, nearly making me go deaf because he was still clinging to me, and his vocal cords were way too close to my eardrums.

"Yeah..." Chris admitted.

"What on earth are you talking about?" Jiwoo asked then.

Chris showed the account from his phone to Jiwoo, who frowned at the sight.

"Well, I shouldn't approve this. At this point though, I'm just glad you have it." Jiwoo said, taking Chris's phone. "Wow, this might actually work," She scrolled faster and faster through some pictures before dialing a number on his phone and lifting it to her ear. It didn't take more than a few words to command someone from the other side of the phone call to "drag his ass here, now."

Two minutes later, someone knocked on the door. I guessed the person Jiwoo had called had already been upstairs; no way someone could appear here that fast otherwise. Jiwoo scurried to the door and opened it. It was LBR Entertainment's best lawyer, Jae-Beom. An older, strict, and conservative-looking man with a profound belly. I had never needed his services before...that was about to change.

Jiwoo recapped the whole blackmailing thing and then summarized our rough draft of a plan. He listened carefully, looking a bit odd while sitting at the floor with his pristine suit getting all wrinkled. After considering the whole thing through, he spoke.

"That would otherwise sound like a fairly good plan, but I don't think we have enough material to make a solid case out of it. We need more proof that this man named Dae is behind this. Maybe a witness. Outsider, or at least other than these two," he said and waved our way. "Otherwise, it's just word against word."

It was Joe's turn to talk. "How about that host lady at the hotel back in Daegu? I mean Dae found out about you two from there, right? Surely she'll know something about it. Also, that gal sounded like a decent person, and she might be a fan. What was her name again?"

"Kim Hyunmi," I said after searching my mind for the nameplate I miraculously had memorized.

"That might work, right? If you two are willing to spend some money and persuade her," Jiwoo added.

The lawyer nodded, and the others hummed in agreement.

"Then, I guess it's up to you two," Tae said, referring to Minjae and me. "Can you take the heat or are we going to disband? I'm definitely not continuing without you two, for sure."

I glanced at Minjae; he had fire in his eyes that were searching mine, so I figured I'd just go with it. It seemed like the only sensible solution at the moment anyway.

"I'm down. Let's destroy that douchebag," I said to the others, with the non-violent plan of taking revenge in the form of a lawsuit in mind. But I wasn't the only one whose opinion mattered. I looked at the man beside me. "Min?"

Minjae took a while to figure out his answer. He looked straight into my eyes like he'd find his answer there. After another strained silence when everyone waited for his confirmation holding their breaths, including me, he said, "I sure ain't going 'self-reflecting' because of love..."

Now we're talking. "Let's do this."

End of a Choker

Dae kept his word.

The video went out when we didn't announce out disbandment, and Minjae and I escaped to Daegu to take over Mom's apartment. It was far enough from all the craziness. Granted, we wouldn't have known all of it—we didn't turn on the TV once and avoided everything else related to any sort of news or social media. To be honest, we had a great time. At least at the times when we both managed to forget we were in the middle of a huge scandal.

Neither of us could face it yet. Besides, escaping was basically the only sane thing to do. To our ultimate relief, the others agreed to it and were willing enough to take most of the heat off our backs. I'd be forever grateful for the guys and Jiwoo. I'm sure Minjae felt likewise. Joe followed us to Daegu, of course, but he spent most of his time alone sulking and whining that he had failed us...it got on my nerves a lot too because it had nothing to do with him; it was Minjae and me who had screwed up. He couldn't have done anything about it. We weren't planning on exiting the building at all except for persuading Kim Hyunmi to our side when Joe found her, so it didn't really matter if he was there or not.

Mom had stayed in Seoul, either to give me and Min some privacy or to spend some time with Seong-gi. I preferred not to know which. It kind of made me sick to think about Mom and Seong-gi together, though their thing seemed more and more obvious every passing day. There was too much flirting and longing glances. At least she took the whole thing with the scandal lightly, stating that she had already prepared mentally for these kinds of things when I had first chosen to pursue music. She understood that it was a big deal for us though and tried not to talk about it too much.

The first couple of days went by fast. It was only Minjae and me enjoying some alone time, not quite grasping the reality of it all. We spent most of it in bed—tried new things and such... granted, I sometimes was afraid of hurting him still. The best part was that I kept learning more and more about him every passing day. Everything I learned just made me fall even harder for him. If possible.

In a way, we were in the eye of the storm where it was all peaceful when everyone else dealt with the damage elsewhere on our behalf.

Well, that was until one morning, when reality decided to slap us hard, right across our faces.

That morning, I woke up alone in the guest room's king size bed. Rubbing the sleepiness off my eyes, I didn't really think anything of it. Minjae must have just woken before me, I figured. Still happened sometimes, no big deal.

Taking my sweet time, I showered, letting the warm water wake me up. Brushed my teeth. Even bothered to shave. Put on some actual clothes instead of sporting the pajamas we both had been loitering in around the house for two days straight.

I finally made my way to the kitchen, probably hoping I'd be hooked up with a nice breakfast and a steaming hot cup of coffee before a steamier hot make-out session with Minjae. But in reality, I don't remember what went through my head back then. Probably nothing. At least, nothing important.

But the kitchen was dark. At first, I didn't even notice Minjae, that's how silent he was. I was almost about to turn on my heels and go look for him elsewhere when I spotted him, on the floor, hugging his knees, while only the light of his phone's screen illuminated his face.

Minjae kept scrolling whatever he was reading on his phone. I stood there, watching him, frozen on the threshold. His eyes scared me. The usual flame in them had completely extinguished; the two formerly most beautiful eyes had lost their spark. They looked dead.

That's when I spotted his other hand, which was scratching his neck below the thick, black band—another choker he had been obsessed with lately. He had scratched the delicate skin so hard he had drawn some blood which spread all over his neck.

The whole time when I watched him break apart in shock, he didn't even notice me. I felt so helpless. I became paralyzed. So utterly and completely scared of the sight, I could do nothing but watch. All I wanted was to help, somehow, but my feet didn't move. So bad, I wanted to tell him that everything was fine and ask him to stop, but my voice stuck to my throat. I knew I'd have to take the phone out of his hand, but I couldn't lift one finger.

Then he started to vigorously tear the necklace like he was actually going to choke on it. That woke me up from my weird trance. My knees were the first to give up, and I crashed hard to the floor. Ignoring the pain, I crawled to him. I had to pry the phone out of his hand as he held it tightly, like his life depended on it. I caught a glimpse of what he had been looking at. The headlines that flashed before my eyes were repulsive.

My hand shook with anger after I threw the phone to the floor with all the strength I had in me. The screen cracked and went blank. The sound of the phone's screen shattering echoed in my ears as I turned my gaze back to Minjae.

He stared right back at me with those dead-looking eyes, still scaring the shit out of me. I couldn't take it anymore, so I pulled him closer and squeezed him tightly against my chest and started rocking us both back and forth. I'd get through to him somehow, I hoped.

"Minjae, shh, it's ok..." I murmured into his ear.

I whispered all kinds of gentle, nice words—any I could think of—trying to get some kind of reaction out of him. Any kind of reaction. But Minjae kept quiet and still. Lifeless, even. Tears started to burn behind my eyes, as I felt so damn helpless. Useless.

I don't even know why I started apologizing, but that was finally what got through to him.

At first, he started screaming. From the top of his lungs. It was a shriek really, erupting from somewhere deep in his chest. But it was a reaction, so I ignored my ringing ears and held him as he kept screaming until his voice gave up.

The screams were then replaced with a heart-breaking sob. He scratched his neck again, so I had no choice but to reach for the scissors on the nearby drawer and cut the damn choker off.

I tossed it to the corner and Minjae let out a long, exhausted but relieved sigh and rested his face against my chest. I kept rocking us and stroking his hair soothingly for probably an hour or two. Right until the sobs died down, and he fell asleep.

As soon as I had made sure his breathing was even, and he was sound asleep, I carried him to the bed. After tugging him under the blankets, I cleaned the blood off his neck with a wet towel and then just watched him sleep. The guilt washed over me again, as I wondered if any of this would have happened if I had been more careful.

When he woke up again, the spark in his eyes was back, though it wasn't nearly as bright as before. I chose to ignore it for the time being... But at the same time, I promised myself I'd do anything to get that full spark back and not let anything like this happen ever again.

We didn't touch another phone that week.

Hyunmi

By the end of the week, Joe finally found Kim Hyunmi. Conveniently enough, she was still in Daegu. What took me by a surprise, was that she no longer worked for Dae's family business.

Nevertheless, I figured it was better to deal with her sooner rather than later due to Minjae's clearly deteriorating mental health; I was hoping that if I'd manage to convince her to join our cause, maybe Minjae would brighten up as well. And it was better if I dealt with her by myself. The last thing I needed was to end up in the tabloids being seen together with Minjae again, especially now.

One early morning I waited at a secluded booth of a packed coffee shop near my Mom's place for Hyunmi-ssi to appear. Joe had arranged the meeting and was waiting for her at the front. I glanced at my wristwatch for the hundredth time—still too early.

My hands shook when I lifted my coffee mug on my lips. To think I would have to put both Minjae's and my own whole future in the hands of a total stranger. I could only hope and pray she would be willing to help us.

The door's bell chimed, and I snapped my eyes up. Hyunmi. Finally. Almost unconsciously, I started playing with the promise -ring again as Joe led her to my table.

She sat in front of me, her face practically a question mark. Taking a deep breath, I offered her a formal greeting while removing my bucket hat and sunglasses. Her face lit up once she fully recognized me. Still, as a well-trained woman in the hospitality industry, she kept herself calm. Good.

"What can I get you?" I asked, handing her the menu.

She ordered a cappuccino. We exchanged some more formal but awkward small-talk while waiting for her coffee to arrive.

"And what do I owe the pleasure of meeting you like this?" she asked when her order arrived, her tone still very polite.

"I need your help." Every word was true. And there was no point in stalling. "Surely you're aware of the shit Minjae and I got ourselves into."

She let out a chiming laugh. "And what does your publicity stunt have to do with me?"

I sighed. "If only it was a mere publicity stunt."

"Care to elaborate?"

"We were blackmailed." I admitted, acknowledging I had no other choice than tell this woman everything. "We didn't want to comply with the terms. Now we are famous…well, even more so than before."

"Either way, I don't know how I can be of any help."

"The one blackmailing us was Daesung. I'm sure you're somehow familiar with him, considering you worked for their family's business for, what…five years?"

She leaned back, slowly stirring her beverage with the spoon. "Oh. I see."

"Look, I can pay you for any information you can give us regarding him violating guests' privacy at their hotels. I can pay you even more if you testify against him in court. If you help us, I'm about to make you a very rich woman. And I'll be forever grate—"

"I don't want your money," she cut me off with a somewhat annoyed tone.

"So, you do have information?"

"I didn't say so. I just said you can't buy me with money."

"But you do have something to sell?"

She shrugged and evaded my eyes. It was a tell-tale sign.

292

"Then, I'll give you whatever you want that I can give," I said, starting to play with the promise ring. "Tickets for every single LBR Entertainment artist's concert for a year? Done. Dreaming of being a big star yourself? I can arrange an audition. Just name your price. *Please.*"

She didn't reply. Instead, she kept staring at her coffee and stirring it, ever so slowly. No matter how much it annoyed me, I couldn't bring myself to say anything more. There wasn't much more I could offer her. She had all the cards in her tiny little manicured hand that was holding the coffee mug, and I could do nothing about it.

I grew more and more nervous by the minute of the strained silence. Soon, I couldn't take it anymore, and pulled out the ring I was playing with completely and started spinning it on the table while waiting for Hyunmi to speak.

That finally ended the silence. "Can I see that?" Hyunmi asked, holding out her hand.

"What? This?" I asked, stopping the still spinning ring.

"Yes."

I considered it for a moment. Admittedly, it was my most treasured belonging...but if she wanted it in exchange for any information that would give us out of this mess, I would gladly give it to her. I just couldn't figure out what she would ever do with that piece of scrap metal that held no monetary value in it. Still, I handed it to her.

To my surprise, she instantly started reading the text on the inside when she got her hands on it. "Yaksok," she whispered to herself, before lifting her deep brown eyes to meet mine. "You did keep it? I never would've thought."

"Wait a minute..." I started, thoroughly shook to the core. It couldn't be. Or could it? "You gave me this ring?"

She smiled, handing me back the ring. "No, it wasn't me."

"Then how did you—"

"I was next in line," she said and smiled even wider. "The one who gave that to you was my now late best friend."

My heart stopped. "Oh. I'm so sorry."

I couldn't believe the girl from years back was just…gone. Knowing that felt like a part of me was ripped out. Through all the years, through all the fights with Minjae, I had come back to this particular ring and promised I'd do better. Be better. Every single time remembering the one human who saw Minjae and I before we saw ourselves. And now she no longer existed.

"Thank you," Hyunmi said, interrupting my internal storm. "And yes, I'll help you."

Blinding Lights

In the end, only our concert in Moscow got canceled, due to their strict views on gay people. Even more conservative countries than Russia had banned us ages ago for a bit of fanservice alone, so that one cancellation wasn't that much of a big deal.

Jiwoo had polished the plan further. We didn't even have to officially come out as a gay couple, surprisingly enough. It was just your "regular" hidden camera scandal now. She had forced our label to give out a statement demanding that their artists' dating was meant to be private and that it was practically no-one's business if we were dating or not. The guys had kept that 'no-comments' policy through the whole ordeal. Chris had opened his vault of material and was constantly bombarding our fans with his no-longer-secret Twitter account. And not just about Minjae and I, Tae and Joonie were included too. It worked like magic, and our fans were as supportive as ever.

Apart from true fans, the reactions varied from deep hate to ultimate support. The diversity of opinions was just...something else entirely. Not one of us could keep up, so we gave up and simply tried to act normal. Of course, I worried about Min, especially after the breakdown he'd had back at Daegu. But in a way, I was also glad it'd already happened there, and not now that we were back at it again. Since clearly that meltdown somehow prepared him for what was coming, and to my knowledge, he never had another after. Though, he didn't wear as many chokers for some reason—not sure if I missed that or not. Slowly but surely, even the almost lost spark in his eyes strengthened a little bit every passing day.

Somehow we made it through. And the best part? We made it through together.

Life had some rays of sunshine again.

Dae was charged with a shit ton of lawsuits. Hyunmi-ssi had a huge part in that—and having her on our side tipped the scale so much that didn't even worry about the outcome. Dae was going down.

Also, it turned out that Dae was a complete psychopath. Hyunmi told us he had harassed and blackmailed most of the staff at Seoul and especially in Daegu where he was from. She stated it was about time someone would try and make it stop. Too bad it had to be us. Hyunmi was actually one fine, laid back woman and a huge fan of GRiD, much to Dae's and his family's business's misfortune. Things were looking good for us.

After another week, we headed to our "Contrast" world tour, starting from South America and continuing straight away to North America. After that, we had about a month-long pause to finish up the repackaging of the album and shoot some music videos with Minjae's and Joonie's songs turned into singles. We had to work on those at the tour, but at that point, it was just a minor detail I was reluctant to think about yet. After that, we headed to Europe. The whole tour concluded in a smaller tour over Asia and Oceania. The final concert was held back at Gocheok Sky Dome, Seoul.

In Sao Paulo, Brazil, we faced the fans directly for the first time since shit hit the fan. We prepared backstage for the evening, which would mark the starting point of our huge tour. Minjae was scared shitless to face the fans after the scandal. So was I. Even my almost-forgotten fear of stages made a huge comeback. Two times, I found myself at the toilet, spilling my guts out. Not my best moments.

Minjae came to my rescue. He informed me we'd have to head to the stage soon. As always, being close to him made everything less...intimidating. I brushed my teeth one last time and let the make-up artist touch up whatever I had ruined before we headed to our starting spot under the stage.

The noise from the audience that chanted our names bombarded my eardrums, even through the earpieces. Still, glancing my Minjae's face under the dim lights, barely letting us see where we were going in the maze under the stage, made the outside world disappear. It was just me and Minjae in that precious second. The tension on my back melted away when I looked in his eyes, and he stared right back. It was almost like he could see straight to my soul. I wondered what he saw there that made him fall in love with me. Let's be honest, I wasn't exactly made out of best relationship material.

Minjae was the complete opposite. In his eyes, I saw kindness. Strength. Trust and genuine sincerity. He took no bullshit from anyone, not even from me. And that made him the perfect match for me.

In that moment, I had confidence that we'd make it through everything life would throw on our way. I only had to endure the rollercoaster ride, hanging on for dear life and meanwhile trying to enjoy the precious moments when everything would be perfect. I was sure there would be both bad and good times, but the short time we had already been together told me the good times outweighed the bad ones by a ton.

It was a spur of a moment thing that I scratched our pre-stage routine completely. Instead, I kneeled in front of him as gracefully I could in the tight space. After making sure both our mics were still turned off, I looked at Minjae dead in his eyes. I yanked the ring that said "promise" from my finger and held it in front of his face. His expression was a weird mix of surprise, questioning, and scolding, but I didn't let that bother me.

"Minjae..." My heart swelled with anticipation and excitement. "Years ago, I fell in love with you when we were cramped similarly under a random stage I can't even remember any longer. It took me many years to accept these feelings, and I will be eternally sorry for that. Being in the army and away from you for over two years made me realize I can't possibly live without you by my side.

"That being said, I know I've made some other mistakes, too. I'm amazed that in the end, you chose me. Despite all my flaws. The best night of my life was that night when you confessed you felt the exact same way for me than I felt for you. I'm not perfect and never will be, so even after that, I've made some mistakes. Can't even promise you that I won't make any mistakes in the future.

"Right now, I'm just asking—hoping—if you still could keep choosing me for an eternity.

"Chang Minjae, will you do the absolute honor of being my husband someday, hopefully in the near future, when it's possible for us back in Korea? Will you marry me?"

There, I said it, I thought and closed my eyes for a brief second.

Through the whole little speech of mine, Minjae stayed silent with his eyes wide open. Halfway through, a single tear escaped his right eye, rolling down his cheek and eventually dropping to the floor. It looked as if he didn't even notice it himself, as he kept staring at me with a mouth hanging slightly open. He sure took his sweet time answering me. My heart raced and some sweat broke on my forehead. What if he didn't want to? Was this too soon?

But then I heard the most beautiful words escape his lips, and all doubts evaporated. "Yes, of course, I will."

Smiling so widely my cheeks hurt, I took his left hand in mine and placed the ring on his ring finger. It wasn't a flashy ring, but we both knew we wouldn't need any diamonds for this. Besides, it still was the text inside that mattered, at least to me. I was sure that after I'd explain the story behind it, it would be all that mattered to Minjae too.

Someone started counting the seconds to mark the stage staff when they'd start lifting us to the stage. I cupped Minjae's face and leaned in to give him a kiss that would hopefully translate all my feelings to him since I couldn't find any more words. It was only a brief kiss on our personal scale, but one of the most important ones on our journey. Parting right when the stage lift started to rise, I turned my mic on and flashed Minjae a brief smile. He smiled right back before closing his eyes for a second and turning his mic on.

We were met with blindingly bright spotlights and a deafening mixture of music and noise from the audience that was welcoming us back, once again.

EPILOGUE: Elsewhere

Chris's point of view
Four months later, Contrast World Tour, Citi Field, New York

We, as in me, Tae, and Joonie, stayed behind to watch Do's and Minjae's performance, although we were supposed to go backstage. The staff had already heaved a huge grand piano on stage, which was now under the spotlight with Do standing in front of it, mic in his hand. Minjae was waiting in the dark for his turn to appear. Everyone could see they were nervous from a mile away—understandably so. But I could also see that they had already lost in their own little world, as Do spared a glance towards Minjae who nodded with a slight smile lingering in his face.

The scandal had finally died down. Sure, some tabloids, especially back in South Korea, were still having a field day, but even those had turned the tone to the more accepting side. Nowadays, it was more like, "Extra! Extra! This and that celebrity has shown their support for Do-hyun and Minjae" rather than "Gay sex scandal shaking the idol world and shocking the nation."

The American leg of our tour had been a success. Venue after venue had been sold out, despite the scandal. We were having the best time of our renewed life after the army. It was almost like our popularity had grown in some parts of the world after the scandal, which had shocked us all. Even the most optimistic one of us, who had surprisingly been Jiwoo, had only dared to hope for a neutral outcome.

It was the last of our American concerts. Just one night away from a much-anticipated break. We were all eager to head back home, even though we knew the work would just continue there right away in the form of filming the music videos for the new tracks which were supposed to be released shortly after our break. But before that, this one night just had to be beyond perfect, for two main reasons:

Firstly, it was being filmed, to later release as the tour recording. It was the last night the tour would be with this show and setlist, as the next time we'd hit the stage we'd have some new material to show. Namely the two new group songs we had added to the repackaged album, that we'd been working through on the days we weren't on stage somewhere. In addition, Minjae and Joonie had finished up some new solos for it in their spare time during the tour so it would add up to four whole new songs for the repackaged album.

Secondly, Do and Minjae were finally going to admit their relationship to the world. They were going to do it by performing the original, Minjae's solo version of "Mad Love," our next single. Though it had gone through some minor changes in lyrics. It was the perfect timing since it would get us some hopefully positive exposure. Technically, this was barely one of the concerts of the world tour, but we all knew this would blow up hugely due to social media and our fans. And it would be taped too. It had been Jiwoo's idea, and man let me tell you Do and Minjae practically worshipped her nowadays for making their scandal all but disappear. So obviously, no one had argued.

It was to be the first time any of us addressed the scandal directly.

After taking a deep breath, Do started to talk. It might've seemed like it was just Do speaking, but we had all participated in the writing. After all, we were a pact—a family.

"I believe all of you have heard about this...scandal...that spread like a wildfire a few months ago. I know we have been a bit silent about that whole ordeal, but that's about to change from this day forward.

"You have been an enormous support to us through all this. That is why Minjae and I are both ready to put that whole thing behind us, now that the investigation has been completed. In return for your endless support, I will be completely honest with you now.

"It's all true what they say in the news. Every part of it. Yes, I am with Minjae. Yes, we are gay. No, we no longer care. At the end of it all, we are just regular people who love. We can't take the fame, money, or our reputation to the afterlife, the next life or whatever happens when the time comes, with us. We must make every day count now, right at this moment. Trust me, I have learned that the hard way.

"But let's put all that aside and enjoy this night together. Minjae will be singing this one song for you, only this one time, ever. We are releasing a group version of this in the repackaged album soon enough, but this is the raw original version. I promise it's completely different.

"Please, enjoy," he concluded and circled to the side to sit down on the piano stool.

Minjae walked slowly under the spotlight, making the crowd go absolutely wild, even after they had been completely silent for the whole speech. Do-hyun started to play. Once again a complete silence fell on the audience when they enjoyed every drop of the music. Minjae started singing. Seemed like from the bottom of his heart.

I glanced at Joonie, who had tears in his eyes and was blinking rapidly to prevent them from falling. My eyes shifted to Tae, who was almost equally moved. Though, it did look like he wanted to give Joonie a hug for a second before he let his hands drop with some conflict showing on his face.

Sure, Tae was smart—no, intelligent—but when it came down to Joonie and him, he was clueless. I'm not sure if they even noticed it themselves, but something had been going on for months now with those two. After wondering for one heartbeat if they had resolved whatever had been throwing off their game, I turned my gaze back at the stage to Do and Min.

By the time they got to the second chorus, the crowd could already sing along a bit. The light sticks were held up high, all tuned to show different colors. Both of them smiled, to the crowd and to each other.

This was clearly Do's and Minjae's moment, but we were all in this together. Maybe someday, we could all show our true colors on stage.

At least, this was a good start.

The Story Continues in

Used to being in control as the leader of GRiD, Tae has his life all figured out. That is, until a drunken love confession from his flamboyantly gay, bold and gorgeous bandmate Joonie sends Tae spiraling down into self-doubt.

It takes some convincing for Tae to relinquish control over his life and realize that he might not be as straight as he thought. But once he does, he slowly warms up to the idea of a romantic relationship…especially with Joonie.

However, fame throws another curveball their way when Tae finds out about the threats Joonie has been receiving from a stalker he has hidden from the rest of the group—threats that just might turn out to be deadly ones.

More From Nami:

www.namiartopit.com